SIN *and* SORROW

MARION CROSLYDON

For Papa.

You told me my first stories but you are my first hero.
Always.
Thank you for d'Artagnan and his Musketeers, Lagardère
and Le Capitan.

Prologue

Scotland, near Culloden ~ April 1746

My nails clawed at the rough wool of the sheet and my heels dug into the bed. My thighs burned. I spread them wide and screamed, a scream loud enough to be heard on the peaks of the Cairngorms.

The old man stood at the foot of the bed. He glanced down at me, his attention briefly diverted from the intimate sight between my legs. "Keep pushing, Marie."

Louis Berthière had been a physician at the French court; Everett had told me so. I did not know much, but I knew—in my heart—that Louis could be trusted. No matter what he was.

Dry wood cracked in the hearth and the sound echoed between my ears. I tried to stop wriggling but a new spasm sliced through me. My hips bucked upwards.

Louis's grasp pinned me to the bed. "We're nearly there, *ma petite.*"

I lifted up my chest and supported myself on my elbows. My eyes roamed over the bare walls that were closing in around my hopes and fears. They settled on the rough surface of the door, where the Scottish dampness had rotten the embossed wood. I prayed for that door to burst open and for the shape of Everett's shoulders wrapped in the north wind. I wanted my husband to return to me. I wanted him to murmur tender words into my ears.

But he could do no such thing because he was dead, slaughtered by MacLeod.

I had wasted so much time fighting my feelings for Everett. He'd been the offspring of the devil, his blood, the blood of innocents sucked and robbed of their lives. I should have cared but my own blood had flushed through my veins, and my heart had pounded with wild haste the moment I met him. I'd fallen in love with his conflicted nature and he'd loved my unbridled faith in his redemption.

Pain exploded inside my belly once again. Mist blurred my vision. Deliverance was now close at hand, so I pushed when the Frenchman prompted me. I could not ignore the form pushing against my thighs, its wetness, its stillness.

"We're almost there. One more time."

"This is too much." I wept the words, loneliness stealing the last remnants of strength that had crawled inside me.

"For him, Marie. For the love of your husband, see this to the end."

I pushed. Our gazes met over my deformed body. The grey glitter in his eyes, so similar to Everett's, reminded me of what I had lost. I could not turn my back on my doomed love for here was a promise of a new beginning. So I emptied my womb with one last howl. All I was left tasting and smelling was the coppery tang of blood.

In front of me, the man tapped gently an unmoving form in his left hand. Silence filled the room. There was a noticeable absence.

"Is it a girl?"

I prayed for a girl. A daughter would be free of the curse her father's lineage bestowed upon boys. She would know the double-edged blessing of old age. She would not thrive on blood.

But Louis didn't answer. I shivered. A dry sob strangled me. He stepped around the bed holding a bundle of sheets against his chest. When he sat down by my side, the mattress sank under his weight. Dread coiled around my throat and I struggled for my next breath.

"It was a boy." A tremor tainted his voice. "You went into labor so early… There was nothing I could do."

My body remained still but I collapsed inside.

I would not accept this. I simply could not. But I did because I knew—I had always known—that God had no care for justice or fairness. He wanted everything I had, everything I cherished, and I hated this God for He had no more goodness in Him than the demon He was supposedly battling.

Anger gave my arms the strength to stretch upwards, begging for what was mine to be returned to me. The old man placed the lifeless form of my child against my breasts. No warmth exuded from his small body. I would have loved him, my little boy, despite his very existence defying the rules of nature. I would have loved him with all the fierceness left in my heart. He would have made a mother of me, but all I was now was a lonely little girl.

The man probed my belly and the inside of my legs. "You are bleeding heavily."

He cared for me but I didn't care about anything anymore. My hold on my child loosened. My eyelids fluttered and threatened to close.

"Marie!" His tone was hard. "I can save you."

"Who says I want to be?"

"You deserve to live. MacLeod has stolen so much from you. Do not let him take your life as well. It's the news of Everett's death that triggered the labor."

I closed my eyes, searching my scattered mind for one last image of my husband, one I could fall asleep forever with. In vain.

"You die and they will die with you again." The man's fingers clasped my shoulders. "Your son and your husband. Everett's murderer will remain free to roam the world and his death will go unpunished."

That avenging angel destroyed us. All Everett and I wanted was to live our lives away from the wars, earthly and unearthly, raging throughout Scotland. But it had not been enough for us to be spared. I did not want MacLeod to win.

3

He should not win.

I lifted my hand towards Louis. My fingers enlaced with his, my own blood already drying under my nails. "I want to make MacLeod pay. I want him dead."

His hold on me tightened. "We will make sure of that, *petite* Marie."

It would not take much from Louis to turn me. He would feed on my blood and give me a few droplets of his before I died. Within hours I would rise again.

So I pulled the body of my child closely against me. "Then do what you have to do."

Chapter 1 — The House on The Scores

St. Andrews University, Scotland ~ Present Day.

The house on the Scores stood proudly upon the cliff overlooking the North Sea.

I'd stared so long at the grey-stoned façade that the weak September sun had heated my skin and depleted my strength. The time had come to ring the bell. I breathed in the salty air rushing in from St. Andrews Bay and took the first step across the road, forcing myself to pay attention to the traffic. Hidden away as I'd been in the Quebec countryside on Fjord Saguenay, I wasn't used to cars anymore, and the Scores was the busiest part of St. Andrews.

I pushed open the iron gate and marched up the stone path that led to the Georgian house. The door was freshly painted in glossy black. There was no bell though, only a large metal knocker. His daughter was inside. I could hear the regular beating of her heart and the blood pulsing through her veins.

Two knocks.

Footsteps cascaded down the stairs. Feet rushed over the marble floor. A hand undid the lock.

"Marie!" she squealed. "Come in."

She opened the door and gestured for me to enter. Her invitation sealed my fate and the fate of those living in the house.

She believed she was my friend but I had no friends left. My sweet Odette, her clumsy sidekick Vincent, and twenty more had been burned on Midsummer's morning three months earlier. Nathaniel MacLeod hadn't lit the fire himself. He'd waited for the first rays of the rising solstice sun to knife through the clouds and ignite their bodies. That day, he'd killed my friends and Louis, the man I called father.

But I still managed to smile at the daughter. Her name was Elizabeth but she'd asked me to call her Lizzie the first time we met on the back bench during Anatomy class.

"I'm so in need of help with this bloody dissertation," she rolled her eyes. She had beautiful eyes, Lizzie did, slanting and sparkling emeralds. She didn't get them from her father. "Seriously, who needs to know about the *anvil*, the *hammer* and the *stapes*? They're in the ear and I doubt breaking them is life-threatening."

"They're the smallest bones in the body." A North American twang stretched my words. More than two centuries spent on the other side of the Atlantic had robbed me of the brogue of my native Edinburgh.

"*That*, my friend, is exactly why I intend to bribe you with gallons of ice creams. You'll have enough energy to write *my* paper as well as yours. Is there something you don't already know anyway? I swear, it feels like you've been through the whole curriculum a dozen times already."

As a matter of fact, I had but only once. Forty years ago, at Princeton, I'd graduated from Med school. I wasn't at St. Andrews for a refresher course.

I gave a pointed look at the vestibule and the double doors that opened onto an L-shaped entrance hall.

"Oh yeah, maybe we should get to work? Follow me." She swiveled around and her height dwarfed me. Her physique was Amazonian, but her manners strangely girly. The mix was attractive, alluring even.

"The house was built by my great-great-something grandfather in the nineteenth century. He was a professor here. Dad had it fully refurbished when my brother and I decided to study at St. Andrews. Our father is all about history so he made sure all the period details were respected." She pointed at the decorative cornice in the entrance hall, but when we moved into the sitting room I understood the extent of the care put into restoring the place.

I oohed and aahed at every detail. "Pity none of the houses I've viewed look half as nice as this."

"Have you found a room yet?"

"Nope. But I'm sure I will soon." I faked a brave smile and a slight wobble of my lips. "It would be too ridiculous to have to leave school for not having anywhere to live."

Would Lizzie take the bait? She only gave me a nod and a smile.

In front of me, the bay windows had upholstered seats looking out over the gardens and across to the sea. An open fireplace with a marble mantelpiece begged to be filled with a homey fire. French doors opened onto the gently-sloping garden outside.

"The kitchen is over there and so are the freezer and my best friends, Ben and Jerry. I know you told me you weren't a big fan of ice-cream, but by the end of the afternoon, I promise you'll be acquainted with those lovely blokes too."

I followed Lizzie across the maple floor and into an extensive kitchen, complete with a marble-topped island and rectangular wooden table by another bay window. The view was the same as in the sitting room with the ink-colored sea spreading as far as the eyes could see. The house was built like a ship ready to launch into the ocean.

"I'm not big at cooking, but my twin brother is." She took two cups from a glass cupboard and placed them on the countertop.

"My father used to cook too." This time the twitch in my cheek wasn't faked.

Lizzie stopped her fidgety tour of the house to rest her eyes on me. I held her gaze, fighting the urge to swallow my words. I didn't want to talk about my father, especially not to *her*. But the girl and I needed to bond.

"Has your dad passed away?" The question was blunt but her tone soft.

Passed away? The memory of his burning flesh, his melting facial features… I shivered and wrapped my arms around my chest. *Passed away* didn't do justice to Louis's final moments.

On that solstice dawn, Lizzy's father had taken everything from me, just like his ancestor had robbed me of Everett and of our child. On the night of Culloden. I only survived thanks to Louis; I survived because he turned me into what I am today.

I'd traveled to Scotland to ensure MacLeod would lose as much as I had. Revenge against his clan had eluded me once, all because I'd been beaten to it. But now had come the time for retribution and I'd start by becoming a permanent fixture in the young MacLeods' lives.

Lizzie bridged the gap between us and laid her hand on my wrist. I jerked back and her eyes widened in surprise. "I'm sorry, Marie. I didn't mean to pry. I—"

"Last spring. He passed away last spring. Cancer. My mother died a long time ago."

"So did mine." I heard the lump in Lizzie's throat. "Car crash."

Her hug was quick but tight. Pink worked over her cheeks. Despite her bubbly and sociable mask, Lizzie was a lonely girl with a deep sense of alienation. I knew this because I was very much like her. Lizzie still yearned for a mother she had no memory of and longed for a father who was never around. And I knew this because I'd spent the past month spying on her.

Her gaze settled on me. Her girly attitude had evaporated and there was kindness and strength in her eyes.

"Dad was so excited about me coming to Scotland to study." I let my gaze roam around the room as if lost in my memories. "Of course, he didn't know rent was so expensive over here."

"Have you looked for a job?"

"I'm still waiting to hear from two restaurants, but it doesn't look great." It was a lie. I had access to unlimited funds since my father's death and didn't need to work. "I'm on the waiting list for one of the rooms in uni. There are quite a few people ahead of me though." Another lie.

"We have a free bedroom." The information escaped her mouth and her eyebrows arched as if she was surprised by her own words.

I gave an invisible fist pump, but my question was full of innocence. "Is it to let?"

A crease formed at the top of her nose. She cleared her throat and her shoulders slumped slightly. I heard her panicked thoughts, her wish to recall the words. But again a warmth radiated from her whole being, a warmth that was entwined to her very soul.

"No."

"Sorry, I thought you were looking for a housemate or something. For a sec, I had my hopes up." I waved a hand as a quick dismissal. "Not that I could afford to live in a house like yours anyway."

"Marie…" Her voice trailed off. Sometimes I wished I could do more than just read thoughts. I'd love to be able to manipulate them too. But I might not have to, after all, and her next words confirmed it. "We're not looking for someone, but my nanny, I mean—" The pink on her cheeks turned beetroot-red. "I mean my governess, who was kind of a housekeeper—I mean, what twenty-year old needs a nanny, hey?" The babbling stopped short. She cleared her throat again. "Anyway, Becca retired last summer, hence the free room."

"Okay, but you've just said you weren't looking for a housemate."

"We aren't but I don't like the idea of you ending up with some random people in a shithole. St. Andrews is an expensive place to live. You said it yourself."

"I don't need your pity, Lizzie." I adjusted the strap of my messenger bag over my shoulder in feign embarrassment. "But it's really nice of you to offer."

"It's not pity. I'd love to have someone else living with us... Another girl would be nice."

"I don't know what to say." I made my voice hesitant yet hopeful.

"What about you have a look at the room first? I'll have to check with my brother if he's okay with it. He's not very welcoming to strangers."

"I'd love to see the room, if that's okay."

We retraced our steps to the hall and climbed the spiral staircase, stopping on the first floor landing.

Lizzie pointed at the door on the left. "That's my brother's room." I gave it a nonchalant glance. I'd have plenty of opportunity to explore it later. "And here is yours, if it all works out."

The bedroom had a lot in common with the one I had in Saguenay. Light, sparsely furnished with care and an educated sense of history. The double bed in the center of the room was low and had an iron headboard. There was a bay window opposite the door. A mahogany desk stood in front of it.

"The bathroom is on the next landing." Lizzie led the way. "You'd have to share it with my brother but there's a freestanding bathtub. Very *fin-de-siècle*."

"I like it very much," I said. "I'd love to stay but I'm pretty sure I can't afford the rent."

"If you stay, you can do it for free." A curl of coppery hair fell over her forehead and she absent-mindedly tucked it back behind her ear. "It's not as if we need the money." Her mouth twitched. "Listen, what about you pay us whatever your budget was? We'll cover the utility bills. And you can tutor me from time to time and share with me all your clever thoughts about anatomy and other exciting subjects that go way over my head."

The girl underestimated herself. She was a smart one.

"Why me?" I couldn't help asking. "I appreciate you're trying to help and your nanny—I mean *housekeeper*—has left, but it's really generous of you."

She shrugged. "I like you. You're different from the other girls I've met so far at uni. You're also not from around here, which is definitely a good thing."

"You don't like it here?"

"I do, but I've never really been anywhere else than Scotland. My father and my brother can be protective. Too much sometimes."

"Maybe that's just because they care." Or maybe that was because they wanted to protect her from the MacLeods' enemies and their victims. Like me. "What about your brother or your dad? They'll surely want to talk to me."

"My brother is with some friends at our country house, Hollaroch, for the weekend. But he's got a game on Wednesday and he'll be focused on that for the next few days. Why don't you come and meet him afterwards? We'll see how you guys get along."

"What about your father?"

"He travels for business from summer 'til Christmas. It's easier not to get him involved."

We walked back onto the landing.

"Will your brother mind having a girl sharing his personal space?"

"I'm pretty sure he'll get used to it. Besides, I could have chosen an ugly one..." She winked at me. "You're half his size but I'm sure he'll find you interesting."

I'd endeavor for her brother to find me more than simply interesting. Payback was long overdue. This time, I'd destroy everything dear and meaningful to the MacLeod Hunter, starting with his son. Only I'd make MacLeod's suffering last. I'd bide my time, befriend, seduce. Once I had his heir infatuated with me, ready to turn his back on his clan, I'd crush him. And make his father watch.

My eyes peered into the young McLeod's room. The

scent emanating from it was familiar but I couldn't place it. I looked at the bed made with military precision and missed my next breath. Panic seeped into me for the first time since I'd devised my plan. Self-loathing too. It had a bitter taste, one I might often experience in this venture.

Would I betray Everett in this bed? Would I betray myself?

And I almost missed what Lizzie said next. "His name is Gabriel, my brother. But everyone calls him Gabe."

I shut my eyes and swallowed hard. I knew his name. His ancestor had borne the same one.

In 1746, Gabriel MacLeod had killed my husband.

Chapter 2 — First XV

The second half of the game had already started when I wended my way along the second row of spectators to reach Lizzie and her friend. His tousled wheat-colored hair fell over the edges of his round-rimmed glasses. I'd seen him before following Lizzie around like a newborn puppy after his mommy.

She grabbed my arm and pulled me into a free seat between them. "You've missed a cracking start. The Saints are on fire and my brother is a god."

University Park is the home of Saints Rugby. Three pitches share the space but the First XV pitch has its own stand, which can seat up to two hundred people. Today, all the bleachers were full for the first game of the season. St. Andrews were playing Edinburgh University. Tomorrow I should be moving into the house on the Scores, provided Gabriel MacLeod didn't veto Lizzie's offer after meeting me.

I turned to the boy next to me and extended my hand. "I'm Marie Aberdein."

"Simon York." His handshake was firmer than I expected.

"Sorry, guys. I should have made the introductions myself." Lizzie didn't look sorry at all. Her sole focus were the thirty burly men on the pitch.

"Are St. Andrews the ones in black and blue?" I faked ignorance. Since I'd spent the past month observing him at his training sessions, I'd already established that.

"Yes. Gabe is their fly-half and captain."

I didn't need to know his position to pick him out. Even caked in mud and surrounded by his teammates, Gabriel MacLeod cut a powerful figure. At least six feet four inches tall, his build was lean and muscular. His gait was determined without being forceful, and next to the other bearlike players, he exuded a feline flair. His hair had the same coppery tone as his sister although his curls were less unruly. Damp with sweat, they clung to his temples as he shouted encouragement to his team. He didn't pay any attention to the spectators and was economical with his commands. His team followed him without question.

Gabriel MacLeod had leadership bursting from the marrow of his bones. Soon he'd have to make use of this gift for ventures other than sports, but for now, he lived in blissful oblivion. I envied him for that.

"This is his fourth conversion of the match. He hasn't missed one yet," Simon commented while Gabriel placed the ball on the ground and measured four paces backwards and two sideways in preparation for his next kick at goal.

The people on the row in front of us stood, forcing us to do the same, but Gabriel's eyes stayed fixed on the ball. The crowd fell still and the chorus of silent heartbeats around me slowed. At my side Lizzie bit her lower lip, her fists clenched with tension.

My attention shifted back to the pitch when Gabriel struck the ball. It traced a perfect arc in the sky, crossing the bar perfectly in the center of the two posts. The crowd applauded, chanting his family name. Each of their shouts stabbed me in the chest and I clasped my hands between my breasts to still the hate boiling there. On either side of me, Lizzie and Simon stamped their feet, bumping into me and threatening my balance. I swayed and my gaze searched forward for a point to anchor itself on.

Over the ten-yard gap, my eyes locked with MacLeod's. His run came to an abrupt end. For the first time he wasn't focused on the game. Instead his feet were rooted into the grass while his teammates jogged past him, congratulating him and patting his back. He didn't even look at them.

He blinked, his eyes so much like his sister's. Slanted and catlike, but his were a shade of green as dark as ink. The frown and square-jawed scowl that followed came unexpectedly. I could hear the heightened speed of blood rushing through his veins. I tasted the bitterness in his mouth, so strong it should make him nauseous. But his skin tingled and I knew, without a doubt, that should my fingers brush his face, I'd feel the heat from within him, heat that had nothing to do with the physical strain of the game. It fed from the sudden tightening of his groin. It was blind desire, both fresh and familiar. In turn, that heat lit up a fire inside his chest. That fire was familiar to me.

It was hate.

He shook his head as if trying to wake himself from a dream. The bond between us was severed and Gabriel rejoined the game.

I plopped back onto the seat and my hand clasped around my neck. Gabriel was still only twenty and the powers that were passed on to the next MacLeod's Hunter would be fully held by his father until the first son turned twenty-one. Gabriel's anointment shouldn't happen until March. He should still be living a perfectly normal existence in total ignorance of my world. Could I have been misinformed about the ways of the MacLeod clan? Had they changed? It was the first time I hadn't hid from Gabriel and already I felt like he'd found out about my true nature.

The MacLeods were the only line left of the Highlands Hunters. One Hunter was anointed in every generation when the adult men of the clan would swear their allegiance to him. Nowadays the fighting members of the MacLeods were trained as hard as Navy SEALs. Individually they couldn't defeat a Stramos, our elite of ancient males. Put three or four of MacLeod's men together and all bets were off. But only the Hunter had the power to single out my kind.

"Are you okay?" Lizzie squeezed my thigh.

"I'm fine. I didn't have lunch, that's all." This wasn't really a lie. I hadn't fed since I visited the house on the Scores three days earlier. Louis used to reprimand me for ignoring the needs of my body, and his death hadn't changed my ways.

Lizzie bent forward, rustled something out of the handbag at her feet and handed me a bar of chocolate. "It'll help." I stared down at the wrapper but didn't take it. She rolled her eyes. "Please don't tell me you're watching your weight. I could probably lift you with one arm."

"Don't overestimate yourself." I smiled, took the bar, and unwrapped it.

My father had always encouraged me to keep a taste for the food I enjoyed as a human, and I'd always loved sugar so I bit into the bar. But no matter how much blood or plain human food I absorbed, the spells and the fainting were becoming more frequent. So was the new disease that affected Turned like me, who refused to bite and feed directly from humans.

Lizzie and I didn't exchange any more words for the rest of the game. From time to time, the crowd jumped to its feet to acclaim another Saints exploit, but I stayed safely seated.

"Simon is going to give us a lift to the pub," Lizzie said after the final whistle. Edinburgh had been humiliated and Gabriel Macleod was the victor. That much I knew.

My neighbors towered over me while the crowd left the stand. I stood and followed Lizzie to the car park. She chatted about her brother's achievements while Simon kept his vigil behind us. We stopped in front of a shiny new Range Rover.

"A gift from my dad. It looks more like a tank than a car, but that makes him feel better," Lizzie said. I'd followed her the day she'd picked it from the car dealer. "Simon will drive as he's not drinking today. Hop in the passenger seat. You look even paler than usual. I don't want you to get carsick and puke on the brand new leather."

She winked and opened the door for me. I sat on the

leather seat and pretended listening to their chitchat for the entire journey. After leaving the city center, we drove north along the coast. The afternoon was approaching its end and the rays of sun were cast in an oblique trajectory over the landscape. Unfortunately the sea mirrored that and intensified the brightness of the sunlight. I kept my head bent down and my eyes half shut.

I relaxed when I saw the World's End for the first time. The name befitted the location. The building was of simple whitewashed stone with blue shutters. It reminded me of the home we'd owned in Newfoundland before we moved to Saguenay. Like our temporary Canadian refuge, the Scottish pub stood at the end of a narrow peninsula. Water and sky filled the horizon.

I stepped out of the shelter of the car, and the wind threw the wisps of my hair in multiple directions. They whipped back against my face.

"Hurry up!" Lizzie took hold of my hand and dragged me inside. As always, Simon was in our wake.

The crowd at University Park had reached the World's End ahead of us so there wasn't much space left for us to negotiate. The air was overloaded with the stale smell of beer, cheap perfume and sweat. However, a working fireplace at the back of the main room produced the smoky scent of gently burning wood. I headed in that direction.

"What would you like to drink?" Lizzie called after me.

I should have stuck to her side rather than acting like a moth to a candle and heading in the opposite direction.

"I'll get this round," I offered, but she gave me a dismissive wave. "I'll have a beer."

"As you please." She didn't get the order herself but instructed Simon of her choice of drink and mine. "There's a table booked for Gabe right next to the fire."

The table could seat around eight people with a bench against the wall and chairs and stools around the other sides. *MacLeod* was handwritten on a small cardboard square placed

17

at its center. We sat next to each other on the bench and discarded our jackets under our seats.

"Are the two of you an item?" I nodded at Simon, who was queuing at the bar to place our order.

Lizzie followed my gaze but for once kept silent. I was about to apologize for my curiosity when she opened her mouth. "We aren't…not *that* way at least." She shuffled on her seat and cleared her throat. "I'm not supposed to date. Simon and I keep it on the down-low so my father doesn't find out."

The MacLeods' rules were strict: Elizabeth had no right to intimacy until her marriage. The clan would choose the man she'd be betrothed to. Should Gabriel die without male progeny, the next Hunter would be her son, therefore particular care would be placed upon the choice of her spouse. And her husband would be Scottish, which Simon wasn't.

Lizzie stretched her left hand over the table. It was adorned with a signet ring embossed with the familiar symbol of her clan at its center: a dirk slashing through a crescent moon. "This is pretty much like a purity ring. Sometimes I hate that bloody ring so much I'd gladly chop my own finger to get rid of it."

"So you've never…"

"Not yet. Simon and I…we kiss and we make out, but I haven't yet taken the big step."

"All that because of your family's rules and that ring?"

Lizzie's gaze drifted away from me and I worried I'd antagonized her. But her thoughts remained calm and placid. She just gave me a shrug. "Partly that and partly because I'm not sure Simon is the one. I like him very much, but it's not a grand-scale, epic, sweeping love." She sighed.

"What about your brother? Does he follow the family's rules?"

Lizzie opened her mouth and I hung as to what she was about to reveal.

"Three beers." Simon cut in.

I mumbled a *thank-you.*

Lizzie raised her pint and threw out a cheerful, *"Slàinte mhòr!"*

My fingers tightened around my glass. I hadn't heard these words since my departure from Scotland. They used to be a disguised toast to Prince Charles Edward Stuart. More than that ring of hers, the girl's words were a reminder to whom she belonged. The MacLeods. And the MacLeods had served the man now known as Bonnie Prince Charlie.

"Cheers!" Both Simon and I shouted back, opting for English.

"Don't forget you're our designated driver." Lizzie pointed at his beer.

"I'm switching to Coke after this cheeky one."

I was about to ask about their summer holidays when the wind rushed through the crowded room and brushed my face. The door of the pub had opened. The salty sea air filled my nostrils, overpowering the human smells. But another scent also reached me, enveloped me. I knew it from my visit to the house on the Scores.

This time I could place it. It belonged to the glens and the moors. It was the scent of the heather that grew there, both floral and earthy.

I stared ahead of me and watched the crowd part. My hands fell flat on the tabletop to steady them. I took in a gulp of air as if I were about to dive into the North Sea. His commanding silhouette filled my sight, slowly coming into focus. The narrow waist. The defined curves of his chest underneath his rugby jersey. The strong line of his neck and fiery curls of hair.

His eyes. Gabriel MacLeod's eyes. They were fixed on me and I recoiled, my back crashing against the bench.

There was fiery anger burning in his stare.

Chapter 3 — Pull and Repel

"You were fantastic!" Lizzie propelled herself into arms that welcomed her in a tight embrace. After a kiss on her temple Gabriel released her, but she stayed cradled against his side.

Standing just a few yards away, I felt him swaying, fighting for his balance. His grip on his sister's shoulder tightened. His nostrils flared, he shut his eyes, and when he opened them again, his sight was blurred. His gaze traced a blazing path over my body, which both confused and unnerved me. I wanted to shrink away and vanish.

I swallowed the lump in my throat and noticed his own throat mirroring my action. The slamming of his heart against his ribcage slowed down and the hostile scowl faded into a frown.

"Gabe, this is Marie," Lizzie volunteered. "Our potential new housemate."

Marie. I heard my name echo in his mind. *Marie.* It was a murmur, a murmur shaped by the gravelly lilt of his voice.

He slowly tilted his head in acknowledgement. "It's nice to meet you, Marie." A forced neutrality was instilled into my name when he said it out loud.

"Nice to meet you too, Gabriel." I caught his gaze. The air between us was so taut I could have pulled it like a rope.

We didn't exchange anything further since his three-men entourage was already taking over our table, dwarfing Simon.

Two of the men could have been interchangeable if it wasn't for their hair color. Hayden and Fergus—as they were introduced to me—had fleshy, rugged faces with the appropriate amount of bruises and cuts required of any respectable rugby player. One was blond, the other had a mane as dark as a moonless night. Both gripped pints of beer with their mighty hands.

Lizzie sat opposite me, remaining at her brother's side. The third man—whom I'd never seen before—took the place next to me on the bench. He winked at me, then ogled my breasts.

"I'm Tobias." The accent was from across the Pond, the drawl furthering the journey to the Southern states. That, the name, and the slanted eyes clarified his identity. I was, after all, very familiar with the MacLeods' family tree and all their affiliates.

"Marie." I nodded at him but kept my expression neutral. I had no intention of flirting back. He wasn't relevant to my plans and hopefully wouldn't become so.

"I'm Lizzie and Gabe's cousin. You just landed in Europe too?"

Apparently I'd already been discussed. Whether that was a good sign was still to be determined.

"I'm from Quebec. And you?"

"Texas."

He shifted his body so that there was no way for me to miss the full expanse of his chest. Human mating rituals definitely sprang from the animal kingdom and I had no interest in partaking. At least not with him.

I shuffled backwards to widen the gap between us. "What are you doing in St. Andrews?"

"What are *you* doing here?"

The question had come in the regular cadence I knew was *his*, but a sharp edge was cut into it. My head turned towards him. Gabriel hadn't missed one word of my introduction to his cousin. Although he wasn't scowling anymore, his voice still hadn't recovered the warmth it had when he'd said my name in the silence of his head. However, he relaxed against the back of his seat. The sleeves of his Oxford blue shirt were rolled up to his elbow. Freckles and hairs, the same red-gold as the rough stubble of his jaw, dotted his sinewy forearms.

No one else at our table uttered a word and, as far as I was concerned, the whole pub could have turned mute because all my senses were drawn to Gabriel.

"I'm studying medicine." I lifted my chin. "What about you?"

"History."

He raised his pint of beer and took a large gulp, his gaze fixed on me over the rim of the glass. With careful precision he laid the glass back on the table. On his index finger was the same signet ring as Lizzie's. From my peripheral vision, I noticed how her head went back-and-forth between her brother and me.

"Besides," Gabriel continued, "I'm a Scot, which is a pretty good reason for me to be at St. Andrews. What's yours?"

Hayden and Fergus's male-giggles punctuated his question. Next to me, Tobias stretched his legs. Doing so, his shoulders touched mine. Gabriel's eyes flickered over his cousin but quickly turned back to rest on me alone.

"My surname is Aberdein," I said without looking away from him. "My family left for Canada during the Highland Clearances."

Fergus did another iteration of the male-giggle followed by a snort. "So you have some Scot in you, lassie."

Hayden contributed with a snort of his own. I wasn't used to dirty banter and my hand moved to my neck. It'd always been my tell.

"I'm glad you look at history through rose-tinted glasses." I bit back at them. "After the Clearances, Gaelic culture was pretty much annihilated and most of the

22

Highlanders were so hungry they had to emigrate. But I guess that's a little bit too far back for you to care."

Gabriel's eyes narrowed on me and I shifted on my seat. His gaze passed to his teammates. It was a pointed look, and without him having to say a word, Hayden broke into a mumbled apology.

"That was a pretty amazing match, guys." Simon opened his mouth for the first time since the newcomers' arrival. *Bless him.* I was grateful for the change of topic.

Gabriel kept glaring at me for stretched seconds but abandoned my interrogation. Instead he launched into a technical summary of the afternoon's game for Simon and Lizzie's benefit. His change of focus left me curiously hollow. On his right, Hayden and Fergus broke into a form of Neanderthal dialogue that they thankfully kept between themselves.

I released a faint sigh—which I hope no one noticed— and leaned my back against the wall. Our first official encounter hadn't exactly turned into the flirtatious banter I'd hoped for.

"Beer shouldn't be drunk warm." Tobias wasn't participating in the detailed game debrief the others were involved in. Instead he was deeply involved in the sizing of my breasts.

My answer was to force a sip of the beverage down my throat followed by another one for good measure. The drink was now at room temperature and left a stale taste in my mouth. I winced.

"Let me get you another one." He started to stand but I stopped him, my hand over his bare forearm.

He stared down at my fingers. They were perfectly formed hands, nothing remarkable about them. Turned ones, like me, don't stand out among humans. There are no anatomical or biological signs that differentiate us, except our peculiar retractable canines. I have a heart that beats, lungs that fill with oxygen, one liver, two kidneys, functioning reproductive organs. Nothing is missing to my human panoply. Stramos like Louis and Fiu like Everett—born from Stramos and humans—can also pass unnoticed.

But Tobias Svenson had no reason to be aware of my world. Still, his gaze lingered over my hand. He slowly sat back down, his gesture robotic.

"Thanks, but there's no need to. I don't drink much anyway."

"Maybe it's better that way." He eyed me again but I didn't shuffle on my seat this time. "You're not built for it."

That was a fact. Louis used to call me his *Toute Petite*, his little one. The nickname was well deserved, if only because of my diminutive height and frame. But what I'd been able to endure from my father felt plain dismissive coming from this boy.

"Is that so?" It was my turn to stare at his beer now. "Maybe you should watch what you're drinking too." I nodded to the rugby players on the other side of the table, whose stature Tobias didn't match. "You might not be built for it either."

Fire flashed across his eyes and the heat reached my face. But he put a mask on it and I switched subject. "Will you be staying at the house on the Scores?"

"The house on the Scores? You make the place sound straight out of a horror movie." Another long sip of beer. "But to answer your question, no. The only guest room isn't going to be available for much longer. Or so I've heard."

"Sorry about that." We both knew I wasn't.

Tobias's cell rang and he took it out of his pocket. After checking the caller ID, he apologized and answered, turning his back on me. Poor sod, he could very well take that call outside and I could still hear every single word he said. But Tobias Svenson was none of my concern and I wouldn't eavesdrop.

That left me on my own, as the rest of the group was gathering on the other side of the table. I kept my hands from reaching to my neck again and glued them tightly on my lap instead.

His laugh rippled throughout my body like a smooth round stone skimming on the River Tweed. Its warmth wrapped around me and in that moment, all I wanted was to bask in it. I couldn't allow myself to do that. I also couldn't keep my gaze from scurrying over the tabletop and stealing a glance at him.

Gabriel's head was thrown backwards, his shoulders more than filling the back of his chair. One hand circled the bottom of his pint, the other rested on Lizzie's shoulder, tucking her tightly in against him, keeping her safe. I fought the sudden and shameful need for that very protection. I looked up at his face to remember who he was. It didn't help because all I noticed next was the dimple creasing his left cheek and the perfectly square white teeth bared by his laugh.

He looked sweet, innocent, and a lingering emotion—doubt?—crept inside me. Here was the monster I'd set out to destroy, not for who he was but what he'd become and who he belonged to.

My enemy.

Did he sense the wave of questions that assaulted me? He straightened up and our gazes clashed and locked. The sparkles in his eyes vanished to be replaced by a stillness—warm and welcoming—that encompassed only me. His genuine strength pulled my spirit to him, and for the next seconds, I let him explore me. I heard him whisper my name again and again as if it were a question. The sound of his all-male rumble dried my mouth, forcing me to lick my lips. The depth of his eyes turned fierce and fiery. Heat swirled in tendrils around us and I wanted them to engulf us and whisk us into oblivion.

A loud crackle exploded near us. My skin burned under the sudden surge in temperature. I recoiled. A pathetic squeal escaped from my mouth. I must have bumped against Tobias because his hands landed on my waist. I searched for the cause of my pain and found the fireplace nearby was filled with flames. They'd found reborn strength. None of them had reached me fortunately. A sigh of relief whizzed from between my parted lips. The burning heat had already receded.

"Are you okay?" Tobias asked.

I summoned back my wits. Lizzie frowned at me with concern. Of course my attention glided sideways to her brother. I wanted—needed—him to see me again. His gaze was cast downwards across the table and riveted on my waist. I felt the increasing pressure of Tobias's fingers on me, branding me like a poker. I pushed them away.

"I'm fine." The statement came in a croak, so I cleared my throat and repeated, "I'm fine. Thank you."

I ignored Hayden and Fergus's bovine expressions, responded to Lizzie and Simon with a tight smile, and caught up with Gabriel. He didn't scowl or challenge me anymore. It was a relief as I wasn't prepared for a mental fight. He simply looked puzzled and—if anything—a bit lost.

I didn't notice the girl approaching either. I should have because she was remarkably pretty. When she opened her mouth I caught a whiff of her sugary perfume. The scent wasn't cheap, more like a child's strawberry-flavored sweet.

"Gabe, I'm so sorry I missed the game." The girl lodged herself against his back, her hands resting on his shoulders. She bent forward, and her silky curtain of blond hair fell along her face. When she kissed his cheek, he stiffened, as if tearing his eyes off me was an effort. Or, more likely, it was because he had to let go of his sister. I still couldn't sneak into his flow of consciousness.

"Alice." Gabriel welcomed her. "It's nice to see you."

I'd seen her before. She was part of the close circle of friends that gravitated around Gabriel. She'd seemed keen to capture his interest but, from what I'd observed so far, he hadn't indulged her. What if she was part of the clique that followed him to their country house, Hollaroch, last weekend?

What if he'd finally decided she was indeed to his liking? This would significantly complicate my prospects here in St. Andrews. Her plump and rosy-cheeked beauty wouldn't be easy to push aside.

Gabriel offered her his seat and took a vacant one from the next table. It meant Fergus and Hayden had to shift further down the bench. I couldn't openly stare at her so I sipped my warmish beer while the rest of them exchanged jokes about their time at the MacLeods' estate. *Yes*, she'd spent the weekend with him.

Alice blushed and kept throwing sideways glances at Gabriel. He hadn't made a move to hold her—or kiss her—but his arm was stretched over the back of her chair. It was hardly a claim, but there was enough ease in it for anyone to acknowledge their connection. The sight of that connection felt like a fist burying into my stomach.

I managed to stay at the table for another hour. From time to time, Gabriel's eyes on me tingled my skin but I chose to ignore him. The World's End had packed up with a thick crowd and the surrounding heat started to overwhelm me. The human noises and smells disturbed me. They filled my mouth with an acrid taste. Far too many hearts thrashed blood through engorged veins. I hadn't fed and Lizzie's chocolate bar hadn't even come close to fulfilling my needs

It was safer to make a break for it. Apologizing to my neighbor, I stood and waved my fingers at Lizzie. "I'll be back in a sec." Hopefully my squeamish behavior hadn't made her question offering me a room.

When I stepped outside, the sun had almost set. The darkness hadn't yet settled over the sea but its somber hues matched those of the cloudless sky. The wind had subsided but had a colder bite to it than in the afternoon. I pulled my arms around my chest and ventured away from the pub's porch towards the rocks that led from the peninsula into the water. I lost track of time, let myself go, and floated away into myself.

Since my return to Scotland, my perception of the past had sharpened and it was a double-edged change. For decades I'd suppressed my memories of Everett, of the short time we'd shared together, of the happiness we'd created for ourselves. After Culloden, I'd forbidden myself to think of him. My quest for vengeance had been my way of remembrance. But I was back to the land of my birth, of my first love, and memories were taking shape and colors again.

His voice cut through my journey down the years. I looked over my shoulder and found him heading towards his car, the same model as his sister's. He wasn't alone; Alice snuggled against his side and his arm slung around her. She stared up at him and the glint in her eyes was close to worship.

She looked at him but he looked at me.

After helping her inside the car, he asked her to wait and closed the door. In ten strides—I counted each of them—he came to stand in front of me. We'd never been so close before and I realized for the first time the large gap between our heights. If I were to take one step towards him, my nose would nestle right in the center of his chest. Was his skin there all soft or covered with russet hairs? I knew it'd feel warm under my touch. I shivered and the cold wasn't the culprit.

Gabriel removed his sleeveless puffed-up jacket, and in one move laid it across my shoulders. He adjusted the collar around my neck, the tips of his fingers and the backs of his thumbs brushing against my jawline, teasing my skin. His hands became still. He stared at them, almost cradled against the curve of my throat, next to my jugular.

The wind whistled around us and was all I could hear. Gabriel's emotions, once again, were veiled to me. So were his thoughts. His expression was neither a scowl nor a smile, and he'd become so still he might have been a statue. But his hair moved with the wind and came and went in front of his eyes. Even in the descending darkness, I couldn't miss the fiery shine of his wild curls. Finally, Gabriel broke the contact, his arms returning to his sides.

"Thank you, but I'm about to go back inside so I won't need it." I forced my voice into a neutral tone.

"Lizzie is very keen on you coming to live with us and I want to make my sister happy. This means your bedroom will be opposite mine. I don't want your sniffing and sneezing to wake me up."

An imaginary green light flashed in front of my eyes. I was *in*. "Good sleep is essential to good health. You should indeed be protective of it."

The corner of his mouth curled and he tilted his head sideways as if he was trying to decipher my mystery. When he spoke, the lilt of his voice had thickened. "I'm a very protective man, Marie. Especially of my wee sister."

He wasn't smiling anymore and I wasn't certain what to read in his words: a promise or a warning? So I let him elaborate.

"Lizzie chose you. I let her because it's important she makes her own choices. Her own mistakes."

"You're calling me a mistake?" I put the right dose of repressed outrage into my question. It was pure acting because I had every intention of indeed being Elizabeth MacLeod's greatest mistake. Perhaps her last one too.

"I'm saying that I look after my sister. She believes you're her friend. Stay one and we'll be as happy as Larry. Disappoint her, betray her—" he paused and inched a fraction closer, "—hurt her, and I will hurt you in return."

"I don't like being threatened."

"That wasn't a threat, lassie. Take it as one of the rules of the house."

He took a quick glance over his shoulder, towards the entrance of the pub, then looked back at me. "You should go back inside. People are getting drunk, and staying outside alone isn't the smartest idea."

"Are you getting protective of me now?"

"You're feisty, Marie, I can already see that. But you're also not much bigger than a kitten, so I'd feel better if you went back to the others."

I let the silence hang between us then nodded.

"Plus, as pissed as some of those guys are tonight, they're bound to go after a pretty girl like you."

"And what do you think they'll like about me?" I think I was flirting. "My *pretty* eyes?"

"They're drunkards, not poets. Likely they'll ogle your tight arse."

Heat journeyed down my throat and spread in the pit of my stomach, then lower. "Would you ogle it too?"

He dismissed my question with a shake of his head. Humor gleamed in his eyes though. "Nah. I'm a poet at all times. Eyes do it for me, and yours are the color of a thirty-year-old Talisker."

"That's all very hypothetical anyway since your girlfriend is waiting for you in your car."

"These were mere conjectures. Of course."

"I'm glad we had that clarified."

I rounded him and started marching back towards the pub. He stayed by my side all the way to the entrance door, which he opened for me. The human smells and noises hit me hard again, but I had to rejoin Lizzie. Gabriel was otherwise occupied and I would have to bide my time where he was concerned.

"You can leave now with a clear conscience. I'll be safe. So will your sister, who, by the way, might not be as defenseless as you think."

"A girl is never too safe."

I heard the underlying sadness in his words. The regret. *There* was my opening, I thought, the fissure I could open wide and explore.

"Good night, Gabriel," I said confidently.

"Good night, *a leanaigh*."

I stepped inside and held his gaze until the door closed between us.

A leanaigh.

My little one.

Chapter 4 — Happening

I hurried along the pavement, flipping up the collar of my coat. Tonight the wind blew straight in from the sea. The tide was high and waves ate at the narrow band of the beach. The marine scent, mixed with that of burnt fireplace wood, engulfed my nose and mouth, filling my lungs. This was what a Scottish autumn should smell like.

The crowd was slowly deserting the Scores. After spending my morning moving my meagre belongings into my new room, I'd spent hours at the library. As a second-year medical student, the focus of my research should have been of a scientific nature. It wasn't, at least if you attached history to humanities. Louis used to recognize in events of the past no more than the recurrence of a limited number of patterns. As to what drove those patterns—pride, lust, hate, and above all love—they were mere impulses born from hormonal imbalances.

In any case I'd spent my afternoon hidden in St. Andrews's library with my favorite modern toy—my laptop—gathering information on those who had inserted themselves into my plans, namely Tobias Svenson and Alice Cameron. I hadn't learned much, unfortunately, except that Alice's pedigree, tracing back to Robert the Bruce, was a perfect contender to become the next Lady MacLeod. The fact she happened to be studying at St. Andrews at the same time as Gabriel was so well-timed I suspected Nathaniel was somehow behind it.

I pushed the gate open on the pathway to the house on the Scores. Tonight would be my first night here, my first night spent a corridor away from him. In front of the door I took the keys out from my bag. My hand was still buried in it, rummaging through the mess inside, when a sense of foreboding crashed over me.

A shiver of dread whipped my bones. My spine stiffened. I didn't need the lantern hanging from the porch to see. I didn't even need to turn around and face him. His scent was one I remembered all too well. Powder and musk, with a touch of lemongrass.

Lawrence Beaumont. The Stramos who stole my vengeance.

Captain Lawrence Beaumont from the 20th Regiment although I doubted he still went by his eighteenth-century rank. The last time I'd had the misfortune to cross his path was on a fateful night in Hollaroch, not long after my siring.

I swiveled round, as nothing good could come from keeping my back to him. Quite frankly, nothing good had ever come from this man whatsoever, whether you looked him in the eyes or not.

"Good evening Lawrence, I'm glad to see you didn't come alone." My voice didn't betray the dread building up from the pit of my stomach. That was a miracle in itself. "We wouldn't want you to feel lonely."

Two brutes escorted him. Judging by the width of their shoulders beneath their long black coats, they would be fierce competition even for Aiden and Fergus. Unlike Lawrence, his acolytes were Turned, but should anything erupt between us, I doubted my wits would be enough to save my skin. My prospects would be even poorer if Lawrence lowered himself and got his Stramos hands—or, rather, fangs—dirty. As they put it nowadays, I was *screwed*.

Where Stramos originated from was a secret never shared with lowly Turned like me. Even Louis had never revealed anything to me. I knew they were older than any living

Turned, *millennium* older. With the exception of the silver hues in their eyes, they didn't differ much from us. At least in appearance.

Like us, they needed blood—although in smaller quantities—and could be killed in the same way: a wooden stake in the heart, a chopping off of the head, or by the first light of the solstice sun. There was also the more time-consuming process of exsanguination. However their physical and mental abilities far surpassed ours. Their senses were even more sharpened than ours. Their strength, speed, resistance to pain made them well-oiled, lethal machines. They also healed faster. Like me, Lawrence could read human minds but he also had the power to manipulate them into doing the most horrendous deeds.

Lawrence took three deliberate steps to join me under the porch. "Good evening, sweet Marie. It has been a while."

How ironic that such a morally debased heart would beat under those perfect features. Lawrence Beaumont was a long-nosed, high-cheeked specimen of beauty, with hair the color of a ripe wheat field. The only feature betraying the darkness inside were his thin, lopsided lips. When he smiled, they almost didn't conceal his sharp canines. He looked ready to drain you to your last drop of blood at any moment…which he was.

"As for friends," he continued with his clipped English accent, "I have heard you lost all of yours last solstice." He raised his hand and brushed the tips of his fingers along my jawline. "That was unfortunate. Be assured you have my fullest sympathy."

He was as dangerous to me as a spike in a Hunter's hand, but the mention of my family's demise lit sparks of anger within me. I batted his hand away. "What do you want?"

The arch of his left eyebrow was engraved in my memory. It would have a certain charm on a less abhorrent being. I loathed it on him.

"I should throw the question straight back at you: What

do *you* want? If I have been informed correctly, the very house you are about to enter was built by a MacLeod, and its current inhabitants are his descendants."

I kept my mouth so tightly shut that my teeth started to grind against each other.

Oblivious to my distress—or perhaps very aware of it—Lawrence forged on. "If my memory serves me right, your dear late husband…what was his name?" He scratched his chin in mock contemplation. "Ah yes, Everett Marsden. That late husband of yours was impaled *then* beheaded by Gabriel MacLeod during that messy day at the Battle of Culloden. Poor chap." He tsked and shook his head, then leaned forward so that the silver of his eyes filled my entire vision. His next breath with its coppery tang struck me. "And it was the current MacLeod who burned your own Maker and his pathetic little tribe of Canadian Turned only three months ago."

"Get to the point." No one gave Lawrence Beaumont orders and he pressed his lips together. For now, he kept his temper on a leash.

"Marie Aberdein, you are confusing me," he purred. "Such a skittish little person you are and still I fear you have set yourself an entirely pointless vendetta."

"Even if you're right, how is it any of your concern? And since we're discussing intentions, what are you doing in Scotland? You used to consider anywhere north of London as a step back into the Dark Ages."

He straightened and I welcomed the newly introduced distance between us.

"Since you emigrated to North America, things changed on this side of the Pond, my dear. How should I put it? MacLeod and I have called a ceasefire. Those reporting to me and following my rules can stop fearing the Hunter and his troops. Those who do not swear allegiance to me or break my rules become fair game. For me *and* Nathaniel."

"What a nice little arrangement you have there. Should I

34

congratulate you on your promotion to ruler of the British underworld?"

"I am keeping our kind safe for the first time in centuries. With that disease eating their blood, Turned are weaker than ever. I will not have one of them—and a female at that—compromise my efforts."

Indeed, a lot had changed while Louis and I had lived hidden in Fjord Saguenay. Stramos had never cared for us Turned, but they needed us to perpetuate their lavish lifestyle. To them, we were no more than enablers, servants, whores, or at best bodyguards. But something as unprecedented as a truce with the MacLeod Hunter, surely we'd have heard about it on the grapevine?

"When did this ceasefire start?" I'd struck a nerve because he narrowed his eyes and didn't answer. "The ink isn't dry, is it?"

This new peace was so fresh and fragile it could be trampled over by someone as insignificant as me. What I didn't understand was why I was still breathing. So I asked again, with an authority I didn't have, "What do you want?"

"You. It is you that I want." Weakness—longing—flashed through his stare.

It didn't last. The flicker in his eyes was gone as soon as I saw it. But I'd been aware of it, so had he. Lawrence cast his gaze downwards and the pull he had on my mind faded. My back bumped against the door. My next exhalation was a rush of air as if it were my last breath. Perhaps it would be.

"I looked for you." He spoke so softly it was almost a whisper. "I looked for you everywhere. I killed him... I hunted the Hunter and I killed him for you. I thought you would stay with me afterwards, but Berthière whisked you away, and after Hollaroch I never heard of you again."

"*I* wanted to be the one killing the Hunter. For what he did to my husband, but you took away my reason for becoming—" I swept a downcast glance over my body, "—*this*."

"I saved your life. Do you think a little thing like you, freshly sired, untrained, had a chance against a Hunter? And in any place, at Hollaroch, the stronghold of his clan?"

"I had everything planned. I'd bought his servant. I had MacLeod drugged. His death was mine. *Mine*. Why?" I yelled, then bit my tongue. I couldn't attract anyone else's attention, so I coaxed my voice under control. "Why would you take that away from me?"

His stare nailed me against the door. "You know why. After Culloden, after Marsden's death, I offered you my protection…my devotion, to you and your unborn child, but you discarded it as if it was no more than a passing fancy of mine. This was my way of proving to you that I—that I…"

I heard Lawrence Beaumont stammer for the first time in our two centuries of shared history.

"That you could kill? Slaughter our race's oldest enemy without so much as a scratch?" The image of Gabriel MacLeod's head torn from the rest of his dismembered body hadn't lost any of its potency despite the passing years. I could still smell the stench of blood and gore.

Once again, his hand was on me, stroking the nape of my neck. "I heard you were looking for a cure with Berthière and others like you who refused to drain humans. I was scared for you. I searched for you, Marie. Everywhere. But I didn't hear about you and your Maker until it was too late. Nathaniel MacLeod had already taken care of your clique."

I grabbed his wrist and felt his lethal strength under my touch. I attempted to pull his hand away from me by yanking his forearm frantically. It didn't move so much as a millimeter. "Get off me!"

His escort appeared in my peripheral vision. Lawrence raised his free hand as a silent order for them to stay back. The mere increased pressure of his fingers on my throat could pulverize my bones, so he had no need for support should he choose to finish me.

I ignored any survival instinct I possessed. My own

weakness morphed my anger into furor, a ball of fire swirling inside my chest, gaining internal momentum.

"Get off me!" I hammered every syllable distinctly. "You don't want me. All you want is power. You killed the Hunter because it got you a seat at the European Council. And you're the reason Everett died, you and your Stramos friends. He died for a cause that wasn't his anymore. He wanted out, out of this dark world you cherish. But he was also your friend and didn't want to look like a coward. So he went and fought."

Lawrence's chivalrous mask evaporated. "I did what I had to do for our kind. Culloden was the perfect opportunity to get rid of the Hunters in the Highlands clans without attracting unwanted human attention. I almost succeeded. Only the Macleod line has survived. Sacrifices had to be made on our side to achieve that purpose."

"Pity you didn't sacrifice yourself." Everett's smile when he bid me goodbye the night before the battle shot in front of my eyes. For once, every detail of him was vivid, colors and features, and the memory stabbed me. "You're a coward and I despise you." I spat at Lawrence, wishing my saliva were acid and would burn his perfect face.

I had no time to dive or flee. My reflexes couldn't match his speed. One second I had my feet firmly rooted to the ground, the next he had me pinned against the door. My legs jerked. I fought for breath as his fingers tightened around my throat. I gasped and croaked a pathetic groan while the light of the lantern above us flickered and died. The two men had turned their backs on us, watching the dark alley leading to the street. The house was empty of all heartbeats.

I was alone.

"Watch your mouth, Marie."

He pounced on mine, his tongue sliding through my lips. I bit it and he swore through the kiss, then broke away. I prayed for him to release me…or kill me—right then, right there. I'd survived many wounds but I wouldn't survive this one. I couldn't survive Lawrence soiling me.

"Tell me, pretty one, how long has it been since you tasted a Stramos's blood? Did that old wrinkled Master of yours indulge you from time to time?"

"He'd never do that."

Louis was my father, my only family. Stramos's blood was a rare aphrodisiac, one that had fueled the lust of my kind for centuries.

"His loss then." Lawrence leaned forward and smeared his blood along the edges of my lips with the tip of his tongue.

Bile rose through my throat. I tried to turn my face away but he cupped my cheeks so tightly that I feared my skull would implode. His knee shot up between my thighs and made me jolt in pain. He was hard against me.

I was a fool. A bloody fool. I'd let my anger take over and now I'd never be able to make the MacLeods pay.

"My turn to taste you, pretty Marie." As his knee moved away, his whole body placated me so forcefully that my back must have left an imprint on the door.

I squirmed and thrashed while his mouth traced a wet path from the corner of my mouth, across my cheek, and down the curve of my neck. When he planted his teeth into the tender skin there, I screamed. It had happened to me before. I'd fed Turned friends in distress with my blood, but I'd never felt the tearing and the burning caused by a Stramos's bite since the night Louis sired me.

I kept trying to wriggle but his body covered me entirely. The blood loss and the Stramos's bite stole my spirit. My eyelids fluttered. My limbs became a dead weight. All I could feel was his hard length against my belly. I'd have thrown up if I'd had enough strength left within me. When his hands reached my breasts, a single tear traipsed down my cheek and tipped over my upper lip.

There was an explosion of noise and more swearing. Not from Lawrence but from his two Turned bodyguards. My eyes had rolled upwards so all I saw was the lattice of branches and leaves formed by the maple tree above us.

Lawrence broke off from his bloodsucking. "What the hell!" He checked over his shoulder. "Dammit."

The Turned's limbs raised and fell in all directions, while a third silhouette pummeled and kicked their powerful bodies. At least that was the perception I had from a recess of my consciousness. Lawrence cradled my chin and lifted my face so that our eyes met. He was searching within me, but my sight was so blurry his features had lost their sharpness.

"Time to let you go, Marie," he whispered. "Do not think for an instant this matter is resolved. Neither you nor your plans for the young MacLeods. I will be in touch soon."

The kiss he gave me was searing and deep, as if he wasn't in a rush to flee. His tongue explored my mouth one last time, and the invasion stole a plaintive moan from someplace deep inside me. It was as if that moan intensified the mess in the front yard. One of the bodyguards doubled over and crashed on the stones of the pathway. Two other shadows continued their fighting dance.

Lawrence deposited my crumpled mass against the door, my head bobbing forward. He was a Stramos and you didn't see a Stramos turn his back on you and move away. One moment he knelt in front of me, the next he'd vanished. I heard his whistle though. The remaining bodyguard lost interest in the fight and circled around his adversary, keeping his defensive stance. He ran as soon as the path to the gate was clear. We—Turned ones—didn't have the ability to disappear in a puff.

My back slid along the door and I was now leaning on my side. The cold stone of the porch against the side of my face calmed my dizziness. Still, I lay there and caught a glimpse of the pair of sneakers sprinting and closing in on me. They made a squishing sound on the stones of the alleyway. A form wearing sports gear crouched down while one hand slid along my neck. The other lifted my shoulders to sit me up.

"Marie." Gabriel's voice was thick with fear. Still he'd said my name with the same wonder as yesterday. "Marie, look at me."

I opened my mouth but no sound escaped. I ordered myself to look up and answer him with my eyes. When I met his gaze, I saw what he saw and it shamed me. I could never be that pathetic clown with the shape of her lips fattened with blood, the red trailing down my neck. I recoiled and pushed him away with despair stronger than the hate I'd shown Lawrence.

"Don't touch me." I curled my body in a ball.

He jumped back as if I'd spat on him. His eyes stayed on me though while he raked his hand through the thick curls of his hair. I was too weak to hear his thoughts but there was no need for the effort. Fear and concern were etched across his face, and the frown between his eyes was so deep it looked like a scar.

His lower lip was cut, releasing a narrow path of blood. I resisted its appealing scent. I was weak, low on my own blood, and craving more. I covered my mouth with my hands and prayed he hadn't heard the threatening click of my canines.

Gabriel swore. It was directed at himself. Very carefully he extended his hands so that they cupped my cheeks to raise my face. It was torture to me with the blood pulsing inside his wrists so close to my mouth. The flushing sound echoed in my head, taking my urge to feed to the most primal depths of my being. I had to fight it to spare his life because bleeding MacLeod dry now wasn't the plan.

I threw his arms away. They came back to circle around my shoulders and quieten me anyway. I kept fighting, pulling and pushing, but he was stronger so I stopped moving with only a stupid hiccup revealing the turmoil within me.

"Hush…" He held me against him and caressed my hair. I let myself focus on the rhythm of his touch. It carried me back to my childhood and my mother. Sometimes, she'd done exactly that. "Hush," he whispered again.

My fangs retracted.

Time passed but I had no idea how much. We could have been there, under the unlit porch of the house on the Scores, for a minute. Or it could just as well have been an hour. Behind us, I heard the retreating steps of the second Turned. Gabriel let him go but kept me against him, his body a warm blanket around my shattered soul. He gently pulled me across his lap, tightening his grip and rocking our bodies together, back and forth. The steady thumping of his heart replaced the buzz between my ears. I matched my breathing to his and my thoughts gradually cleared.

"Marie?"

"Yes." I was surprised to still be able to find my voice.

"I need to look at you and check you're okay." His mouth moved against my hair. "Will you let me?"

"The blood isn't mine." My reply was steeped in panic. I couldn't risk a journey to the hospital. As a doctor—yes—but never as a patient. They might run tests on my blood and that would be most problematic.

"I need to make sure."

He sat me down effortlessly in front of him. His hand started probing the back of my skull, my shoulders, the lengths of my arms, and finally settled back on my neck. He extracted his cell from his front pocket and lit up the area where the dried blood was caked on my skin. Depending on the exact amount of time that had elapsed since the attack, what he would find beneath it could cause mayhem. I resisted his attempt to bend my neck, but then I took a chance and let him do it. His fingers picked the dried blood away while he inspected the skin underneath.

Whatever he expected to find, it wasn't there. He exhaled, making his chest curve inward and his shoulders slump. I mirrored his reaction. I must have already healed and the marks of the bite had disappeared. That was how Stramos bites worked.

"Can you stand up?"

I nodded and let him bring me back on my feet. He wound his arm around my waist to keep me from collapsing. "It's warm inside. Once we're there, we can decide what to do next."

Next? I didn't intend to do anything except pretend nothing had happened. I'd drawn attention on myself in a manner that wasn't appropriate. After all, one doesn't set out on the path of seduction with tangled hair, a face smeared with blood, and marred virtue.

I let him carry me across the hallway into the kitchen anyway, my arms looped around his neck. Carefully, as if he still feared I'd broken something, he deposited me on one of the stools around the island. He switched on the two pendant lamps hanging from the wood-paneled ceiling over us. I was grateful the light they dispensed wasn't too harsh over my miserable appearance. Vanity can show the top of its head at the most surprising moments.

Gabriel busied himself, taking a folded napkin from one of the drawers and wetting it under the tap. He walked back to me and I stiffened, keeping my eyes glued on my hands joined over my lap. His scent was a mix of sweat, cologne and blood. I already knew his would taste sweet. But I had to control my thirst. I had to bridle my true nature, until my body recovered.

"Marie, will you let me clean the blood away?" The gravel of his voice washed over me with warmth.

I was thirsty for more than his blood and it was simply from him talking.

I lifted my eyes from the center of his chest up to his square chin. His jaw was locked but his eyes were begging. I thought I saw guilt in their slanted shapes, as if he were the one who'd attacked me.

"You saved me." The words tumbled out of my mouth. My eyes followed my fingers when they touched the split corner of his lip. It was swollen but it wasn't bleeding anymore. But his eyelid had swollen into a red puff. "You're the one in need of care."

His shrug was boyish and his smile creased the dimple in his right cheek. "I was at rugby practice tonight. That counts for most of the damage."

"You sure know how to fight, Gabriel MacLeod."

Although the MacLeods' heir was to be kept oblivious to the underworld until his twenty-first birthday, he'd been trained from an early age. It had always been that way.

The tip of my index finger climbed from his mouth to his bruised eye. The skin underneath felt rough and scratched. I brushed the line of his cheekbone, and his whole being became still under my touch. Heat radiated from him and tingled my skin. We shared our next breath as if sipping the air from the same cup. Standing opposite me, he was a mountain of energy, buzzing and threatening to break through and engulf me.

Gabriel had his sight fixed on the base of my neck, the exact spot where the Stramos's bite had healed. His eyelashes stretched like the wings of a butterfly and threw shadows over his own cuts and bruises. My fingers left the curves of his face and reached for his hand that still clenched the wet napkins. I pulled it towards me. He let me but the tendons on the back of his hand tensed under my command.

He took one step towards me, filling my space in front of the chair, his legs on either side of mine, and brought his free hand to rest on my thigh. A faint current sprang up from under his palm and ran up to light up warm sparkles between my legs. I leaned my head sideways and welcomed the fresh touch of the cloth. With deliberate precision, he started wiping the blood from my neck. Drops of water dripped down the valley between my breasts. When he'd completed his task, he turned the cloth between his fingers. With the clean part of it, he padded the contours of my mouth, where were drawn the traces of Lawrence's kiss. I shut my eyes to hide my shame but let Gabriel pursue his ministrations.

The shameful truth of that moment was that I never wanted it to end. I wanted this boy—this man—to care for me and attend to every parcel of me that was broken or cut or shattered. I wanted him to heal and cure the disease destroying my blood. I wanted him to fix me. I wanted him to make me live again. If he had to make me forget my purpose or those whose memories I had sworn to avenge…so be it.

But Gabriel retreated and the new emptiness between us cut a ravine I almost tumbled into. My eyes opened wide as I searched for a point to anchor myself on. I found none and let out a helpless cry. Gabriel held me by my shoulders and kept me from falling.

"Right, I'm taking you to the hospital." Fear quickened his speech.

His grip on me had replaced my spine, but I shook him away nevertheless. "Don't! Please don't. I'll be fine."

"You want to be a doctor but you squeal like a skinned rabbit each time I mention the hospital."

"I'm not squealing. Don't ask again."

Gabriel kept holding me, his fingers clasped under my arms to support me, the lengths of his thumbs in line with my collarbones. I touched his wrists but made no effort to yank them away as I had done earlier with Lawrence. Gabriel froze. His mouth twitched as if my touch had hurt him. I tried to drill into his soul. Once again, nothing.

Nothing.

All I could spy in Gabriel Macleod were fleeting spurts of emotions or thoughts so loud they rippled like a voice inside his mind, but soon vanished. That was about it, and it was certainly unusual. Had his father make him ingest Stramos blood without his knowledge? Stramos blood had that temporary effect. In my two hundred and fifty years, there wasn't a single human being whose soul I hadn't been able to read. The only exceptions were the Hunters, who were beyond our reach.

Was he one already? That couldn't be. If I had any doubts, my encounter with Lawrence and the *ceasefire* news had confirmed that Nathaniel was still in charge, and there never were two acting Hunters in the same clan.

"You can't live here." Gabriel's statement fell between us like the guillotine.

It must have looked like I'd regained enough control because he stopped holding me up, took two steps back, threw the cloth on the countertop, and strode around the island to stand opposite me.

The mass of granite blocked my access to him. I held on to it so tightly my knuckles turned white. "Why not?"

"Because of what happened tonight."

"What do you think happened tonight?" I might very well have opened the proverbial can of worms.

He escaped the hold of my gaze. "I don't know yet, but this place isn't safe anymore."

"Maybe we should call the police."

This idea had the merit of pulling his attention back to me. There was nowhere to hide from his authority. "We won't."

"They attacked—"

"I'll make them pay." He leaned against the island. His posture emphasized the width of his shoulders and the weight of his words. "I promise you, Marie Aberdein, whoever attacked you tonight will regret it. I *swear* to you: I'll make them pay. But in the meantime, you must get away from here. I'll talk to Lizzie. I'll expl—"

"I'm not going anywhere." I jumped to my feet and my sudden drive helped me maintain my stance.

"You're being stubborn, lass. What is it about you anyway? I felt it…I felt it back at the World's End, you—"

"Hi guys!" Down the hallway, a door slammed. Footsteps closed in. "I'm late, sorry. This study group is driving me nuts. They can't get to the point and…" Lizzie's blabbering went on and on.

We didn't listen, too occupied as we were with our private duel. A muscle on Gabriel's jaw started to pulse.

"Lizzie must not know about tonight," he ordered, but I heard his uncertainty. "She'll get upset. All I want is to protect her. I—"

"I won't tell her."

His shoulders drooped. "Thank you."

"I need a place to live and here is better than anywhere

else. If you really think I'm not safe, then we should go to the police. If you don't want that, then let me stay." I took a big inhale to recover from my ultimatum. "Deal?"

A bolt of anger flashed through his eyes but Lizzie's voice was drawing closer.

"Deal."

When she entered the kitchen, I took the now bloody cloth from the top of the island and buried it in the pocket of my coat, all the time watching him. I read defeat in the bend of his neck and his now clenched fists.

Gabriel Macleod and I now shared a secret.

Chapter 5 — Memories.

The morning after Lawrence's attack started with an early swoon.

I dragged myself out of bed, my neck still stiff from the bite, my head spinning. From the bottom of the dresser, inside my traveling bag, I dug out my favorite pick-me-up: a pack of O-negative. I snapped the cap away and brought it to my lips. It tasted stale and rancid but I had no choice so I sipped the entire pack in under a minute.

I placed the empty pack in a plastic bag. It'll be disposed in a public bin on my way to my lectures. After rinsing my mouth with water from the tap, I texted my supplier at St. Andrews Hospital and scheduled a meeting for later that day. But showering and getting dressed were such a struggle that I doubled the order. It wouldn't solve my problem but it might buy me some time.

Forty years ago, we found out that the only blood sustaining Turned is the one we drain ourselves directly from humans. And by *directly* I mean *fangs-in-flesh*. Animal or blood packs we get from hospitals or blood banks don't do the trick anymore. We can feed on it but the disease keeps spreading if we do, and with it its symptoms: weakness, somnolence, weight loss, anemia…until cell degeneration starts and we die. Why? That was what we'd tried to figure out for decades in Saguenay.

The risk went beyond the simple wellbeing of Turned.

We could feed from humans without killing them, but *accidents* were frequent with Turned losing control and sucking their prey dry. Not the best way to keep our kind under-the-radar in a social-media world. Instagram could be our curse.

The dizzy spells had started shortly after I graduated from Princeton and so had the unending tests Louis ran on my blood. We moved north, to Newfoundland, and then Quebec where some sick Turned ones hid with us to seek the cure Louis and I worked on.

I kicked the memories into a corner and set my mind on coffee. While human food doesn't satisfy Turned, caffeine has an undeniable effect on us. Blimey, so does alcohol. I needed another pick-me-up and it was my chance to test the coffee machine I'd admired in the MacLeod's kitchen. The ability to produce the perfectly bitter and coarse beverage topped with fluffy cream at the mere touch of a button fascinated my eighteenth-century self. I was deliberating between a cappuccino and a mocha latte when the dizziness struck again.

I doubled over and placed my hands flat on the kitchen counter to support myself. Louis's voice echoed in my head. *Don't forget to breathe, Little One. In and Out.* I applied myself to inhaling and exhaling. *Always through your nose,* I heard him say as if he were right there next to me. My nostrils flared to follow his advice.

Unfortunately, that morning, it wasn't enough. The weakness didn't recede. I opened my eyes but my sight was still filled with a thousand stars flashing at its periphery. I leaned further forward, resting my forehead on the cold granite of the countertop. It helped even so slightly until my stomach lurched. I swallowed hard to fight back the retching movement.

I was so overwhelmed I didn't pay attention to the steps behind me. Hands circled my waist from behind. Heat enveloped me. His palms moved up to curl around my shoulders and carefully pull my upper body back into full standing position. I felt the hardness of his chest against my back, and my head relaxed against it, finding a safe place beneath his jaw. I wanted the warmth there to uncoil along my muscles, but he led me back to the stool where I'd recovered only the night before. He left my side and it felt like a desertion.

Gabriel came back holding a glass of water. "Take a sip." He seized my shaking hand, lodging the glass in it, and brought it to my lips.

I took one generous gulp followed by another one. The fresh liquid pouring inside my mouth, down my throat, diverted my senses from the landslide shaking my stomach. I was so eager to get over the dizziness that I knocked my head back. The next sip spilled over the edge of the glass. I sputtered and coughed.

"Go easy, lass." The corners of his mouth curled and I expected it to morph into a fully-formed smile. It didn't. Instead, he took hold of the glass and placed it on the countertop. In an uncanny reenactment of last night, he searched for another clean napkin and dried the water dribbling from my chin onto my neck.

I was either regressing to a toddler or heading at a fast and furious pace towards senility.

"Sorry." The heat on my cheeks made me fear I was blushing. I couldn't remember the last time I'd blushed. I didn't even know I still could.

"I should have taken you to the hospital." With the tip of his index finger, he tilted up my chin so that I couldn't escape his gaze. "It's still not too late."

"If we go, I'll have to tell them about what happened last night, and the police will get involved. I believe you don't want that."

His jaw set hard and he ducked his head as if he was conceding the point but both his eyes and his fingers stayed on me. His attention made me straighten up and forget all about swooning. Apparently Gabriel MacLeod worked better on me than any breathing techniques.

"I didn't thank you." I modulated my voice to roll it into a rasp. "You might have saved my life last night and my honor for certain."

All I got from him was a loose shrug.

I pursued, "It was courageous of you to go it alone against three men."

"Men who take advantage of their size over girls—women—they're worth nothing. I wish I had killed them."

His sentiments were shared without the slightest touch of guilt. Gabriel hadn't been anointed yet but his killer instinct was already as sharp as the stake he'd soon use to slaughter my kind.

The thought made me shrivel, my shoulders curling inwards, and I stifled a shiver. My diminutive stature emphasized his own height. It reminded me of my first visit to New York City, when tracing the sides of skyscrapers to their tops had made me stumble backwards. Maybe he feared I was about to faint—yet again—and his palms embraced my cheeks.

"Marie." He pronounced my name in a rushed breath

I held on to him by circling my fingers around his wrists. The symmetric spots within beat under my touch, the stream of blood flowing with increased speed through his veins. Curiously, that acute knowledge didn't unsettle me as it had the night before, and my fangs remained safely hidden.

Gabriel stepped closer, his fingers reached out into the thickness of my hair, his scent—like the wind blowing from the moors—permeated every parcel of my skin. My lips tingled at the sight of his, so bluntly wide and full. How I wanted to taste those lips. They'd have the aroma of chocolate and the touch of velvet against mine. I couldn't help how my chin tipped up in an open invite for a kiss. Like the night before, the muscles at the edge of his jaw pulsated. His pupils had dilated and his eyes drowned in mine.

I let him enter my soul, my heart, and that small portion of me that would always crave the light. We shared our next breath, our next heartbeat, and the space between us narrowed to a few small inches.

He swallowed hard and released a ragged exhalation. The pressure on the sides of my face relaxed while his hands slowly slid away to hang back at his sides. I resented the coolness of my uncovered skin. Gabriel stepped back. He brushed the curls back off his forehead and shut his eyes. Five seconds ticked by until he switched his sights back on me.

His voice was strained but his next request was crystal clear. "I'm going to ask you one more time. Leave this place, Marie, please leave."

"I like it here."

"What happened last night could happen again. You make everything more complicated."

"Life should never get boring."

His fists curled, stretching the skin over his knuckles. They were scratched from the fight.

"Very well." It didn't sound much like a concession. "You've been warned."

Gabriel marched away without another word. The space he'd occupied in front of me was now so empty and deserted I wanted to cast it away with one fell swoop.

Apparently, both my breathing and seducing techniques needed some work.

***

That Friday morning was my last meaningful interaction with Gabriel MacLeod for the next six weeks. I saw him every day but mostly in Lizzie's presence. The extent of our exchanges was limited to polite greetings.

He was always perfectly civilized, never forgetting his *good mornings* or *good nights*. We even managed to have three shared Scores-Sunday Roast—as named by Lizzie— where he succeeded in entertaining lengthy conversations with his sister without once involving me. He was subtle about it and she didn't pick up on anything. I found myself relegated to the role of bystander to their sibling intimacy.

I resented their bond while—really—I shouldn't have. I hadn't stepped into the house on the Scores to forge truthful bonds. My intentions stemmed from a dark past and would lead the three of us into a darker, if shorter-lived, future. But each of their shared jokes, each of their laughs and playful hugs, reminded me of what I'd lost with my own father. Even the silly nicknames they had for each other made me feel left out.

The MacLeod siblings belonged: to a family, a past, to Scotland, but more than anything else, they belonged to each other. Since the Saguenay solstice massacre I'd been reduced to no more than a free electron.

What I resented more than their bond itself was that my determination to destroy them didn't strengthen. It softened. It softened when I started laughing at their jokes, sharing their movie nights, and arguing about the choice of takeaway food. It softened when I realized my failure to break through Gabriel's barriers hurt more than just my desire for revenge. It hurt *me*. He'd put his life on the line to rescue me. Although he couldn't have known about the true nature of Beaumont & Co., he'd taken on three men to save me. But it seemed that now I didn't…matter. At all. It was like nothing had happened whatsoever. Worse, he wanted me out.

I'd never been vain, not even when I fell for Everett. My love for him had been turned so entirely towards his torments, his doubts, his needs, I hadn't factored myself into the equation of our love. However, Gabriel's lack of interest made me question my charms for the first time. Was I lacking any?

While I kept addressing that question to the mirror of our shared bathroom—lifting a strand of hair in an attempt at a new hairstyle, or glaring at my face from the least favorable angle—Gabriel shone mostly by his absence. Between the rugby practices, games, or studying, he was hardly ever at home.

Alice Cameron, however, showed her plump face from time to time. I wouldn't have hesitated spying on whatever was going on in Gabriel's bedroom but he never took her there. All I could say for certain was that he spent every single night in his own bed. Alone.

My confidence in my ability to seduce him followed the seasonal temperature. By late October it had plummeted and was close to zero. Nathaniel MacLeod would be back from the hunting season shortly before Christmas, therefore time wasn't my ally. I was deliberating about booking an appointment at the hairdresser, hoping a make-over might trigger my prey's interest, when I bumped into Simon.

I was on my way up the revolving staircase and he was leaving Lizzie's bedroom. However distracted I was with my own issues, I should have picked up on his internal turmoil. Frustration spun inside him, hot and bitter.

"Sorry, Simon."

"Don't worry." He stepped sideways and trotted down a couple of steps. There he stopped and called back to me. "Marie?"

"Yes."

"I was wondering—Well, I thought that maybe… There's the MacIntosh Hall Ball next week."

"Yes." I'd seen the poster at the library but the uni's social calendar wasn't something I paid much attention to. Attending classes was as much as I was ready to go to protect my cover. "What about it?" I heard the thought before he uttered the question and I was positively gobsmacked.

"Would you like to go with me?"

I climbed down the two steps that separated us and stopped intruding into his mind. I asked instead in a low tone as if we were sharing a secret, "What about Lizzie?"

Simon pushed his glasses up his nose and worried his lower lip. "What do you mean?" I tilted my head sideways and my scowl made him blush. "Lizzie doesn't want to go with me and I'm tired of being her dirty little secret."

"Oh." Surely a simple ball wouldn't break the MacLeods' dating ban? It was unlikely Lizzie and Simon would end up copulating right in the center of the dance floor. I laid my hand on Simon's forearm and mustered my most reassuring smile. "Let me talk to her."

"Sorry, Marie." He answered with a sheepish shrug. "It was rude to ask you out like that. You're not a consolation-prize type of girl...like..." Pink blotches dotted his cheeks. "Like not at all." He actually meant it, and simply for his faith in me, I was determined to champion his cause. My ego was in dire need of a pat on the back. Scrapping the MacLeods' rules in the process was an added benefit.

Lizzie's room occupied the top floor. It was far bigger than my own but the lower ceiling was slanted, giving it a pokier feeling. I knocked at her door.

"Can I come in?"

"Sure."

I turned the doorknob and entered her room. It was lit only by candlelight. Shadows danced around me. Night was already falling outside in the Scottish autumn afternoon. She was spread over her duvet, her head buried in the bend of her arm. Textbooks and notepads were spread all over her bed. I blocked her thoughts since I had the best intentions to find them out by myself.

"You're upset." Her hiccups were an easy giveaway. I cautiously circled around the bed as if the girl was an alligator I planned to wrestle with.

She sat up without a remote attempt at being graceful. Lizzie was a tall girl with limbs that went on forever. Once she'd managed to fold herself into a cross-legged posture, she patted the space next to her. I sat down.

"You're crying because Simon stormed off after you refused to be his date. Again."

"Jeez, girl, don't use gloves." Apparently more polishing would be needed on my part. "Did he get it out to you in the five minutes since he left my bedroom?"

I chose the diplomatic route and kept for myself that the boy had asked me out. Girls could be unpredictable and I didn't feel like dealing with that trickiest of things: jealousy.

"He's hurt because you want to keep your relationship in the dark."

"There's no other way." Lizzie opened her hands palms-up while her face contorted into a powerless frown.

"Says who?"

"There's no guy for me until I'm ready to marry…and I'm not there yet."

"We're in the twenty-first century, and you're twenty years old. You have the right to be with a boy." The MacLeod household was still playing catch-up with feminism. "And from what you told me, you and Simon haven't been purely platonic."

"I don't want to hurt him. It doesn't change anything for me anyway. There'll never be a *more* until I'm married. My father and my brother, they are my whole world, my everything. And I've been raised with the idea that sex before marriage would make me impure."

"Are you being serious?"

Impure was what the Hunters called my race. Turned, in particular; we were the lowest, the dirtiest of all, the only thing below us was any progeny we shared with a human. Nathaniel had spat out the adjective at my friends in the seconds before the sun ignited their bodies. Hearing it from the mouth of his daughter—his dutiful, pristine daughter—lit the fight inside me.

"Being with Simon or anyone else doesn't make you impure. He's a good guy and he loves you."

"You're wrong." She sniffed. "Simon doesn't love me."

Yes, he very much did. *I love you* was a recurring phrase in the commentary running inside York's mind. I was a reliable witness but I couldn't share that piece of information with the object of his affection. Instead I ducked my head sideways in a silent challenge. It had the merit of making the corner of her mouth twitch in embarrassment.

"You know what his feelings are for you. You went to boarding school together, and since you've started college, he's been constantly asking you out. Simon's waited a year for you to make it public. It might start getting him down."

"We're friends. I feel a lot for him but it's not like passion." She repeated at a higher pitch. "Simon and I, it's more like a sweet infatuation."

"You know he wants more. And I wonder, I wonder…" I let my sentence hang between us.

"What?"

"I wonder how much longer he'll be prepared to wait. What if he asks another girl to the ball?"

Lizzie's face paled. Her mouth turned so dry, her tongue so heavy, I shared the sensation. "He can't… I—I…"

Pity tugged at my heart. Young love could be so utterly sweet and it was hard not to root for it. I covered her wriggling hands with mine and said in almost a whisper, "I know you do. But you have to make a decision. You either give him a chance or you let him go."

Under mine, her hands turned so that her palms rested against mine, and I expected her to take back ownership of them. Perhaps I shouldn't have interfered with the matters of her heart. They were not directly relevant to my plans.

"You're right. I'm not being fair to him. I should try to have a real relationship with him. Not some secret make-out sessions as soon as Gabe turns his back on us." She sighed. "It's so good to have a girlfriend to talk to. I mean, I have some girls to talk to, like Alice, but with you I don't feel like I'm being judged."

"So will you accept his invitation?"

"I'll think about it. I have to stop leading him on."

"Well, let me know when you've made up your mind." Preferably sooner rather than later. "And anyway, Gabriel is dating Alice, so why shouldn't you have the same right?" That was where I wanted to get.

Lizzie stretched to pull a paper tissue from the box on her

side table and blew her nose in the most undignified way. When she'd finished, she threw it into the bin next to her desk.

"Gabriel has always dated. He just knows where to stop."

What a sibylline statement. One that definitely required clarification. "And where is that?"

She shrugged and blood flushed across her high cheeks. "At the baby-making point. I'm not sure I'll have as much self-control."

Was Gabriel MacLeod a *virgin*?

The concept was so anachronistic I stifled the laughter that threatened to erupt from my throat.

I didn't see the small peck Lizzie dropped on my cheek coming. "Thanks, Marie."

I crawled out from the bed and muttered a *You're welcome*. "I'm going now." As if my declaration wasn't explicit enough, I also pointed at the door.

"See you later. Why don't we have a pint at the World's End tonight. I'll drive."

"Yes, let's do that." I walked out backwards and disappeared after one last clumsy wave.

The door clicked and guilt pierced through me, grasping my guts. What was I doing? Who had I become? She was just a girl. Two centuries had elapsed since I'd been one. A girl. I'd never had the same opportunities Lizzie enjoyed, despite her clan's hold over her. But I'd dreamed. I'd fallen in love. I'd built romantic fantasies with knights and princesses. My knight had come, but he'd fed on blood.

I pressed my fingers against my closed eyelids. There was no time to indulge in scruples. Innocents were always the first casualties in war. It was a known fact. I'd been an innocent myself and Odette and Vincent had been too. MacLeod hadn't flinched with doubt when he burned them. They'd begged him, professed their belief in a peaceful life. He hadn't listened.

I had to repeat this thought, but out loud this time so that there was no escaping its truth. "He burned them." I summoned the memory of the fire, its smoky pungent taste, the roughness of its heat over my skin. Hidden in the woods, I'd watched it from far away but felt it as if a match had been struck one inch from my face. I summoned the sight of their bodies, no more than piles of ashes. Their pathetic shapes had soon been scattered by the wind.

I had to remember my Saguenay friends. I had to remember Louis. Everett. My love for them. Their love for me.

I exhaled and forced my feet down the stairs because I'd heard him coming back. Now was the time to break through the icy façade of Gabriel Macleod. I located him in the living room where the absence of light made me slow down. The fireplace was filled with cheery flames.

He stood in the center of the bay window, his back to me, and beyond him, the sun was setting over the North Sea in a canvas of vivid purple hues. The colors flooded the room around the silhouette of his broad shoulders and the rays of the dying sun reflected off the curls of his golden hair.

I glided across the room, hoping the rug would muffle my footsteps. When I reached his side, surprise made him flinch. His Adam's apple bobbed up and down as if he'd swallowed something sour and lumpy. I didn't let his reaction deter me and edged closer to him. My eyes wandered into the night that was descending. Our shoulders weren't touching but the narrow space between us buzzed with electricity that prickled my skin. I didn't say anything; neither did he. It didn't come as a surprise given how he'd treated me over the past weeks.

On the other side of the garden, the cliff fell into St. Andrews Bay, waves breaking at regular intervals against it. I wondered if he could hear them too. Or the wind whispering through the trees.

I waited.

The limbo stretched on for a minute, seemed like hours. But the air around us was not charged with animosity or loaded with suspicion. On the contrary, there was a companionship between us. His breathing followed a soft and steady cadence that I soon made mine. His chest rose regularly. His shoulders were relaxed. I didn't try to sneak inside his mind since I knew by then it was a lost cause. I didn't need to anyway. Gabriel welcomed me inside him even though the greeting was a passive one. That was all that mattered.

Finally I stole a glance at him and he stole my breath from me. His profile was unchanged, the crest of the nose long and sharp, the eyelashes curled up, the chin a square end to his jaw. But what I'd seen in Gabriel so far, the relentless energy and drive, was gone. The contours of his face had slackened. His neck was slightly bent as if the crown of light over his head was too heavy to carry. There were more curves than sharp lines about him now. For the first time, I didn't expect his next word to be another rebuttal.

And, for the first time, I didn't know what my next word should be.

I feared I'd break the peace he was letting me share with him. I couldn't indulge in the sight of him either, because if I did, if only for another second, the ancient hollow in my chest would open up and fill. Perhaps it was my heart there.

So I lowered my gaze along his arm. His fingers held a square paper tightly and, without hesitation, I took it and met no resistance. He simply loosened his grip on it. I had to turn it over to allow the fading light to reveal that it was an old photo. Figuring out who was on the discolored picture didn't require any clarification. Two flame-haired toddlers snuggled against a beautiful woman who shared their coloring and, I presumed, the same freckles. I knew her from my own research. She was Hannah Macleod, née Svenson. Gabriel's mother.

The picture I'd seen of her before didn't do justice to her beauty, to the aura of warmth that radiated from her heart-shaped face and slanting eyes. Maybe because she hadn't been holding her children close to her heart, her arms tight around their wriggling, chubby bodies. My palms turned clammy. I ran my tongue over my lips. They felt dry and chafed. I had the conviction I held a crucial piece of a jigsaw in my hand, and not only of Gabriel's life.

"There's no photo of her in the house. Why is that?"

Gabriel blinked as if my words had dragged him out of a deep slumber. He tore his gaze away from the near darkness outside and settled it on me. His eyes ran over my face like agile fingers: my hairline, my earlobes, the tip of my chin. They found their final destination on my lips. He frowned as if they posed him a metaphysical challenge. Maybe he realized he wouldn't find an answer there because he shook his head in surrender.

"It's easier to live without reminders of what we don't have. What we'll never have."

Would a picture of Everett make me suffer more than I already did? Yes, it definitely would.

"There's no solace in memories," he continued. His voice was broken and I knew the statement was born from intimate knowledge.

"No, but you can find strength in them, and strength is what you need to live without what you've lost."

He tilted his head slightly as if I'd shone a new light on a much-pondered issue. I had a two-century surplus of memories but I wished I had none, as they meant I was the only one left to remember.

"How much have you lost, Marie Aberdein?"

He wanted to know, he really did. His genuine curiosity was in the slow cadence of his words that went their way into a recess of my soul. Persistent and truthful, so was Gabriel MacLeod.

I fought this knowledge of him. Whoever he now was wouldn't last. "What makes you think I've lost someone?"

"Because whenever I look at you, it's only you I see. You are your own world."

"Are you saying I'm lonely?"

"You're always on your own and you don't seem to mind. It makes those around you want to…" He pressed his lips together, locking his thoughts inside.

"What does it make them want?"

"To find a way in." His strained voice quickened my heartbeat.

"I was an only child. We learn to be self-sufficient at an early age."

The corner of his mouth twisted as if I'd just said a joke. But only a mildly funny one. "No one is entirely self-sufficient, nor should they be. There's no meaning in life if it's not shared with someone: a sister, a friend…or a lover."

"Lizzie is my friend and perhaps I do have a lover."

His chuckle was low and it would have annoyed me if he hadn't stretched out his hand and rested the tip of his index finger on an invisible point right in the center of my breastbone. To the right of my heart.

I forgot to breathe.

Slowly—deliberately—he traced an upward path that led him away from the portion of my skin covered with the soft wool of my pullover to the skin at the base of my neck. He stopped at the depression there, increased the pressure, and I knew he could feel the staccato of my heartbeat. A veil covered my vision and I remembered my need for oxygen. My next breath was rushed and raspy, but it was his nostrils that flared and his chest that curved inwards.

When he'd recovered, the journey along the central line of my neck resumed until he reached my chin. His hand pivoted so that it was now the pad of his finger touching me. He pulled me towards him. I stumbled against him as graciously as a ragdoll. His free hand came and rested on my hip to balance me, slid to the small of my back. Our sole points of contact were the tips of my breasts against his chest and the tip of his finger under my chin. And his palm firmly splayed across my spine.

Once again, Gabriel reverted his attention to my lips.

They parted and there was a remote chance I might have been gawping like a witless fish. He bent his head so that *his* lips were inches away from mine. When he talked, his breath smelled of cherry and all I wanted was to take in another deep breath of it.

"Marie Aberdein, would you like a lover?"

Contradictions ricocheted inside my brain. No, I didn't want a lover. I wanted *him*, Gabriel MacLeod. I wanted to engulf his soul and his body so deep inside me that he would forget and deny his allegiance to his clan. To his father.

It was the truth, but only one side of it.

A slam of the entrance door saved me from contemplating its full spectrum.

"Anyone here?" Tobias Svenson's voice resonated across the hallway.

MacLeod and I jumped back to create a gap between us.

"In the living room." His voice boomed, but there was a cutting edge to it.

I was still clutching the photo and handed it back to him. He stared down at it as if he considered letting me keep it. Which wouldn't make any sense. Finally he took it from me and slid it into the back pocket of his jeans.

His cousin was closing in but there was one thing I still needed to know. "Why are you remembering her today?"

"Are you saving on electricity or something?" Svenson sounded annoyed. He switched the light on in the hall and a bright halo filtered towards us.

Gabriel ignored his cousin's complaint and kept his focus on me. I shuffled on my feet because I was being assessed by his far-too-insightful eyes. He answered, so I assumed I'd passed the test.

"She died eighteen years ago today. It's the one day in the year I let myself miss her."

I hated the intrusion of the light now switched on in the living room. Annoyance took full bloom inside me when I noticed the quiet presence behind Tobias. Alice Cameron had entered in her full doe-eyed-and-golden-curled glory. My gaze rushed back to Gabriel because I needed to know... I needed to see how he'd look at her. Would the flames in his eyes burn for her? Would the muscles twitch at the edge of his jaw when she approached him?

There was no flame. The muscles of his jaw remained still. Relief wrapped over me but there was no comfort in its prickly blanket. It stung my skin and chilled my heart.

Alice passed Tobias to come and nestle her shapely body against Gabriel's, her arms snaked around his narrow waist. She went on tiptoes and kissed him on the mouth. It wasn't an indecent kiss by any means. But it was a real one nonetheless. He didn't touch her. His lips didn't move under hers. He straightened and cut the kiss short by curling his hands on her shoulders. His expression was puzzled as if he wondered about what had just happened.

Me? I knew exactly what had happened. Alice Cameron had marked her territory, and I craved to tear the barrier to shreds.

Jealousy was indeed a tricky thing.

Chapter 6 — Wet Dream

Tonight hadn't been entirely wasted. I had to repeat this to myself and cling to the moment I'd shared with Gabriel in the afternoon.

Water cascaded down my naked body. I increased the temperature of the shower as high as I could without burning myself. After ten minutes, the skin on my shoulders had turned pink.

For the whole evening I'd grappled with the unrest inside me. It was born from an absence and I wouldn't lie to myself any longer. I missed Gabriel. How could I come to depend on him in such a short time? Maybe it was because he was an elusive prey. Or maybe it was because I'd allowed myself to look at him like I hadn't done with any other man since Everett. I'd opened the dam of desire and here I was drowning under its rushing flow.

When Tobias and Lizzie had suggested we all drive to the World's End, I'd expected Gabriel to go too. Alice had other plans, or rather, she quickly made some that didn't include the rest of us. And I knew why. The girl wasn't clueless and she'd picked up on the underlying current between Gabriel and me. After all, she'd found us alone in an unlit room.

So she'd come up with a sudden need to watch a movie and had begged—whined—Gabriel to take her there. And he'd indulged her. Hence an entire evening spent pretending a liking for beer and Tobias's company. The boy wasn't unpleasant, to talk to or to look at, but he wasn't the one I had to be with.

However a couple of things had come out from the night. First, I'd now secured a date for the MacIntosh Ball. With Tobias. I didn't think too long about accepting his offer. I had to go to the ball and remain in Gabriel's field of vision. Going alone would have been slightly embarrassing. Second, I realized Tobias wasn't the straightforward character I'd assumed him to be.

Far from it. While I could connect with most of his thoughts or emotions, there was a part of him I couldn't access. I kept hitting a wall. It wasn't the blank page Gabriel disclosed to my probing again and again, but it wasn't far off. I'd noticed this before. Given how Tobias was my companion of misfortune that night, it was confirmed to me. Svenson had nothing to do with the Hunter's line though.

At the time of her marriage, his aunt had been an unexpected choice for Nathaniel, one that hadn't pleased the rest of the family. The MacLeods had always chosen a spouse from the Highland clans. Hannah had been American, from Norwegian descent, and therefore an outsider. Not that she was given much time to settle and make Scotland her home, since she gave birth to the twins within a year of getting married and died before her children's second birthday.

I couldn't exclude some rare mental makeup brought by the Svenson bloodline. However, Lizzie didn't show any signs of it. I kept returning to the only other explanation. Had Gabriel and Tobias drunk Stramos blood?

It was becoming clear I had to up my game on all levels. Not only in my campaign to conquer Gabriel, but also in whatever was happening in St. Andrews. Something was off. Lawrence hadn't reappeared since that fateful night but I'd caught glimpses of his acolytes on my way to lectures with Lizzie or glaring at me from the other sides of the Scores. I was under surveillance.

I also couldn't shake off the memory of Gabriel MacLeod frantically searching my neck after the attack and his relief when the skin there was unscathed. Had he been looking for puncture wounds? The implications were too wide to contemplate. And tonight I was tired. So tired.

I'd been in the shower for too long, and if I hadn't boiled yet, the tips of my fingers were now all shriveled. I rinsed the shampoo out of my hair and applied some conditioner. While I let it run over my hair, I eyed the bottles of shower gel standing on the metal stand in the walk-in shower. One belonged to Gabriel, the other was mine. I extended my hand and considered for a couple of seconds the simple option. The truth was that I had already made up my mind.

I grabbed the cheap-looking, no-nonsense one, which was his, and opened the cap. I brought the bottle to my nose and breathed in the blunt, soapy scent. Longing punched me hard. His real scent was more earthy and complex than this but it was the closest I could get to him.

I poured a generous dollop of the liquid into my palm and lathered it between my hands. I closed my eyes and placed my palm over the spot Gabriel had touched earlier. Right between my breasts. I imagined it was his hand on me and the illusion tricked my body. The beads of my nipples puckered when my fingers brushed over them, the touch as featherlight as I imagined Gabriel's would be. I cupped my breasts and drew damp air into my lungs, my palms now fully filled. A warm, satisfying jolt traveled down my belly and spread between my legs. I traced its journey with the tips of my fingers and reached that part of me I'd wanted to forget since Everett. With his death, I'd grieved lust and pleasure. I'd buried them with him in the same grave.

I shut my eyes and explored myself. I welcomed the very present instead: a face, a dimpled smile and two big, masculine hands. They were callous and rough from too many rugby practices but they'd be expert and skilled on me. Inside me.

I climbed a ladder of sensation, closing on the summit with each stroke. I hoped the water splashing against the tiles would cover my whimpers. It was a journey inside myself I took, a discovery of valleys and crests all chiseled by the pleasure born from my own touch. Born from the scent of him now instilled into the perfumed steam. I quickened the pace, thrumming the little nub of nerves inside me. My breathing matched this new rhythm. I imagined his solid chest against my back, cradling me from behind. His hairs there would prickle my skin.

The empty space between my thighs filled with heat, pulsing and throbbing. When I crashed, my knees were so wobbly I had to lean against the tiled wall of the shower. I struggled to breathe. Surprise surged through my conscience and tampered any residual aftershocks.

I turned off the tap, stepped out of the shower, and wrapped a towel around my body. I swiped off the steamed mirror and gave a hard look at the face of the girl eying me back. That girl looked smug, her cheeks pink from more than the hot water, her lips swollen. That girl needed a good night's sleep, and her self-control would be restored by morning. I opened the door wide.

And it opened wide on him. The floor dipped beneath me.

The landing was dark, the only source of light coming from the bathroom. It was enough for the contours of his body to stand out and overwhelm me at first sight. I tilted my head to meet his gaze. Had he heard me in the shower? Even the possibility of it made me want to rush to my bedroom and hide underneath the blanket.

There was no mockery or disgust in his eyes and I addressed a silent *thank you* to God despite my absolute lack of belief in Him. Gabriel's bemused stare simultaneously engulfed all of me and focused on every single part of my body. I tightened the towel around me to keep myself from leaping out and wrapping my naked self around his. My thighs were now glued together to contain the pulsing at their core.

"I—" My voice peaked and I cleared my throat. "I must have used all the hot water. Sorry."

My apology jerked him out of his apparent fog. He shook his head. "No worries." It was as if his words sucked up all the air between us.

He made no move to enter so I stepped aside to free the way. Without a word, he walked forward but stopped beside me, offering me a full view of his profile. He wore a tight shirt whose short sleeves covered the bulges of his muscles snaking across his shoulders and biceps. The tension of his jaw was unmistakable, the familiar muscle throbbing there. My fingers twitched as they burned to reach out for his face and soothe his trouble away.

Gabriel had still not entered the bathroom. We stayed immobile at its threshold. I was half-naked, still warm and shaky from his imagined touch. Here was my opportunity to make a move on him. I'd waited far too long. My fingers started to relax their grip on the towel. I exhorted myself to commit the deed, to strip naked and throw my assets at the MacLeod heir. That had been the plan all along and now had come the perfect moment to implement it.

But I did nothing. Nothing at all.

I glared at an invisible point in the center of his chest, one that didn't cease to fascinate and beg me to snuggle my face against it. My mouth dried and I pressed my lips together. He inched forward and narrowed the space between us. His scent, all earth and musk, made me light-headed. In a stumble, I mirrored his move, my back soon hitting the doorjamb. He stopped. His forearm came to rest over my head so that he enveloped me entirely, without our bodies touching.

I dared look at him and what I saw in his eyes was a blow to my heart. A deep vein of pain and sparkles of lust were at war with each other. I crossed my legs at the ankles to temper the flush of longing that shot through me.

What should I do? Go on tiptoes and kiss him? Flick my fingertips over his nipples? I'd summoned the courage to do exactly that when he dipped his head, his forehead resting against mine. The tip of his nose brushed the tip of mine. I knew of tribes for which that gesture was a sign of affection or even greeting. Gabriel's touch had nothing in common with this ritual. We breathed the same air, our lungs sharing a rhythm that was ours alone, as if life had always flown from one to the other. His next exhale was a rasp, and the warm air tingled the softer skin of my lips. His stare on me was burning and covetous.

"*A leanaigh,* you're worse than a memory."

"Why's that?"

"Because I can choose to look at a picture to remember, but I can't choose to look at you." He let out a short chuckle. "I have to. The whole bloody time."

"Why is that so bad?"

"Because I've lost you before even having a chance to have you…to know you."

"Do you want to know me, Gabriel MacLeod?"

"Aye. I do." He swallowed and my hand reached for his Adam's apple. He flinched under my touch but didn't move away. "And so to clarify, I mean that in an entirely biblical way. I want to have you too. Very much so."

I went up on tiptoes now, my lips reaching for his. They were an inch apart when he made a sound in the back of his throat and wrenched his head to the side. Next he was inside the bathroom, his hand on the side of the door rushing to close it.

Was Gabriel about to slam the door in my face? Panic struck me. Anger too. My fangs dropped. I covered my mouth.

"I'm sorry, Marie. This shouldn't have happened."

This was long overdue, but I couldn't argue my case without revealing my needle-sharp canines. I willed them back into my gum. They obeyed, and I swallowed in relief.

"If there's one thing I've learned from my father—" his tone was shot through with steel, "—it's that lust isn't always love. And for me, one can't go without the other."

I wriggled my fingers as I fought the desire to slap him across the face. "Why can't you love me?" I spat at him. "Am I too *impure* for you?"

"Why would you use that word?"

"Your sister told me about your family's value system."

"I see." He paused. "There's nothing impure about you. But my thoughts about you very much are."

"So must be those you have for Alice, but I don't see you backing off."

"Not so much for her, no." His mouth twitched and the tips of his cheeks reddened. "With you, it's like my brain shuts down. I'm not thinking straight anymore. But I can't lose myself in you, *a leanaigh*. I can't lose myself in wanting you."

"Sex isn't a battle, you know. Nobody has to lose or win. Just let yourself be." How hypocritical coming from someone with a two-century-old fear of intimacy. And here I was discussing the virtues of casual sex.

He cast his gaze downwards and shook his head. "I can't, Marie. Right now, I must stay in charge...in control. Of my dick and of my heart. I have no choice."

I don't like crude words. They made me shuffle my feet. "Maybe you should give the brief to that girlfriend of yours. She might have other plans for both those parts of your anatomy."

"Alice knows how far I'm ready to go. But you're right. I shouldn't think of another girl while I'm with her. I'm going to take care of it."

He didn't look too heartbroken by the prospect of breaking it to Alice, whatever it was they had. I drew fleeting comfort from that thought. Where did it leave me though? Not much further advanced. One thing was certain: better to retreat before he closed that damned door in my face. I lifted my chin and re-tightened the towel around myself as goose bumps broke over my forearms.

"Good night, Gabriel."

I was two steps down the stairs leading back to the landing we shared when he called after me. I watched him over my shoulder, forcing my face into the most regal expression I could manage, hoping I was convincing enough. His was troubled, his gaze lost somewhere inside himself.

"I'm not just attracted to you, it's like my body recognizes you, *a leanaigh*. It scares the hell out of me but I can't be a coward about it."

Would he soon recognize the enemy in me?

"I don't know what to do with you." His fingers clenched on the doorjamb. "I don't know what to do with myself anymore."

I had a couple of suggestions with regards to his next actions though. First, he should start by ditching the girlfriend. Second, he should forget about the obsolete MacLeod value system. Above all, he should surrender to me.

Of course, I didn't suggest any of the above. "Maybe you should play more rugby. I've heard exercise helps with your predicament."

He chuckled. "I've already tried that, lass. But Hayden and Fergus aren't really who I want to tackle."

"That's too bad."

On that note, I made my way down to my bedroom. I heard the door of the bathroom click shut only after I was back inside my own space.

I slid under the covers and switched off the light. Tucking the duvet under my chin, I forced my body to relax and my mind to disengage from the sexually charged conversation. Nothing was going the way I wanted to, but at least I knew Gabriel was attracted to me. All I had to do was devise a plan to manipulate this desire.

Could I manage to do so before the Hunter's return? I focused on that thought when I heard the water starting to flow through the pipes. He was showering, standing right on the same spot I'd been minutes ago, and I wondered if he'd seek the same release I had. The possibility made me bury my flushed face in the pillow, moaning in frustration.

After several long minutes, I welcomed the sound of his steps on our shared landing. When they stopped, I sucked in some air. My eyes were fixed on the light filtering underneath my door. His feet blocked some of it so I knew he was right there, weighing up the pros and cons. I heard a rough mumble, a muffled swear word.

Duty won. The shadow disappeared. The door of his own bedroom clicked.

Disappointment kicked a big exhale out of me. Nothing would happen tonight. I tossed and turned for far too long, looking for a sleep that eluded me. I summoned up my happy place and imagined myself in my lab in Fjord Saguenay. I used to relish its antiseptic smell because it told me the place was clean of the outside world and all its filthiness. The memory calmed me. The tightness in my muscles disappeared, my eyelids fluttered, then closed. I fell asleep.

I dreamed *the* dream. *My* dream, where every second of that night is replayed, dissected, and colored with so much vividness my mind is in Technicolor.

And I tasted the fear, acid and pungent, all over again.

Chapter 7 - Nightmare

Odette was right. I needed to get out of our closed-up community.

With the spring now morphing into a bright and sunny summer, I have to wear long sleeves and Vincent's cap to protect my skin from the burn of the sun. It's the Red Sox cap he gave me last Christmas. Until we formed our little settlement here in this remote part of Quebec, Louis and I had never celebrated Christmas. The friends we made here—sick Turneds who joined our community—are different from us. They've all been turned not so long ago and they still have this hope inside them, this humanity they cling to, which I can't be entitled to anymore. But we want to please them, therefore we celebrate with them.

I readjust my backpack and speed up my descent towards the valley where we've built our refuge. Stones shift from under my hiking shoes, and I follow the path across the pine trees. I've been hiking the whole day and Louis must be worried by now. He always worries about me, right from the moment he sired me and even more so now since my health started to deteriorate. If I cough or clear my throat, he hovers over me and checks my vitals. I never miss teasing him about it. Sometimes it makes me smile and warms my heart to see him like that, so protective and caring. My biological parents never fussed like he does.

Sometimes I also see the guilt my disease causes him. I

never wanted to be what I am but he's been the one who convinced me to choose life whatever the price to my soul. I don't hold anything against Louis Berthière; I hold everything against myself. I still chose to live after the Hunter was killed by someone else than me, so really the guilt is all mine.

The sun is setting down behind the hills when I reach our home on the shore of the fjord. Its waters are navy blue with lighter strands spread through it. I'm already looking forward to seeing Louis and my friends. Our life here can feel claustrophobic but I like it. Actually I like it here more than I've liked anywhere else since I was turned. I found myself in Saguenay and if we lose our fight against the disease, I'd be happy to die and find my final peace here.

Before hiding here forty years ago, we'd never stayed at the same place more than a decade. First, there'd been the Carolinas after we'd left Scotland with so many others during the Clearances. But even in the midst of people desperate to survive, we stood out. I didn't age. Neither did Louis. Plus he didn't care much for the rough life of a colonist. Even for the sake of blending in, he had no intention of pretending we grew our own food, hauling water from the well, or making our own soap, candles or dyes. So we moved north to Boston and its more urban comfort.

There we kept a low profile during the Revolution, while Louis's endless funds kept replenishing the finances of the rebels. Even once the English King was kicked out, we kept moving states every ten years or so, taking new names and posing as low gentry, a widower very protective of his shy daughter.

Over the years, Louis shared with me his knowledge, of science, history, philosophy. He taught me French which I now speak very badly. But I'd grown bored. Bored, purposeless, restless. Finally, I set my mind on becoming a physician and attended Princeton. I even had the dorm experience. By the time I got my medical degree, I was already suffering from the spells, nausea, and fainting. They've been particularly bad over the past week. But a full day of fresh air has filled me with positive energy. I don't want to think about the past. I even feel like whistling.

That's when I see the Hummers and I know something is off. They form a circle around the scattered wooden buildings that make up our community. None of those vehicles belong to us or to the few associates who visit us from time to time. They're huge, black with tinted windows. I'm certain the diameter of each of their wheels matches my full height. I swallow hard but my saliva is frozen in my throat, all sharp and cutting.

The cars are one thing, but the men who march around are something else altogether. They're warriors, built for killing. The arsenal of blunt weapons at their waists and the guns they carry on their shoulders only make them more lethal. These men could kill any one of us with their bare hands. There's one Stramos here—Louis—and he's the only one with a chance to escape if this troop wants to terminate us.

From the turn in the descending slope down towards the valley, I have a clear vantage point. I'm also in plain view. I scrunch down and hide behind a human-size rock. What am I supposed to do? There's a remote chance Louis, Vincent or Odette have gone out and therefore aren't in the house. Or perhaps these men aren't who I dread they are. It's easy to check. I extract my cell phone from my backpack. No signal. We do normally have one. Have they scrambled it?

Tears sting my eyes. I steal another glance over the tip of the rock at the small army now occupying my home. With the exception of five men holding their automatic rifles as if ready to use them any second, the rest of the troop are now inside the house. The ones outside are patrolling the area around the buildings.

The night slowly settles over the fjord and I grab the blanket from my bag. I must keep warm. I mustn't lose strength because, while my phone isn't working, I have other means of reaching Louis. I wrap myself in the blanket, welcoming the growing darkness around me, and seek our bond. One of the few abilities I gained when I turned was the link with my Maker. We can communicate without words. Because of my poor health, distance now hinders it but I'm only two hundred yards from the house. If Louis is there, he should be able to hear me.

I call his name. Once. Twice. Nothing. I force my body to relax against the hard surface of the rock. I let my shoulder drop and call his name again.

"Get away!"

The sound of his voice with that persisting accent of his undoes me.

"Louis," I call in the silence of my head. "Louis."

"Get away," he repeats. "If I can hear you, it means you're close and you mustn't be."

"Are these men with—"

"The Hunter. He's here. That's why you must leave now."

"I can't...I can't leave you. I have to do something."

"There's nothing you can do, *ma petite*. Nothing except save yourself. Tomorrow is the solstice. When the sun rises, we'll be dead."

While Stramos, Fiu, and Turned can sustain under the sunlight, the solstice dawn burns us. Unless we've been trained, Turned are fair game for MacLeod and his men. Stramos—even a gentle one like Louis—are the real deal. But there are at least twenty men here in addition to the Hunter, there was not much he could have done to fight back.

"I can reach someone. I can run to the highway and ask for help."

"What use would that be? It'll take too long for any other vampires to rally enough power to take on the Hunter and those men. His brother is here too. No Stramos will come to the rescue of mere Turned anyway. And if you drag humans into this, if you expose us to them, you'll be chased and killed on the Council's order."

"I don't care." I'm dying anyway. "I don't care. We can deal with the Council once you're all safe."

The North American Council regulates our lives and conflicts. It's made of the five most senior Stramos on this side of the Atlantic. But whatever the location of the councils, Europe, South America, their priority is the well-being of Stramos and Fiu. Turned, not so much. They also have a zero tolerance for anyone involving humans in our business.

"We're going to die. There's nothing you can do except save yourself."

"I don't want to live without—"

"You must live and keep searching for a cure, Marie. You must."

The anguish boils up inside me. I swallow a sob. "I won't be able to do it without your guidance, Master."

There's a smile in his next words. "Don't underestimate yourself. You're far more resourceful than you give yourself credit for. All the data is saved electronically and you know how to access all our offshore accounts to fund another lab."

I shake my head. I've never been on my own, ever. I've come from Everett's protection to Louis's. I can't lead a project like the one Louis has undertaken.

"Our future is in your hands. Keep working on the cure and you'll save thousands of Turned. They'll be able to live without having to feed on humans. They won't be monsters. That's what you want for yourself, for them."

I clench my fists so tight my nails draw blood from my palms. "I don't care. All I want is for you to live. There must be a way."

"Leave now." His order cuts through me.

I pull the blanket tighter around me. The temperature drops and I don't hear from Louis again. I should follow his orders and get as far away from Saguenay as I can. But I stay at the same place, hidden by the rock. The patrol walks a perimeter around the building. Twice one of the mercenaries moves close to me. As highly trained as they are, they're not the Hunter. They can't feel and smell us from afar.

With the passing hours, I start retreating farther behind

the boulder, where I give in to sleep at short intervals. Soon the night softens. Dawn is approaching. East is on the other side of the rock so it should protect me from the rising sun. I could also just walk towards the home, right into one of the guards and surrender myself. I'd face the same fate as my friends. I'll be dead soon anyway, but at least I'll die with them and they'll die with me.

Odette is so scared of death—she's told me so many times—but I'm not. I could be next to her, smile at her, comfort her when the morning comes. That will make her end better. I know that. Slowly, I rise to my feet.

"Marie, don't move!" I don't answer. I don't sit back. How can he know? "Don't do anything reckless."

"That's my choice to make, not yours."

"You have my responsibilities now. You must continue what I have started. Dying today here…would be selfish."

I want to scream and argue and cry. I want to see him again. One last time. "Father, I love you." Tears are running down my cheeks.

I hide again.

Noise comes up from the occupied buildings. Doors open and armed men start pouring out of them. The line of horizon is now burning red. It's going to happen now. My stomach sinks. My heart races.

My friends, the twenty of them, are escorted outside. Most of them keep their heads lowered. Odette and Vincent are holding hands. She's crying, her frail shoulders shaking, and Vincent watches her. I hope he had the time to tell her how he feels. I should have pushed him to do so each time he confided in me. It's too late now for them. From all the waste that is about to unfold, that lost love is the most tragic.

Vincent tries and hugs Odette but a man, whose face I recognize from photos Louis showed me, knocks him down with the butt of his rifle. The man's name is Malcom MacLeod. He's the Hunter's brother.

Louis is the last prisoner to step outside. As soon as I see him, I know he can see me too, at least sense my proximity. He tilts his head towards the boulder, and a smile flies over his wise face, but the movement soon vanishes. He doesn't want to attract the attention of his captor to my hiding place.

Behind him, the Hunter comes into full view. Nathaniel MacLeod, so close in features and coloring to his ancestor, Gabriel. I see him and I want to kill him with my bare hands, suck his blood to the last droplet, and then rip out his throat and feast on his flesh. If I'd managed to kill Gabriel earlier, he wouldn't have had time to procreate the next Hunter, and the line would now be extinct. I didn't find Gabriel MacLeod on time and the tragedy playing before my eyes is the result of that failure.

The guards form a circle around the Turned and the one Stramos. Their weapons are aiming at my friends and I cover my panicked giggle with my hand. What do they expect? My friends can't fight. They're scientists. They're geeks who were only trying to survive without hurting any humans. My skin itches and I bring the blanket tighter over my head. The sun is about to appear. It's about to happen.

"*Ma petite*, are you still there?"

"Yes, Father." I sound like a frightened child. I'm one.

"Promise me you'll live. Promise."

"I will."

"Good." The Hunter pushes him forward with the point of his rifle. Louis stumbles. He comes to stand in the front row of my family. They're all facing east. "It's coming now."

"Master…"

"You made a father of me, Marie, and I've cherished every second spent with you. You gave me happiness and purpose. I want to thank you for all you have given me."

The air around me shifts as the first rays slice through the sky. Sparkles crack all over the bodies of my friends, and flames uncoil from them. I hear screams. I bite my fist so that I don't echo them.

"Father!" I shout in my mind.

"I love you, Marie. I will always love you."

"Father, don't go. Please, please don't leave me."

"Father, don't go. Please don't leave me."

The fire that burned his body raged now from the pit of my stomach, but my skin was as cold as a Saguenay stream at spring. My heart slammed against my ribcage. The memories of that dawn stabbed through my soul.

"I'm here."

Two steely arms encircled me. I tried to escape but his power overwhelmed me, his muscular legs encasing mine. I stopped the struggle, but the sobs kept rocking my body.

"I'm here, *a leanaigh*, I'm here for you. Whatever scared you, it's gone."

His breath tickled the tiny hair on my temple and I drank up his words like an elixir...or some Valium. The dream had never taken me so far out of my mind. I was desperate for some peace. He pulled me on my back, my legs still tangled with the sheet. His hand came to rest over my stomach, his palm warm and heavy. The effect on the ragged fall and rise of my chest was immediate. It slowed down and slowly got back to a more regular rhythm. *His* rhythm.

I shut my mind to Saguenay. I had to or I'd die of grief and Louis had begged me to live. Begged me to live and honor his legacy. Not to seek vengeance and kill humans. Humans like the one who was touching me.

"What are you doing in my bedroom?"

"You were screaming blue murder and I had to check if you were okay."

"It was a nightmare." How informative of me.

"That or you're a total wacko. Please give me hope it's not the latter, since we're sharing the same house."

I heard the smile in his tease. He hadn't really teased me since that night at the World's End. Gabriel MacLeod was the epitome of impassive and stern. Most of the time. His fingers moved away the strands of hair covering my face. Sweat covered my temples and I hoped he wouldn't notice. If he did, it didn't bother him because he started curling and uncurling a wisp of my hair around his index finger.

"You dreamed of your father," he said in the ghost of a whisper, his mouth moving against the crown of my head.

It wasn't a question and didn't demand an answer. I was grateful for that as there was no chance I'd discuss Louis with Gabriel.

"When did he die?"

I wasn't going there… "Last June."

"Is that why you came to Scotland? To escape?"

A bitter chuckle erupted from my mouth. "In a way."

Seconds ticked away in silence until he—very slowly—laid the wisp of my hair over my chest and wrapped his hand around my waist. He pulled me against his side so that my head snuggled under his chin. My hand landed on the solid swell of his chest. His heart thrummed harder against his ribcage. His warmth slithered into me and I welcomed it because the Saguenay night had chilled my bones.

"I'm glad you came here." His voice was gruff. The admission cost him.

I flinched, stared up but his grip on me tightened, restraining my movement. I willed myself into total stillness.

But not muteness. "Strange coming from someone who wanted to kick me out of his house not so long ago."

He tensed against me. "You should have left. My life would be much easier."

"How so?"

"I have to make sure you're safe and sometimes it feels kind of creepy."

"Are you stalking me?"

"I don't *stalk* you. I'm only keeping an eye on you. At all times."

"You can't be everywhere."

"I have help, but with you I don't trust anyone. You're so small you can sneak out anytime you want."

My trips to St. Andrews Hospital popped in my head. Had I been under scrutiny when I went there?

"I wonder what your girlfriend would think about that new obsession of yours?"

In one swift movement, he flipped and rolled over me. He rested his forearms on either side of my face so that his weight didn't press on me. Between us there was only the flimsy sheet and every hard part of him, every muscle, mirrored my curves. His lips were inches from mine. A lock of his hair tickled my forehead.

"I made a promise to you, Marie Aberdein. I said I'd keep you safe, that those who attacked you would be punished. I plan to keep that promise. They've gone after you once, they'll try again."

"Why do you care?"

"I don't want any harm to come to you."

"You've been rude to me since we met. You've ignored me and made me feel unwelcome for weeks now. I don't think you care about me at all."

"I don't trust myself when I'm around you. We discussed that a couple of hours ago. Remember? Or maybe you being half-naked and all played a trick on your memory."

"I remember everything you said. But why don't you trust me?"

"I told you. I want you."

"And when you want, you bark?"

"I bark to keep my hands off you." He said that while his very hand came to cup my cheek. "Lust and love aren't the same—"

My eyes rolled up. "And you can't have one without the other, I know. Is that what happened to your father?"

I knew almost nothing about Nathaniel's love life. It hadn't been of any interest to me so far. Judging by how it seemed to affect his son, maybe it should have been. But Gabriel wasn't talking anymore. I didn't push him. He rolled back on his side but his hand took a firm grip on my hip. I turned to face him. After he hooked his free arm to lay his head on, our bodies were in line with each other.

"My father—" His voice broke and he cleared his throat. "My father wanted my mother badly. It went against all that his family wanted for him, for our clan. She fell head over heels too, and they were married after only a few months of knowing each other. I guess it was what they call a whirlwind romance…or maybe my father couldn't keep it in his pants and marriage was the only way to have her."

"Did things change once they got married?"

His fingers shifted and settled on the small of my back. Little swirls, all warm and fuzzy, climbed up my spine. Even in the darkness of the room, I could see the glimmer in his eyes. "They had us, Lizzie and I. They must have found out quickly after that they didn't share the same ideas for raising us. At least, that's what I know now."

"What did they disagree on?"

Silence stretched for several heartbeats and I wasn't expecting an answer. But it came nevertheless.

"There's not much choice about how you live your life when you're a MacLeod. We have a long history behind us."

"What do you think your mother wanted for you?"

"Freedom. I know…" His jaw locked. "I know she wanted me to make my own choices."

"And what do you want for yourself?"

He buried his gaze downwards, somewhere into the narrow space between us.

"Freedom?"

"It's too late for that."

"You're twenty. You can do whatever you want."

The shake of his head was almost unnoticeable. But I noticed everything in that boy, from the shadows thrown by his eyelashes to the dimple at the left corner of his mouth. My attention to every detail of him edged on painful. When he hid his face in the crook of his elbow and released a full breath, I curled my fists and killed the need to run my hand through the curls of his hair.

Finally his eyes came back on me. "I'm doing what I want but it doesn't make me free."

"That's because you're not doing what you want but what you must."

What were we discussing precisely? His sexual freedom, his choice of university, of major...or much, much more. The MacLeod legacy.

Only he should know nothing about the last one.

His thumb traced small patterns on the tip of my cheekbone. He seemed more preoccupied with touching me than acknowledging my last comment. And I didn't mind. I'd fallen asleep with dreams of manipulations and exerting revenge, I was now awake with a brain and a body in surrendering mode.

"Now, now, *a leanaigh*, when did my nightly rescue turn into full-on therapy?"

"I'm awake now and I feel like talking."

"Well, it's 3 in the morning. You'll thank me tomorrow when your head doesn't hit your desk during one of those boring tutorials you and my sister attend. You know the ones when you spend hours learning about every one of our 206 bones."

He disengaged from me, sat up, his feet now touching the floor on the side of the bed. Without thinking, I half sat up, taking support on my elbow, my other arm stretching towards him and reaching his side. Under my touch, the hard-packed muscles of his abdomen clenched. His breath hitched.

"Stay," I begged in a hush.

"That's not a good idea."

"I don't want to be alone." The revelation struck me. It was a truth I'd never had the strength to face, even less to express. Not that I had anyone to listen anyway. "I'm scared I'll have the same dream again. I need a friend."

My palm followed the quickened pace of his breathing. I spied on his heartbeat and hoped its mad staccato would mean a *yes*. It must have, because slowly he resumed his lying position and I reverted to snuggling against him, welcoming his warmth with shame-tainted relief.

"As a friend then," he pulled me back against him, though, with my head resting on his chest.

Do friends get that close? Or does a friend kiss another one on the tip of the nose? Maybe that was what brothers do. I didn't want for him to be either of those. The sound of his blood rushing through his veins threatened to overcome my self-control but I pushed the temptation away. My fangs stayed put.

There was so much more to resist right then than the simple appeal of his blood.

His eyes were fixed on the ceiling, but his fingers were on my bare shoulder, reverting to tracing small circles on my skin. I relaxed in his embrace, Gabriel's hard body a barrier between me and the memory of Saguenay. Of his father. Although a sleepy fog seeped into my brain, I couldn't miss the irony.

I chose to keep him close to me.

Chapter 8 — A Treat

It was midday and Lizzie and I were heading out of St. Andrews' Medical Department. Our morning had been spent in the dissection room and my housemate looked the worse for wear. That was what a first full-body postmortem did to most people.

"Some dried apricots?" I offered.

I'd refilled the pouch I kept in my handbag that very morning. If it did the trick for my dizzy self, it should help with her temporary one. She opened her palm and I poured a handful into it.

"Thank you." She brought one fruit to her lips and bit into it.

"We can sit down if you want." There was a plastic bench lining the wall.

She shook her head, but it was a very faint gesture. "I'll be fine." And then threw the rest of the apricots into her mouth, chewed and swallowed. "How do you do it anyway? You looked almost perky throughout the whole shebang. Even Kerr threw up…" Her mouth drew a downcast curve in disgust. "God, the guy must have puked everything he's ingested since last Hogmanay. If Professor Donaldson didn't have him escorted out, his intestines would have splashed all over the tiles."

Kerr was in our year and one of Gabriel's teammates. His open display of weakness wouldn't improve his tough-guy credentials.

"I won't tell my brother about it. He doesn't deal well with weakness."

I'd have openly disagreed with Lizzie. However doing so would lead me to reveal her brother had spent last night with me. Not that anything inappropriate had happened between us, at least by twenty-first-century standards. But it'd been enough for me to establish that Gabriel MacLeod could show a great deal of compassion when he felt so inclined.

"Speak of the devil." We'd stepped outside and Lizzie gave a loose wave in front of us.

I followed the direction of the gesture. My heart made a strange contortion—half somersault, half recoil—within my ribcage. Twenty yards away from us Gabriel leaned against his Range Rover, his legs crossed at the ankles, his arms folded over his chest. His gaze was downcast but swung up towards our duo when Lizzie yelled his name.

The speed at which she darted towards her brother would have made any Stramos take note. Forgotten were the autopsies and Y-incisions. You wouldn't have thought she'd seen her brother only the day before. Her race ended in his arms and in more squeals. Unlike her brother, Lizzie wasn't the silent type. She generously made up for Gabriel's economy with words.

I followed her at a more recreational pace, holding my books so tightly against my chest I'd have suffocated them had they been alive. She had her head buried in his chest when I reached them. Gabriel didn't acknowledge my presence but kept ruffling Lizzie's crazy curls. My books officially drew their last breath.

I'd woken up that morning alone, with the dip in the pillow next to mine the only proof of his overnight presence. That and the new warmth buzzing under my skin from the hours snugged against his body. Right that instant—standing next to the twins—I had no clue what would be the next twist in my already topsy-turvy relationship with Gabriel.

I waited and waited. The truth was that I probably didn't

wait that long for him to look at me, but eagerness had altered my time-awareness. Never had I been so keen for someone to stare at my face. The air froze inside my lungs when his chin started lifting up. I tracked the movement inch by inch. From the top of Lizzie's head to the vertical line of his neck. Even then he was still looking down, his eyelashes a thick shadow fanning over his cheekbones.

Finally, he glanced up.

And when he did, it looked like the sight of me hurt him. There were creases at the corners of his eyes and the now familiar point along his jaw started throbbing once again. Maybe it was more anticipated pain, like a child who's been naughty and is about to be told off. With his gaze now on me, I remembered to breathe. With that next breath I identified the exact emotion troubling him.

Fear.

Gabriel MacLeod feared me as if our shared—but very proper—night had given me some mysterious upper hand over him. The thought was so ludicrous I smiled. That smile acted like a spell because his jaw relaxed and the wrinkles vanished. His lips twitched and curved into one of those rare smiles of his, if tinged with shyness. His grip on his sister slackened.

He let go of Lizzie but kept smiling at me. My own smile widened in turn because he was focused on me and oblivious to her and her babbling. I didn't have an inflated ego but I cherished being Gabriel MacLeod's sole point of focus for once. I enjoyed it very much. Even for a handful of seconds. A taut line stretched between us, energy rushing back and forth, tingling at my skin and ratcheting up my heartbeat. And his.

"Gabe, I've asked, *what are you doing here?*" Lizzie pulled at the collar of his jacket, startling him. When he stared down at her, it was with a frown.

His gaze on me must have acted as some invisible blanket because cold sneaked through my own coat and slithered over my whole body. I shivered.

"I thought I'd spare my sister and my housemate a walk back home. The weather forecast announced more rain."

Lizzie stole a quick upward glance at the sky, which was of a clear azure, or as *azury* as a Scottish autumn would allow.

"Well, I guess the weather forecast was done from London because it's as dry as a bone up here."

Gabriel replied with a shrug and buried his hands deep in his jean pockets. He'd just been caught in a lie and he knew it. Lizzie didn't comment any more on the state of the weather. Instead she stared at her brother. Suspicion was sketched in the wrinkle between her eyes. Her attention shifted to me and I scored my face into a neutral mask. Then her focus switched between Gabriel and me a couple more times until she spoke again.

Her voice solidified. "I'm sorry, guys, but I have other plans."

"Do you?" I blurted as it was news to me. I hadn't sensed any preliminary thoughts hinting at her new agenda.

"I'm going to Simon's." It was delivered as a challenge.

A challenge that Gabriel entirely missed. "Okay." He straightened up, cleared his throat, and then cleared it again. "Marie, would you like a lift then?" His question was accompanied with a daring glance in my direction.

"That's nice of you. Thanks." *Casual* was what I'd been aiming for. My answer was far too high-pitched to fulfill that goal.

There was nothing casual in Lizzie's next statement. "I'm going to ask Simon to be my date to the MacIntosh Ball."

This time her brother didn't miss anything and I was so grateful Gabriel's scowl wasn't pointed at me. It wasn't enough to deter Lizzie, though, and she forged on, "Actually I want to date Simon. Full stop."

Gabriel's profile hardened. I wished she'd consulted me: a car parked outside the Medical Science building wasn't the place for stamping over centuries-old rules. I stepped forward to slide between the two of them. I would go with her, chaperon her, do whatever was necessary to avoid a confrontation for which she hadn't yet sharpened her weapons.

As it was, I didn't make it further than the tips of my toes.

"I'm happy for you."

Well, well, that was unexpected. I scanned Gabriel's face for a trace of underlying anger, anger that couldn't fail to burst forth. Nothing at all. He pushed even further. "Simon is a good guy and I know he'll treat you well."

Lizzie tipped her head forward, stretching her neck as if to search her brother's face for any telltale signs. I had to refrain from mirroring her gesture.

"You mean that?"

"I do." He swept his gaze over the parking lot. "Lizzie, no one should set the rules for how you live your life. I'm sorry if I've made you feel that way."

She grimaced in disbelief. "So you're not going to shit a brick?"

Gabriel rolled his eyes. He *rolled* his eyes. "No, Elizabeth, I will do no such thing."

"Will you tell dad then?"

"It's none of his business unless you want it to be."

"I don't," she rushed out. "So you trust me?"

Behind me, someone shouted Gabriel's name. I recognized Kerr's guttural voice. Apparently, the boy had recovered from his earlier weakness. Gabriel waved at him, then reverted his attention to his sister, his eyes meeting mine on the way back.

I heard his question, not one he'd spoken out loud but in the silence of his head. The fact I was privy to his thoughts was such a rare occurrence, that in itself should have knocked me down.

Do you trust me?

I bit my lower lip to mute my answer to him, but *YES* resounded inside my head. He'd rescued me. He'd cared for me, comforted me. I knew, I *knew*, I could trust him with my life. Guilt, shame, helplessness clashed with each other and made my shoulders hunch.

My very presence here meant he could never trust me with his.

"Sis, it's not about my trust in you but about the trust you have in yourself." He wasn't talking only about Lizzie.

"What are you saying?" It came from her but that could have been my line.

"Do you trust yourself to make what you have with Simon meaningful?"

I swallowed my remorse. I'd never mean anything good to Gabriel MacLeod.

"I'll try. You know how well Simon and I get along. We'll be happy as Larry." Lizzie was already sauntering backwards and wriggling her fingers at us. "Thanks! I'll see you both later once I've broken the news to Simon." I wriggled back at her. "And by the way, bro, I do trust you to make it *very* meaningful too." She winked and swiveled away.

That left the two of us swarming in a charged silence until Gabriel opened the passenger door.

He cleared his throat. "Still interested in a lift?"

"Sure." I climbed into the Range Rover. By the time he'd circled the hood, I'd fastened my seatbelt. On the backseat lay the massive bag containing his rugby gear. "You're going to practice." Stating the obvious was my only way to fight my jiggling nerves.

"Aye. But I've plenty of time before that."

Gabriel started the engine and drove out of the car park. It was St. Andrews after all so any journey within the city would be a short one. I glanced through the window but didn't register details of any of the familiar streets on the way home. Meanwhile I wasn't entertained by my companion's mad conversation skills either. It was a myth that all Scots were born storytellers. I didn't expect anything else from a man who ruled a team of fifteen men in a ninety-minute rugby game with no more than a dozen words.

Therefore I was the first one to speak again when he stopped the Range Rover on Campbell Street. I turned on the seat to face him. "Do you have an errand to run?"

His answer was a shake of his head. A smile flew over his face. He leaned over the wheel, raked his hand through his curls, but one of them stubbornly fell back over his forehead.

"After last night...I mean, after your nightmare, I thought..." He searched for some inspiration on the windshield and found it. "I thought you'd like a treat."

"A treat?"

He got out of the car and made his way round to my door. I stepped out, waves of giddiness swirling through my stomach, and took his hand. When my feet touched the sidewalk, it was tempting to leave my hand in his. I didn't though and we walked side by side until he stopped in front of a shop with a wide glass window.

I stared up at the sign above and read out. "Gelateria Cassini."

"Everyone likes ice cream."

Did I? A pack of O-negative was more what I had in mind as a pick-me-up. "I guess so."

"Come on in." He opened the door for me and we entered the diner-like shop, his hand on the small of my back.

The bell rang when the door closed behind me. A counter displaying two rows of ice-cream flavors lined the back of the shop. There was a dark-haired, burly man behind it, with a paper-white hat planted on his head.

"Good to see you, Gabriel." For someone so blatantly Italian-looking, from the olive skin and the black mustache curled at its ends to the green-white-red flag on his apron, his English had the robust diction of the Highlands.

"Good to see you too, Giacomo."

Gabriel waved his hand in my direction. "This is my friend, Marie."

His smile stretched his mustache further. "It's nice to see this young man with a lady he's not related to for once."

The tips of Gabriel's cheekbones had reddened. He swung from one foot to the other while scratching the back of his neck. A fluttering feeling spread in the pit of my stomach as I ordered two flavors at random: Eton Mess and maple syrup. Gabriel's choices were more classic: vanilla and coffee. When I offered to pay, I was silently dismissed. We sat at one of the square tables along the glass window. The giddiness had subsided and I was training my brain to pause. I didn't want to think anymore. What I wanted was time shared with the boy who'd held me the night before.

"I'm sorry I left before you woke up."

My mini plastic spoon froze midway between the cup and my mouth. "You don't have to apologize."

"I promised Hayden I'd go for a run with him. We'd agreed to meet at six and you were still out for the count. It felt wrong to wake you."

I took my first taste of the maple-syrup ice cream. A mix of caramel and brown sugar melted on my tongue with a hint of nut. It took me back to Saguenay and the pancakes Odette used to cook. I'd always been very liberal with the maple syrup topping. Gabriel approached his vanilla scoop with the deliberate care that was his and we went through the next three bites in silence.

I stared through the glass window feigning interest in the crowd outside, mostly young mothers pushing buggies and office workers heading out to lunch. A couple of students stood out, simply because they were the only ones seemingly not in a hurry.

On the other side of the street, hidden behind a delivery van, I saw the now all-too-familiar shoulder and half-profile of one of Lawrence's men. He or his colleague were never far away any time I stepped out of the house on the Scores. I played along and never confronted them.

I was about to start on my Eton Mess when I decided to take a risk. With an introvert like Gabriel, we might go through Giacomo's entire ice-cream display and not manage a word. I didn't pace my words, the whole sentence blurting out. "It meant a lot to Lizzie, what you said about Simon."

Gabriel's head bobbed slightly. He twisted the handle of the mini spoon between two of his fingers and I feared his focus would return to the remaining scoop of vanilla.

It didn't. "I should have had that conversation with her long ago."

"Why didn't you?"

The twist of the spoon ceased. He dropped it in the cup. Leaning on his elbow, he buried his fingers in his hair. The gesture bared his forehead, lifting the curtain of auburn curls that usually covered it. The skin there had a golden glow and was devoid of the freckles dotting the sides of his nose. The bone structure underneath it was sharp. My gaze caressed the angles marking his temples and the straight line of his eyebrows.

"It would have been hypocritical for me to say anything." His voice was low as if there were other people in the shop. We were on our own except for Giacomo, who busied himself behind the counter.

"How so?" I matched his tone.

"I couldn't tell her to ignore rules I didn't have the courage to ignore myself."

The memory of the MacLeod signet on Lizzie's ring finger sprang to my mind, a dirk slicing through a moon, but for her nothing else than a chastity ring. Gabriel's finger was bare. I could have sworn it'd been there the night before.

"Are you able to ignore them now?"

His hand came to rest on the table, palm down, his thumb an inch from my little finger. The curls tumbled back over his eyes as he leaned backwards, his shoulders wider than the chair. He released a breath, opened his mouth, shut it, only to open it again.

A new hoarseness grated his words. "Ignoring them is the easy part. It's setting my own rules that takes more time."

I didn't have the chance to ask him about what these new

rules were. Behind me World War III had broken out. I could have sworn a tank had burst into the gelateria. The cold gushed in from the outside. It splashed on my face when I spun on my chair to check what was causing that level of noise. Not for one second did I fear an attack from my Turned stalkers. When they came to end my life, I trusted them to be more inconspicuous about it.

It wasn't a Turned bodyguard but a heavily pregnant lady pushing the door open with her back and pulling a buggy over the steps. There was some huffing and puffing and some mild swearing that Gabriel interrupted.

"Let me help you."

He took a firm grip on the handle of the buggy and with his other hand opened the door wide. The woman stepped inside by ducking under his extended arm. With dexterity, Gabriel made it pivot on its back wheel and swung the buggy around.

"Where do you want to sit?" he asked her.

Of the half-dozen tables she chose the one next to us. It had a lateral space on each side of it where Gabriel parked the pushchair. He helped her out of her oversized jacket. It wasn't an easy task as the lady's due date had to be imminent and because of the many layers protecting her from the November cold.

She was the chatty type and launched into a full rendition of her shopping adventures to which Gabriel reacted with polite nodding and appropriate words of commiseration. Their voices frazzled and tangled with each other, so much I couldn't distinguish any syllables. The sparkles that had lit up my mind since I'd seen Gabriel outside the Medicine Building stilled, shrank and died. My throat dried up. When I next swallowed, my saliva burned and pricked my throat.

There was a toddler in the pram, a boy of not even two years. The crisp air had reddened the tip of his nose. His eyes were oversized pools of navy blue edged by lashes that could compete with Gabriel's. His mother pulled the woolly hat from his head, and thick wisps of hair as black as obsidian topped his round face.

While I took in these details, I forgot to breathe. When I did again, the air forced its way down my throat. I doubled over and took support from my hands to avoid toppling over.

Gabriel sat back on his seat, still at the receiving end of the talkative mother's attention, but his gaze weighed on me. I had to be performing quite a show, a show triggered by an innocent toddler. A child whose features had the same delicacy as the man I'd married. The father of my own baby boy.

"Can I ask you one last favor?" the mother asked Gabriel. "Can you look after the little one? Just the time for me to use the facilities."

"No problem."

And we were left in charge of the boy. And I was left staring at him, fighting the yearning, wrestling with the loss that I'd never buried. My heart pumped sorrow, filling my veins with the bitterness of loss and my mouth with death, the taste of it stale and acidic. I gathered the strength to straighten my spine and revert to a normal sitting position. But my chest kept rising and falling so abruptly it was like hiccups rocking my body.

The child frowned at me, human enough already to feel the danger and darkness hidden inside me. This is the thing: the younger they are, the more tuned humans are to my species. They see through that veil of civility we have artfully threaded. Any second now and he'd unmask me. I had to run away. I wanted to jump to my feet but my legs were like knots of wool.

The boy grimaced. His lower lip started to tremble. The howl that followed was disproportionate to the size of the child. It threatened to pierce my eardrums. Tiny hairs rose all over my body. His reaction was not a fake tantrum. The fat tears running down his chubby cheeks were authentic. I had scared the little boy.

I extended my arm to comfort him. My shaking hand crashed over my lap, struck by its own uselessness. The howling increased in volume and Giacomo popped his head from the back room. I had to leave or cause permanent damage to the child's vocal cords.

"Come on, champion, where are your manners?" Gabriel's tone cut through the drama, low and playful. The howling stopped but the child's face was still distorted as if ready to revert to his shrieking performance. "That's no way to charm a lady."

I doubted seduction had been on the cards. However the child tipped his head as if deliberating whether to listen to whatever Gabriel had to say or revert to his antics. I took advantage of the attention diverted from me and leaned back in my chair. Numbness burdened my limbs. Something pricked behind my eyelids. I was stuck in a moment and it was urgent for me to disengage from it.

Gabriel covered his face with his palms, bent towards the child and started lifting one finger after the other. "Peek-a-boo!"

The boy giggled.

Gabriel's hands flew back to his face and he repeated the same gesture. "Peek-a-boo!"

Another giggle followed, one that bounced and rippled with delight this time.

By the time he'd repeated it three more times, the toddler had forgotten all about me. My gaze kept flying back and forth between him and the man sitting opposite me, a man who'd dropped his own mask.

"Thanks ever so much." The lady was finally back. "Things as simple as going to the loo can be so complicated with a pushchair. Plus, right now, I need to pee the *whooole* time." She pointed at her stretched stomach in a conspiring way.

The smile Gabriel gave to her was tight with embarrassment. "You're welcome. Should we go?" he asked me with a pull of one eyebrow and a clearing of his throat.

"Sure." By the time I'd said the word, I was on my feet holding my coat.

I bolted outside and was rolling on the back of my heels when he joined me. He didn't say anything, but took my coat out of my hands and threw it over my shoulders. His arm lingered there. He pulled me gently against his side while we strode back to his car.

I heard the beep signaling the remote-opening of the passenger door and relief bubbled inside my chest. It wouldn't take long—five minutes at most—to drive back to the house on the Scores. Gabriel would be his usual stern and silent self and I wouldn't have to think of any conversation topics to fill the silence.

Only Gabriel didn't open the door of the car while we stood next to the Range Rover. Our bodies were at an awkward angle to each other. His hands curved around my shoulders, applying gentle pressure that anchored me to him. My legs were still wobbly and I needed the support. He positioned me so that we faced each other and stared down at me. There was no judgment or concern in his eyes, just a kind, intense curiosity.

I think the term these days for what I had done inside Gelateria Cassini was *freaking out*. I had just freaked out, *big time*. "I don't know what happened in there. I swear I don't hate children, I—"

"Don't," he cut in, the pad of his thumb covering my lips, rubbing the lower one in a gentle back-and-forth. He was so close I could smell the vanilla of the ice-cream in his breath. "Don't tell me now, *a leanaigh*. But when you're ready, I'd like to know why it hurt so much."

My next breath was a rasp that morphed into a wheezing breath. He kissed my forehead but I might as well have dreamed his touch because, in the next moment, he'd lifted me up onto the leather seat of his car.

We made it back to the house in the expected five minutes without exchanging another word. We didn't come back to Gelateria Cassini but Gabriel picked me up after class every single day for the rest of the week.

It never rained.

Chapter 9 — The Hall Ball

Each beat of the music was a punch to my solar plexus.

The flashing spotlights blinded me. The air was thick with the smell of sweat, cologne, and sugary perfume. I forced myself to suck in short gasps of air through my slightly parted lips. The MacIntosh Hall Ball was unlike any event I had ever attended. It was certainly wilder than those I'd been invited to with Everett in the short time we'd spent together in Edinburgh and Inverness. As far as the few parties I joined during my college days back in the '70's, they'd been all about Flower Power and smoking weed, and far more economical with electricity.

"Something wrong with the wine?" Next to me, Tobias drawled the question.

I checked the untouched content of my glass. "Not at all. I'm pacing myself."

Tobias shot me a look that edged on bored. What could I say? I'd never qualified as the life and soul of a party. I forced myself to sip some of the amber liquid while my eyes caught the disturbing sight of Fergus and Hayden somersaulting in their kilts. The drumming sounds bursting from the giant speakers and assaulting my eardrums inspired them to launch into a high-five of their torsos. They were wearing kilts—and nothing underneath—like pretty much every male at the party. At least that was if the guests stayed true to tradition.

"Those guys were already shit-faced when they arrived. I

bet they'll be leaving here feet-first. Gabe and I will be doing the heavy lifting."

"I don't envy you the task." Forget the option of carrying them, which would qualify as the thirteenth Labor of Hercules. They'd need a truck to load those two onto.

My gaze flicked back to the dance floor. Lizzie and Simon were holding their own with some acrobatic moves that resembled rock' n' roll. They'd come as a date. At last.

Cold kept rushing in shivers down my spine. Since I'd arrived at the party, it had alternated with heat simmering under my skin and beads of sweat rolling between my shoulder blades down to the small of my back. I wasn't wearing much, though, a simple off-the-shoulder black dress that shouldn't cause such an excessive amount of perspiration. My senses were on overdrive and it was more than the proximity of an overload of humans that caused it.

"You seem off. Do you want to walk outside?" My date laid his hand around the nape of my neck.

I assumed it was meant as a protective gesture, but I stiffened nevertheless. "I'm fine. Too many people, that's all."

Accepting Tobias's invitation had been a mistake. Over the past week, things had changed between Gabriel and me. We'd established a rapport. The only time he reverted to his old ways was when I told him Tobias was my date at the ball. Could a hint of jealousy be what made this new friendship tip into something more? In any case, my plan was heading in the right direction.

A *plan*. That was how I still referred to my presence in St. Andrews. No more than a carefully drawn and executed plan.

However, Gabriel, who towered over the crowd and stared at me from the far corner of the packed room, didn't make me feel much in control at all. I resented every single person standing between us. To be frank, I resented Tobias's company too. This wasn't fair on him though. Gabriel wasn't on his own anyway, the ever-present Alice stuck to his side like a tattoo. Unfortunately, with the deafening sound of the music I couldn't eavesdrop on their conversation. Not that they'd exchanged more than a few words. The crowd and my weakness prevented me from entering her thoughts. Alice's usually rosy complexion was ashen.

"Alice seems in even more discomfort than me."

"I guess that's what a broken heart looks like."

My chin snapped up. "What do you mean?"

Tobias smirked; had I sounded too keen? He took a generous gulp of his beer, while maintaining his watch on me over its brim. Tobias Svenson was a handsome specimen, if you were partial to dark and Southern. The first gulp of beer was followed by another and it wasn't until he finished his pint that he finally graced me with an answer.

"Gabe broke up with her."

I suspect the revelation made my eyes as round as marbles. Gabriel had done what he said he would. He'd hinted at it during our bathroom interlude but I wasn't expecting him to stand by his word. "Do you know why?"

"My cousin has some real old-fashioned values about dating...or the lack of it, in his case. Maybe sweet Alice was getting too frisky and he had to preserve his virtue."

"You make it sound like it's wrong." And I definitely sounded defensive.

That brought on another of Tobias's signature smirks. "Not wrong, but a bit of a waste if you ask me. Abstinence wasn't a good move for his father and my aunt. They rushed into marriage to commit the deed and she ended up miserable."

And dead. But, after all, don't all humans?

Tobias's mood switched with his words. Gone was his nonchalance. Tension squared his shoulders instead. His gaze roamed the room as if he'd felt a threat. I followed his gaze but didn't see anything suspicious. Lizzie and Simon had now joined Gabriel and Alice and were making the most of the conversation. Gabriel focused entirely on finishing his beer.

"I need to go to the restroom."

I thought Tobias said *okay*, or at least that was what I deduced from the stiff nod and the mumble he addressed in my direction. I zigzagged between inebriated couples, entwined couples, and embracing couples. It was past midnight and pheromones filled the air. The brouhaha of dirty thoughts disrupted any semblance of order in my mind. I had to seek refuge. The first restroom I entered was filled with girls competing for a fragment of the wall mirror to make themselves up. I went down the corridor that led to the reception of the hotel where the party was taking place. With every step, the music softened. Past the reception desk, I climbed up the central staircase with its threadbare carpet and found an empty restroom on the first floor.

There I sighed. It was partly due to the welcoming silence and coolness of the windowless place, and partly to the poor reflection the mirror over the sink threw back at me. I'd never be the poster child for a healthy tan, but tonight my skin was so translucent the twin veins at each side of my eyes were visible. My lips were chafed, only two shades less pale than the rest of my face. While the tight evening dress had seemed a flattering choice when I'd bought it two days before, it hung now from my bare, bony shoulders and loosely covered my stomach. At least it was short enough that there was no risk of me trampling on it.

I turned on the tap and splashed my face with water, unconcerned about smearing any makeup. It was either that or spend the rest of the night curled up on the not-so-spotless tiles of the restroom. After a couple more water remedies, I'd returned to my almost normal self—which didn't mean much given my overall health. But mascara colored now in two black half-circles under my eyes. I pulled a sheet of paper from the dispenser on the wall and applied myself to correcting the damage. Once I was presentable enough, I made my way along the first floor corridor, room doors dotting the walls on either sides.

The lights flickered, taking me to—and back from—

darkness. I stalled. A gust of air brushed against the bare skin between my shoulder blades. The lights steadied. I did a 180. Behind me the corridor was empty.

My steps quickened and carried me back to the landing overlooking the reception area. There my eyes darted downwards, straight to Gabriel's profile. He was talking to the employee at the reception desk. The girl was blonde and her eyelashes kept fluttering. The movement had nothing to do with the late hour and everything to do with the sight of Gabriel wearing a kilt.

My memories of eighteenth century Scotland didn't do justice to this item of clothing. There was also the possibility I hadn't met anyone who wore one like Gabriel did. Was it because of the defined calves and the muscular legs he planted apart like the captain of a ship? Was it because his shoulders stood wide and square, ready to take any blow for your sake? Or perhaps it had everything to do with how his gaze always seemed to make you want to stand straighter and be better. I ticked all of the above.

He looked good in a kilt. No, he looked *great* in a kilt.

I had to focus to hear what he was saying. He talked faster than usual, as if in hurry, describing someone who looked a lot like me to the receptionist, asking if she'd seen me. I knew she had, but I could also hear her inner monologue: She'd stretch her one-on-one with the hottie out as long as it'd take for the petite dark-haired girlfriend to get her butt the hell away. Then she could have this sexy guy all to herself. The night had just begun after all and she'd clock out at midnight. After that, they could get back—

I shook myself out of her head.

"Parties are still not your thing, are they?"

A polar wind swept through my veins. I shuddered and my heart, my stomach and every single one of my organs shriveled. My feet didn't betray me though. They managed to turn on their heels and bring me face-to-face with Lawrence Beaumont. Him and his Turned bodyguards. He wore a sharply cut tuxedo. Although his frozen features were those of a man in his late twenties, he could mingle with the student crowd without standing out.

"What are you—?" I remembered Gabriel. If he happened to look up the stairs, he'd see me, he'd see *us*. I moved out of Gabriel's eyeshot and grabbed the Stramos by the elbow to drag him farther back into the corridor. "We can't be seen together."

In my world, such familiarity would be frowned upon and probably punished. Louis even told me stories from the olden days when Turned were beheaded for having touched Stramos without their consent. However, Lawrence didn't seem to mind the contact. His arm looped around my waist and he was soon the one propelling me forward. His acolyte opened a door and the four of us entered one of the hotel rooms. One of the more expensive ones, judging by size. The lock clicked behind me.

I extracted myself from Lawrence's grip and hurried to the opposite wall where the closed curtains blocked the only window.

"What do you want?"

Demanding answers from a Stramos wasn't the thing to do either. He extracted a gold cigarette box from his jacket while checking out the decor. With its washed-out paint and vomit-green bed covers, I doubted the room met his exacting standards. Lawrence took out a cigarette and clicked the holder shut, then tapped its butt against it. I had already been impertinent enough and kept myself from reminding him the room was nonsmoking. From the pocket of his tuxedo jacket he grabbed a lighter and soon was enjoying a first drag. I was treated to a couple more smoky exhalations until he spoke. When he did, the sharpness in his voice contradicted his relaxed pose.

"Every time I look at you, I want to be someone else." Lawrence's gaze brushed over my whole body.

I wished I could grab the comforter from the bed and wrap myself in it. No matter how filthy it smelled.

"I don't understand."

He took two deliberate steps towards me. "When you were human, I longed to be one too. Now that you have been turned, I want to share your nature."

This is blasphemy. A Stramos has the purest blood through its veins. They are few but powerful enough to inspire fear and submission in those who know of their true nature. They rarely venture into the mortal world. When they do, it's to turn a female and use her as a sexual companion. Any male offspring will be born a Fiu, any baby girl human. Stramos will turn men too, if they meet their sexual inclinations, or like these two here, if their physical abilities make them able fighters.

To put it bluntly, a Stramos is at the top of the food chain. They don't *long* to belong to substandard strata.

"I still don't understand." I repeated, clueless, and it bothered me greatly.

The corner of Lawrence's eyes twitched as if he had fought off a jolt of pain. "You never did, even when both Marsden and I were courting you and you assumed we were just English gentry. You only paid attention to him."

"I never assumed anything about you, Lawrence, because you never mattered enough to me."

His lips tightened, disrupting his lopsided smile. "Marsden had all that troubled and vulnerable charm going for him. I will give that to him. You fell for it but you chose the wrong mate."

"Don't say his name. I forbid you."

"Why?" Lawrence now stood inches from me, stooping to bring his eyes level with mine. His breath smelled minty despite the cigarette. "Because you cannot face the truth?"

"What truth?"

"That he did not love you enough to survive the Hunter."

My palms landed on his chest and I pushed him away. In vain.

"Because *I* loved you enough to kill him."

Bile erupted from the pit of my stomach. The acid taste filled my mouth and burned my tongue. I had to flee. I had to before he made me doubt. I circled around Lawrence but the two bodyguards barred my way.

"Marie, stay."

I sidestepped the giant on the left but hit the wall of his chest. I tried to exploit the space now left open between them. His companion moved and blocked my escape route.

Behind me, Lawrence repeated, "Please stay."

I huffed and puffed. Finally I swiveled to face him. I didn't want to pretend anymore or defy him. I just wanted to know. "What is it you want from me?"

He started to talk but changed his mind. Instead he took another pull on his cigarette. The tendrils of smoke swirled to the ceiling and I prayed they wouldn't trigger the fire alarm. I didn't want to be found in the present company.

"I don't believe for one second you're able to feel anything at all. Not for me, not for anyone. Still you haven't killed me while I've openly ignored your orders, I must be of some use to you. What is it?"

His mouth froze into a smirk. "Your faith in me, sweet Marie, humbles me." He faked a bow. The silver of his eyes lost the glow his earlier declarations had put there and reverted to their flat, chilling matte. "Times are trying, as you know. The Hunter has inflicted some symbolic and tactical blows on our world. He keeps rallying warriors from other clans, winning more allegiances. He trains his men better than ever and we are weakened. Especially now that so many Turned have to drink from humans again because of that disease. Your kind keeps over-indulging and dropping corpses behind them. So much of the Councils' time is wasted covering their tracks. Not only here in Europe, but also in America and everywhere else." Another pull on his cigarette. "The mass execution of your Master and his clique last June was only one of the Hunter's recent successes. In the meantime, on this side of the Pond, we are reduced to begging for a truce in order to survive." Another inhale-exhale. "We discussed that truce the last time we met. I cannot let this temporary situation turn into a permanent balance of power."

"I'm neither a politician nor one of your trained warriors." I nodded at one of the Turned now sandwiching my sides. "I'm not a pawn important enough to gather so much attention from you."

"On the contrary, Marie. You might be my best bet at destroying MacLeod. Since your interests are now aligned with mine, you should join me." I opened my mouth but he cut me off. "Please do not insult my intelligence once again by saying that you are here in St. Andrews to perfect your medical knowledge."

There was no point pretending indeed. "The last time we talked, you were all about preserving that ceasefire. Now you're all set on destroying the Hunter. I'm confused as to what you're exactly trying to achieve."

"Nathaniel MacLeod slaughtered the whole North American Council."

I felt my mouth gape wide but recovered. "When?"

"Last week." Lawrence turned towards the window and pulled the curtains open. He then opened the window and threw out his cigarette. When his attention reverted to me, I didn't step back. His face had a predatory focus. "He started on Monday. One council member each day. By Friday, he had beheaded all five of them. They were some of the most prominent Stramos ever to walk the earth."

This was unheard of. Turneds were fair game for the Hunter and his men, but Stramos kills were few and far between, and council members were the most powerful Stramos. They were lethal and well-protected, their whereabouts carefully guarded.

"How did the Hunter do it?"

"Various tactics. He bribed some of the Turned charged to protect Council's member. MacLeod's latest round of recruitment has also been particularly successful: he seems to have access to unlimited funds. The *bouquet final* was no less than a drone attack: the Stramos's car was bombed. Of course, the poor chap was burned alive."

"That's unprecedented." I didn't have any sympathy for the Stramos. They weren't victims. They were mass murderers doubling into psychopaths. All except Louis.

"Not quite, 269 years ago our race was under similarly powerful attacks from the Highland Hunters. So we orchestrated Culloden, where we knew all of the clans would fight. They did and we killed all of the Hunters and their heirs except one: MacLeod."

"And here you are again, Lawrence Beaumont, living in fear for your head."

"There's only one person I fear, Marie, and it is not Nathaniel."

I didn't remember Lawrence speaking in riddles, but I had no time to decipher them now. My concerns were self-centered. "Again, I'm asking: What do you want from me?"

"I want you to be my Trojan Horse."

"Be more specific, will you?"

"I want you to befriend the MacLeod girl, seduce the heir, turn them against their father, and when I tell you to do so, kill them."

Chapter 10 — Trojan Horse

This was *my* plan.

I'd used these exact words in the silence of my revenge-seeking soul. I'd sharpened them during the sleepless nights since Louis's execution. I'd matched them with bloody mental pictures while I spied on the young MacLeods. I'd let the words drum inside me at the same pace as my heartbeat.

I'd fed on them, survived because of them.

But tonight, spoken out loud by Lawrence Beaumont, they didn't bring me any solace. Instead, they twisted my guts and ripped out my heart. *Seven weeks.* Seven weeks, that was how long it'd taken for the MacLeod heirs to become Lizzie and Gabe to me.

The truth is, killing is a far more gruesome task when you're on first-name basis.

Lawrence approached and extended his hand, tracing my jawline with the tips of his fingers. I should have batted them away, even if it broke our racial etiquette. I let him because the scaffolding that had kept me standing after Louis's death had started crumbling within me.

"You have never killed, have you?"

I neither confirmed nor denied the question, but no, I'd never killed. After I was turned and my thirst for blood had overpowered my humanity, it was Louis who kept me from dirtying my hands and my soul. He'd provided animal blood and taught me how to hunt for it. It was before the blessed days of blood banks. Before the disease hit my kind.

It'd been his promise to me on that night after Culloden, the night my son died: Louis would make sure I'd never take a life. I'd made a similar promise to him the very night he burned in Saguenay: Not to take but to save lives.

And here I was. Back in Scotland to wound and kill.

My lips parted and I shook my head but not as an answer to Lawrence's question. It was a still unarticulated no to his plan and mine.

Noise erupted outside the room. A voice I knew all too well was calling my name.

"Someone is coming for you," Lawrence said and I sensed the bitterness. "Why do men always assume you are a damsel in distress? They do not see you for who you really are, Marie Aberdein." I had no intention of asking and he continued anyway, now in a whisper. "You're the one who ends up saving them from themselves."

"At least they're not asking me to prostitute myself. What you're asking me to do makes you a *pimp*."

During sex, most Stramos experienced no feeling, no bond, nothing; it was a mere gratifying exchange of bodily fluids. I'd lied to myself thinking I could ever be like them and use pleasure as a mean to an end.

Pain sizzled on my cheek where Lawrence's fingers had been seconds before. I screamed. He glided in a flash back to the open window. Moistness rolled down from the cut to the corner of my mouth. I could taste the tang of blood.

"What are you trying to—" My question sounded like a yelp.

"Marie!" Furious fists banged at the door. "Marie!"

Panic crashed over me. Excuses piled inside my head for the reason Gabriel would find me in this room alone with three men.

"Make sure MacLeod doesn't get her," Lawrence ordered his bodyguards. "Protect her with your lives."

Fighting and killing was the Turneds' purpose. Or dying trying. As trained as he was, Gabriel wouldn't survive a second fight with them. He'd already pushed his luck the first time. The two warriors stared at me with appetite, at the blood now flowing down my neck. Their fangs were on full display.

"Please, Lawrence, take them with you. If you wanted the MacLeod heir dead, you'd already have committed the deed. He has no chance against—"

"Have faith in your savior. He might be more resourceful than you expect. Besides, being saved again will improve your credentials as the innocent roommate."

Lawrence climbed onto the windowsill, the wind causing his dinner jacket to billow like a sail.

"I will be in touch very soon." He bowed again in mock salute and jumped into the night.

Behind me, the doorframe exploded and Gabriel burst into the room.

"Go away, Gabriel." Tears strangled my voice. "Now!"

His gaze flicked over the scene as it registered every detail: the layout of the room, my position, and the two military-looking men guarding me.

Their fangs.

His face didn't betray any surprise. "Marie, in the bathroom, *now*, and lock the door." If only for its slight gravelly edge, his voice sounded as it always did. Not the reaction I expected to exposure of the Turneds' unusual dentistry.

The Turned who stood at my right threw himself at Gabriel only to be jabbed back in the jaw. He doubled over and—I think—spat blood while the other Turned reinforced the attack. Gabriel whipped a stake out of his dinner jacket and impaled the Turned, using his whole body for the momentum. I heard nothing more than a breathless gurgle.

The Turned stumbled backwards and crashed against a chair. He ended up on the carpet at my feet, his grip tight on the wooden stake protruding from his heart. By the time my gaze reverted to his eyes, they were already covered with the opaque filter of death. Louis often praised my quick mind. He wouldn't have done so then because I stood witless above the corpse.

When I whirled around towards the fight, blood was running from Gabriel's nose. He and the surviving Turned were circling each other in the narrow standing area, their legs bent slightly at the knees, their hands curled into fists. A couple of attacks were initiated from both sides and aborted or avoided. The next one—a vicious upper-cut—did reach its target, Gabriel's chin. His head hit the wall behind him. The plaster cracked behind the impact.

"Son of a bitch." For the first time I heard Gabriel swear.

Next the Turned had his hands tight around Gabriel's neck, crushing his whole body with his.

The pressure prevented the air from reaching Gabriel's lungs. He tried to disentangle the thick fingers out of their deathly grip. His nostrils flared. His eyes started bulging, his veins sticking out. I had no doubt the Turned could already smell and taste the blood gorging Gabriel's blocked jugular. I knew I could.

Come on. Come on. What the hell could I do?

The solution was at my feet. I planted the heel of my stiletto on the chest of the dead Turned, bent forward, and seized the stake. I pulled it out. There it was in my hand, its pointy end covered with blood. Gabriel watched me over the shoulder of his attacker. He nodded in approval.

First, we needed something to act as a diversion. Lawrence's man believed he was defending me—perhaps against my own will—but the order had been clear. The Turned couldn't fail a Stramos twice. The action would be worse than death.

"Help," I yelped.

By reflex the Turned checked over his shoulder and offered the opening Gabriel needed. He jerked his knee between the Turned's legs. He screamed in pain—and in a high pitch—but was silent when Gabriel's fist buried into his stomach. Gabriel stepped away, extended his arm towards me.

This was my cue. I threw the stake to him. He grabbed it and, with the same movement, forced it into the heart of the Turned. It wasn't enough to kill him so Gabriel pushed it further into his chest so that the point came out through his back. With another shove, Lawrence's man was nailed to the wall. His head bobbed forward like an unarticulated doll.

Seconds ticked by. I stared at Gabriel's back, how the heaving caused by the fight made it rise and fall. He retrieved the stake. The man crumpled onto the floor, his tongue protruding from between his fangs. There was absolutely no dignity in death. Whoever said the contrary had never seen the end of life.

After hiding the stake back inside his dinner jacket, Gabriel turned towards me and the movement felt like it was in slow motion. I think I squinted and squinted again. This was my reaction to this new vision of him. Gone was the stern boy I'd come to know. The man who replaced him wasn't unknown to me though. I'd stolen glimpses of him before, on the night of the first attack for certain. But here he was with me again, not a flicker in my memory but steady and omnipresent in this closed space.

Sweat made his curls cling to the sides of his forehead. There was as much fire in the highlights of his hair as in the depths of his eyes. With the sleeve of his dinner jacket he dried the blood trickling from his nose. It didn't help; the blood ended up smeared across his cheek but I doubt he cared. His entire focus was on me.

I wanted to recoil but killed the gesture. Had I been found out? Did he know what I was? I had to think. Maybe the time had come for a new plan. *Flight*. I considered the window behind me which had served as Lawrence's escape route. Unfortunately landing one floor below wouldn't be as harmless for me as for the Stramos. My brain and blood would coat the pavement. I wouldn't die—and eventually would heal—but I'd probably lose consciousness. Not long but long enough for Gabriel to catch up with me.

Perhaps he heard my thoughts because he launched forward, then stopped as if he'd hit an invisible wall a yard away from me. He pressed his arms tight against his sides as if to keep them from committing a murderous deed. Such as strangling me. But his shoulders slouched, his neck bent, and his chin touched his chest.

His voice was coarse, his speech slurred when he said the word I expected the least. "Sorry."

My mouth opened and rounded, one eyebrow arched, but the rest of me remained geared for a quick escape.

"I failed you, Marie. I told you they'd never lay their hands on you again, but they did and they—they were about to—"

"They didn't kill me." Stating the obvious was as much as my adrenaline level would allow.

His submissive posture didn't alter. Guilt splashed out of him like blood from a slashed artery. Guilt for what? Saving a girl whose life purpose was *his* death? I had to lift the weight from his shoulders.

I narrowed the gap between us to stand one foot away from him. I wriggled my fingers to check that fear hadn't frozen the nerves there. They were still functioning and with that knowledge came the call of duty. I had to tell him the truth. I lifted my hand and with my curled index finger tipped his chin up. He repressed a shudder but next his head was again holding itself high, the way a warrior should stand. His gaze was still downcast but it shifted to stare at me through the thickness of his eyelashes.

"I'm alive, Gabe." And it was the truth. Not simply because Lawrence hadn't killed me tonight but because Gabriel made me so.

He awoke inside me the girl who died after Culloden. Or perhaps that girl died the day her path led her to Everett Marsden and his world of darkness and blood.

In St. Andrews I was twenty years old again and I'd fallen for the strong, silent boy who already had the world listening to his command. My feelings might have been born from lust and loneliness. In fact, they definitely were, but they also fed on recognition. My soul had been acquainted with him from the very first moment he saw me.

But I'd never get the chance to learn him, and from him, and that knowledge dug a sour pit deep within my heart.

The realization stole a whimper out of me. His gaze flicked back to my face, and his arms wrapped around me. I shuddered out of grief. "I'm so scared of—"

But Gabriel misunderstood. "Please don't be scared, Marie. They can't hurt you anymore." His promise was muffled in my hair. "I won't leave your side again. I'll take you somewhere safe, somewhere they won't know about you anymore."

"Thanks for taking such good care of my date, cousin."

Tobias.

Gabriel's stance strengthened, but he kept me in his arms. "You were right. The Stramos from Edinburgh was here tonight with the same men who attacked her the last time. We need to clean up this mess fast."

I had to admit: Gabriel could keep a cool head. Me? Not so much.

"Hayden and Fergus are smashed. They're not up to the task," he continued. "I'll call for some outside help." He sounded awfully matter-of fact given they were discussing a double homicide.

"Why? The two of us can—"

"That one is for you, cuz. Sorry but I want Marie out of here ASAP."

Silence stretched after Gabriel's statement while the buzz in my head died down. He turned around, still making a barrier of his body.

"And you're going to be the one extracting her." Tobias didn't put much affection in that last word. Gabriel's fists curled. "Fine. She'll need to be debriefed anyway."

I circled around my new protector and hopped over the

body of the first Turned to have died. With my stiletto on, I swayed upon landing, only for Gabriel to gather me back against his side, his arm a hook hard as steel.

"I can find my way home. They didn't hurt me."

"You're bleeding." Gabriel's tone was accusatory as if I'd inflicted the wound directly to myself. In a way, I had.

I probed the cut on my cheek with the tips of my fingers. "That? It's only superficial. I won't even need stitches."

His gaze followed my hand to the wound and he flinched when it touched my cheek. "I'm taking you home."

There was no point arguing, and to be frank, I didn't want to stay in that small space with the two corpses, the too-familiar smell of blood spreading into the air. So I nodded and before I knew it, Gabriel had taken ownership of my hand and we were heading into the corridor.

Tobias stepped aside but I didn't miss the weight of his eyes on me when I passed him by. Again, I hit a wall when I tried and reached for his thoughts. They were not amicable, that much I could say.

"Meet me at home," Gabriel ordered him before he led me down the corridor and back to the hotel entrance hall. "Did you have a coat?"

I nodded and extracted the wardrobe ticket from the built-in bra in my dress. Heat flickered in his eyes and his mouth twitched as if in a smile. But he took the ticket without commenting on my improvised purse. The tip of his thumb kept rubbing the surface of the ticket while we waited for my coat.

The same blonde from the reception was handling the cloakroom. She looked positively disheartened to see her *hottie* leave with that *midget bitch*—and here I cut short the sampling of her thoughts once again. Gabriel held my coat and I hurried my arms into the sleeves. I wanted out of the MacIntosh Ball.

The next minutes would determine whether I'd be out of Gabriel MacLeod's life as well.

Chapter 11 — Pivotal Point

Outside the wind had died down. It'd been blowing in from the sea when we arrived at the venue. There was now a stillness in the air that the biting cold crystallized. I flipped up the collar of my coat and silently cursed my choice not to wear tights.

"I didn't drive here. Do you think you can walk back home?"

The Scores were a five-minute walk from the hotel— double that in high heels—but entirely feasible. "I'll be fine."

"We can order a cab."

"I'll be fine."

Gabriel's arm was back around my shoulder, pulling me to his side. We marched through the darkness, passed a couple of pubs from where last customers were departing. A couple was kissing on the pavement. Since I'd left the party in search of a restroom I'd lost track of time. I assumed it was around one.

My companion didn't seem inclined to talk to me. That left me with the necessary time to decide what I should do, what I should tell, and how much. I had to tell him the truth. That had to be the only starting point. But what next? Would I meet the same fate as Lawrence's Turned with a stake through my heart? Or would Gabriel take pity on me and let me go?

I didn't want to leave him. I couldn't.

His hand curled on my shoulder as if he'd heard my

thoughts of escape and ordered me to stay put. I wished I could have tested his eyes but he had his attention on the pavement ahead of us. With our proximity, the tension of his body was tangible. At regular intervals, his gaze swept over our surroundings in a 180-degree arch. As for the hand that wasn't locked on me, it was hidden inside his vest, no doubt clasping the stake. I doubted Lawrence would try another attack tonight though.

Finally, we turned into the Scores, the howl of the waves welcoming us. He was leading me back *home*. His home. Mine. Ours. But I couldn't just let him take me in with lies, omissions, and half-truths blocking the way.

I dug in my heels, stopping us.

Concern was sketched over his face. "Are you—"

I shuffled backwards, shaking him off. "We need to talk about what happened."

"What about we talk about it inside?"

"No, here." *Here*, I still had a chance to flee. *Here*, I wasn't soiling his home with the filth that was my life. I had to come clean first.

Whatever he thought about my request, he agreed to it with a stiff nod. We were standing in the dark midway between two halos of light created by streetlights. He looped his hand over my hip and made me cross the street to an esplanade overlooking the sea. It was abundantly lit and we were clearly visible. Should we get slaughtered, everyone would see.

I leaned over the railing and faked a renewed focus on the sea. But all I could see beyond the slither of sand right below us was the black wall of the night. I laid my hands flat on the cold stone and struggled to find the first words. Gabriel stood behind me, his body against mine. He bent forward as if to envelop me, his arms locked around my shoulders. Given the potential outcome of this conversation—namely, my death—I should have resented his tight hold on me. But I relaxed and enjoyed his warmth seeping back into my bones. I trusted him to give me the sweetest end.

Should I start with the beginning or the end? Tonight's MacIntosh Ball or that ball in Edinburgh two centuries earlier when I'd met Everett and Lawrence? The morning I became betrothed to one of them?

Or perhaps I should expose the pivotal scene that precipitated my fate, that seizure in time and fracture of my heart, the night I lost my baby son. I'd lived for so long and still there were only a handful of seconds that really mattered.

As it happened I wouldn't be the one speaking first.

"The MacLeods have never brought much happiness to those who befriended them." His voice rolled like the waves eating the shore below me. "I didn't want you to know about me and my family, or about those monsters. I should have made you leave but I was weak. Now your life will never be the same."

"Gabriel, I'm not—"

"The truth is that as much as I hate you to be part of this, I'm also relieved. And *that* makes me the most selfish SOB of the MacLeod line. And believe me, there were quite few of them before me, starting with my father." The heat of his words hid a streak of bitterness.

I should have continued my confession but I was a coward. So I asked instead, "Why selfish?"

"Because I don't want to be alone anymore."

"How can you be alone, Gabriel? So many people love you."

"They don't know me."

"Tobias seems to be very aware of what's happening in your life."

"But he doesn't know I'm scared. He doesn't know *I* don't know."

"What is it that you don't know?"

"If what I'm doing is right or wrong, or whether I'm the good or the bad guy. If I should live or if I should die."

"You *must* live." I swiveled inside his embrace and my hands cupped his cheeks. "Whatever the story you're going to

119

share with me, Gabriel MacLeod, you must live. You must thrive and laugh and love. I won't allow it otherwise." Relief flooded over me just by being able to say it out loud.

I wanted Gabriel alive with the same determination I'd wanted him dead. If there was one truth I'd learned since becoming a creature of death, it was how much I valued life. I was no killer, no angel of justice or vengeance. Quite frankly, if the past two months were any indication, I hardly excelled at the role anyway. My quest for revenge against Gabriel's ancestor had also been a resounding failure. What I was, was a doctor, a healer.

At that moment I knew that if Louis had found peace in some parallel universe, he'd be looking down at me with a smile. For the first time since he died.

Gabriel's hand buried into the tight mass of my bun. He flattened his palm around the back of my head as if to gather and control all my thoughts. His hungry glare roamed over my face, from my eyes, to my earlobe, and ended its journey on my lips. My mouth was dry under the heat of his gaze and I ran my tongue over my lower lip. His taste replaced mine when he kissed me. Earthy and floral like the scent of the wind blowing over the glen. His kiss wasn't inviting or tentative. It was his claim on me. My hands slid over his chest where his heart kept bumping against his ribcage out of fear for me. Not *of* me.

I lifted myself up on my tiptoes to meet him. His tongue reached out for mine. I gladly gave in and the dance started. A celebratory dance for finding our way to each other. His head angled and it deepened the kiss even more. My whole body flushed tighter against his, my stomach rubbing, teasing, and making him harder. A low rumble came from the back of his throat, vibrated through our locked lips, and echoed inside me. My ego sang with pride. The curve between my thighs filled with heat and pulsed. I had to break the kiss because it was too much, too fast. And I did. He kept his eyes shut and rested his forehead against mine. I heard his sharp intake of air.

I knew then that I'd keep Gabriel MacLeod alive or die trying.

"Do you really want to hear my story, Marie?"

"I do, but before you start, tell me why you are relieved."

He winced and shut his eyes. "The first time we met, that afternoon at the game, I saw myself in you. I saw the questions, the doubts, the fine line I tread between truth and lies. I felt you saw them in me too and suddenly I was standing in front of that beautiful girl naked like a newborn. I panicked and I was a bit of a moron to you."

When he opened his eyes to check my reaction, I smiled at the cheekiness in his stare and the curve at one corner of his mouth.

"Only slightly."

"Aye, definitely a moron. But the more time I spent around you, the more I realized how easy—how easy it is to stop pretending around you."

"What were you pretending?"

"To obey my father, to love him." His unveiled hate made his jaw shake. "Living a normal life when I bloody well know nightmares can come true and that they have fangs." Ice curled around my throat. "To pretend not to lust after you."

"I thought we'd established you did. Remember me half-naked outside our bathroom?"

A low chuckle rolled from his throat. His hands fell along the length of my body to cover my bottom. He pulled me against his groin, and I considered abandoning myself to the delicious throbbing between my legs.

"The truth, *a leanaigh*, is that I wasn't only lusting after your body, but after the whole of you. I might be a horny twenty-year old rugger bugger, but believe me when I say it's even more difficult to resist the appeal of your soul than your body."

"Don't try then."

"Resist your body or your soul?"

"Both."

He didn't catch my invitation and it fell between us. Worse, he disengaged and stepped back, opening a rift I almost tumbled into. The wind rushed inside my coat but the cold didn't dampen my need for him. Gabriel glared at me, gauged me. I lifted up my chin to meet his challenge.

"Do you want to see me naked?" From someone so protective of his virtue, the question came unexpectedly and my mouth gaped open in surprise. "What about we get back to the house? I can bare all to you then, Marie Aberdein." He pointed his index finger at his forehead, "My soul." Then at his chest. "My heart. And if you still want to, you can try the rest of me."

He extended his hand and kept his eyes on it, avoiding mine. A couple of minutes earlier, I'd wondered about the pivotal moments in my life. The night I'd lost my child had been the switch from the mortal to the immortal path. As turning points go, it's a difficult one to compete with.

My hand, tiny and breakable, came to fit into Gabe's. It closed on mine and he nodded in approval, still not looking at me. We strode back to the main road. I knew then that the night I chose to follow Gabriel MacLeod into the house on the Scores was another of those pivotal moments. Not only would I be seeing his naked truth, but I followed him hiding mine.

Chapter 12 —Truths be Told...or not

Flames burst from the logs Gabriel had placed in the fireplace. The wood crackled and warmth spread throughout his bedroom.

"I don't like central heating, so I never turn on the radiators." He sat next to me on the thick rug and placed his comforter around me. Its motif was his clan's tartan of dark green and red stripes. I didn't miss the irony of how I now enjoyed the protection of what I'd learned to fear for centuries.

He'd changed into jeans and one of his rugby jerseys. I found myself missing the kilt though.

"I didn't expect to have company," he continued with a shrug that bordered on boyish. He took a long gulp of whisky from the tumbler at his side.

"Not even Alice?"

With deliberate care, he put the tumbler back on the wooden floor between the fireplace and the rug. "Alice has never come here. I broke up with her last week. I told you I would—" he searched my gaze, "—and I did."

"Tobias mentioned something like that." The arch of Gabriel's eyebrow made me shrink a little. "I guess nothing beats hearing it from the horse's mouth."

"Should I be flattered by the equine analogy?"

Talkative wouldn't define me. I'd never been scared of speaking my mind, but I didn't babble. If I'd talked then, I'd have babbled. So, instead of answering his question, I let my gaze roam over the military format of his room, from the desk where books were lined up in alphabetical order, to his bed with the duvet tucked tightly at each corner, and the noticeable absence of any memorabilia.

"Where do you want me to start?" Gabriel sat cross-legged opposite me, his arms hooked behind his knees. He'd left a respectable distance between us. I resented it after having him so close to me. I stared at him while I finalized my new plan and, to his credit, he didn't waver under my scrutiny.

If I told him the truth about what I was, he might kick me out or even kill me. I had no intention of dying quite yet because I'd made two promises. The first to Louis—one I had forgotten in favor of blind revenge—had been to keep looking for a cure to the disease plaguing Turned. The second had been to myself and was still fresh from my confrontation with Lawrence. I wouldn't let him use and destroy the young MacLeods for the sake of politics.

My hand flew to my throat because my conscience had turned fidgety. There was another reason why I wouldn't tell Gabriel what I was: I wanted to stay with him. I wanted to share his life, breathe the same air as him, and drink his rare smiles, those I inspired in him. Eventually—a few weeks, no more—the Hunter would return to Scotland and I would have to leave. With one look, Nathaniel MacLeod would know what I was, being the Hunter and all that.

"Why do you hate your father so much?" It wasn't the most logical starting point, but the father-son relationship was at the heart of the problem. Of that I was convinced.

"Because he killed my mum."

I felt my forehead crease. My eyes squinted. "Lizzie told me your mother had been in a car crash." So had Louis. I wasn't even trying to reassemble a puzzle here. It seemed as if I'd been given a brand new one to play with.

"The brakes had been tampered with. As had the wheels."

"And you know that how?"

"Tobias. He came to me with the truth last summer. His father found out about what happened a long time ago but chose to stay silent. Apparently Mum was about to take us to Texas, back to her family. Uncle Nils kept his mouth shut for years but he needed money. That was when he had the bad idea to get some by blackmailing my father. One month later, Tobias's dad had an unfortunate shooting accident. On the day of his funeral, my cousin was given a letter from his father. Posthumous, of course. It told the whole story."

The words had been delivered with an even tone, so matter-of-factly, as if he'd practiced them before.

"Does Lizzie know?"

"No and she never will if I have anything to do with it."

For once, I had to agree with his wish to protect his sister. There were some truths that didn't have to be shared or faced.

By birth, the Hunter was a murderer, but I always assumed his killing range excluded humans. "Why? You told me your parents didn't agree with how to raise you, but murder seems extreme for a simple divergence of opinions on education."

The fire crackled. Gabriel grabbed the poker and prodded the logs and twigs. I couldn't miss the tension in the muscles of his jaw that sharpened the lines of his cheekbones. He jabbed the fire some more, then put the poker back in its stand.

When he sat back, his fists kept tensing and un-tensing. His gaze was lost somewhere on the Persian rug and I wanted to attract it again. I moved onto my knees, holding the comforter tightly around me with one hand, the other covered his fist. He froze under my touch, then relaxed. I shuffled even closer so that, if I leaned a couple more inches forward, my chest would brush against his arms.

"You said you'd bare it all and I want to know everything." It should be a truth for a truth but once again, I

125

chose to pass on the chance to tell him mine. "I *need* to know everything."

Gabriel gave me a stiff nod. "In each Highland clan, there used to be one Hunter. Often in one of the minor lines. He was anointed on his twenty-first birthday and powers were bestowed upon him. Not just more strength or better fighting skills than his clansmen, but the ability to recognize, to *feel* the monsters hidden among us."

"Monsters like the ones I saw tonight?"

"Yes. For a long time, only the Highland Hunters and a close-knit group of warriors in their clans knew about them. Things changed after Culloden. The clans were exterminated, not only by the English but by those monsters. They had infiltrated the king's troops. After Culloden, only one line remained. The MacLeods. It took my ancestors decades to rebuild an army and establish their authority over not only their clansmen but men from other clans who hadn't leaders of their own anymore. It wasn't until a whole century after the battle that the MacLeod Hunter had fully trained enough men to fight by his side again."

I let him speak without interrupting. There was nothing in his tale I didn't already know for my kind was proficient with the history of the Highlands Clans. Preys and predators have had ample opportunities to learn about each other over centuries of playing cat and mouse.

"How do you know all this?" I asked when he was done.

"There was a diary with the letter Tobias got from his father. My mother's. She'd sent them to her brother in case something happened to her."

I hurt for Hannah MacLeod. She'd trusted her brother to do the right thing for her and her children, but Good Uncle Nils had betrayed her.

"Your mother didn't want you to become the next Hunter. That's what your parents were arguing about."

He nodded.

"When she decided to take matters in her own hands, she

was killed." I squeezed his hand gently. "Was anyone else involved?"

"His brother, Malcolm." Gabriel spat out the name.

The violence of his tone matched the memory I had of the man, of how he'd knocked down Vincent with the butt of his rifle back in Saguenay.

"Your family would hold its own to any Greek tragedy." My feeble attempt at humor earned a smile from him. There was gratitude in that smile and more so in the kiss he dropped on one of my knuckles.

"By definition, tragedies don't have a happy ending." His lips returned to my knuckle, then moved on to the next one, and the next.

His actions left a faint trail of sweet tingles on my skin. It was a much-welcomed diversion, one I'd have loved to seize, but, "The men who attacked me, do you know who they are?"

"Not their names, but I've seen the tall blond one with my dad before." *Lawrence.* "After Tobias crashed in Scotland last spring with that big reveal of his, I spied on my father for weeks. Skipped lectures to follow him to Edinburgh. That was where they met. Why my dad didn't kill him then, I have no idea. Maybe they have some kind of agreement." *The truce.* "Only whatever they've agreed on doesn't seem to include my fate." Gabriel stretched his arm to fiddle with my earlobe, brushing the tip of it with the pad of his thumb.

I ducked my head sideways like a kitten begging for more cream.

"It doesn't seem to include me or those I care for," Gabriel continued, each word like an unctuous layer of honey over my senses, "in particular the one person who makes me wild, who makes me dream and yearn."

I still wouldn't babble so I kept my mouth shut until I could articulate a valid question. "What about Hayden and Fergus?"

"They're in on it. We've been best friends since we were toddlers. Their fathers are part of my own father's guard, but they've proved loyal to me."

"As long as they keep the boozing under control."

He chuckled. I resisted asking him if the two giants would be part of his own guard once Gabriel himself became the Hunter. In fact, I resisted asking anything about his intentions regarding his own future. Now that he knew the price paid by his mother would he still follow in the steps of his ancestors?

The underside of his thumb traveled along my cheekbone then down to my lower lip, tracing its line. Gently back and forth. And again. I fought the urge to sway. My eyelids fluttered and his face turned blurry. All I could make out were the shadows cast by the fire over the crest of his nose and how they drew amber-colored valleys across his face.

"Do you believe me?" His question kicked me out of my daze. "This sounds a lot like crazy talk."

His finger deserted my lip. I was about to ask him to revert his attention to that part of me, but the time had come to act in character.

"These guys have attacked me twice now and I didn't dream either the size or the shape of their canines. So, yes, I do believe you."

He exhaled in a sigh. "You have a choice to make."

I tightened the comforter around me, bracing myself for the choice Gabriel intended to make mine. His Adam's apple bobbed and he sought inspiration somewhere over my shoulder.

When his eyes darted back to me, flames now seemed to inhabit them, flickers of hope and fear. "Do you still want to stay in St. Andrews? With me?"

"Gab—"

"Before you answer, I want you to know that I'll cover your costs if you choose to relocate. I'll get access to my mum's trust fund when I turn twenty-one, but I can get an advance on it. It's only a few months until my birthday anyway."

"I don't need your money."

He forged on, seemingly oblivious. "I don't see them following you across the Atlantic, so if you leave before the end of the term—"

I cut him off with a kiss. Actually it was more a caress, as I didn't dare to go beyond his lips. As much a test as a taste. I kept my eyes open so that I could gauge his reaction. His pupils dilated, growing black dots within green incandescent pools, and his mouth relaxed under mine. Longing filled my lungs as I raised my hands to reach for the wall of his chest. His head jerked back, severing the bond.

"Don't—" Gabriel took hold of my shoulders and carefully sat me back down. Rejection slapped me and my cheeks burned with shame. "Don't underestimate the threat. This is real and, if you stay with me, this might happen again." He swallowed. "If you stay with me here, this *will* happen again. You'll never be safe."

"They attacked me twice already and still here I am."

"They hurt you." He stared at the plaster that covered the cut Lawrence had inflicted earlier that night. "Twice. What will happen next time if I can't find you?"

His concern for me stirred my guilt even more. Babbling became a far better alternative than wrestling with my lie, so I jumped on the first thought splashing through my mind. "What about Alice? You knew you were putting her at risk by going out with her. That didn't stop you."

He lowered his head. "That's not the same."

"How so?"

"Alice and I…we're kind of betrothed."

"You'll need to qualify 'kind of.'"

"Her father died when she was still a wee girl. He was by my father's side. I guess it happened in the line of duty, as they say."

"How did the betrothal kick in?"

He raked his hand through his hair and my lips twitched. He was able to recount to me the most unbelievable tale—by human standards—without stumbling on a single word. However relationships appeared to be a far bumpier road for him.

"It's always been assumed we would end up together. My dad made it clear last summer."

"You're just like your sister then. It doesn't even cross your mind to question your family's rules."

His eyes narrowed and the crests of his cheeks reddened. "You are right, lassie." He nodded but it cost him to concede the point and I heard it in each syllable. "I didn't question anything until Tobias handed me my mother's journals. And even then I had my doubts. I didn't believe in this whole madness until I followed my dad and saw with my own eyes who he was fighting, what those creatures are capable of." For the second time I saw the shadow of fear troubling the fierceness I always read on his face. "And then I guess I started questioning everything."

"Still you went after Alice."

"*I* didn't *go* after her. *She*—" He stopped there and it took him a moment to choose his next words. "It was easier to give in to her."

"Why?"

"Because Alice is safe. She belongs to my world. She isn't an outsider and I'm not dragging her into this shit. I was attracted to her but like with other girls, I can put words on it. When you crashed into my life, it left me as mute as a fish. And here we are with another animal analogy."

"Will you go back to her? If I leave, will you go back to her?"

Gabriel half turned away from me. The gesture was brusque and I refrained from dragging his heavy body to face me again. He feigned a renewed interest in the fire but his movements were jerky and didn't improve the intensity of the flames. He laid the poker against the wall of the fireplace but didn't look back at me. How I wished I could access the secret realm of his thoughts. Instead, I was reduced to waiting for an answer.

"The Hunters marry young so that they can further the line before they get killed. Their life expectancy doesn't usually meet the national average."

We'd reached the point I'd been avoiding. The point that mattered above all else. "Is that what you still want to be? The MacLeod Hunter?"

He looped his arms around his knees as if bracing himself against an incoming blow. "Right now, I want to make my father and my uncle pay for what they did to my mum. Once they have, I'll decide what to do with the rest of my life, however long it ends up being."

If he chose to follow his ancestors, it was likely his life would be on the short side. "What about what your mother wanted for you?" What Hannah had died trying to achieve. "She was taking you and your sister away from this bloodbath when they murdered her."

His gaze shot back at me. "Exactly. Me *and* my sister. What do you think will happen if I bugger off before the anointment? The Hunter's line will move from me to Lizzie. Any son she'll give birth to will be the next Hunter. If I haven't killed them, my father or Malcolm will stand in until his twenty-first birthday, but eventually Lizzie's son will be the Hunter. That's not something I'd wish on anyone, mother or son."

Anger brewed inside me, rising from my heart up to my throat. My voice took on a higher pitch, "But here you are talking about your own children and how you'll need a wife to give birth to them. Quite the contradiction, isn't it?"

He grabbed the whisky tumbler and threw its contents onto the fire. The flames growled and stretched upwards. I recoiled at the sudden heat.

Gabriel's eyes were now drilling through me. I held on to my position. "I haven't figured out everything yet. All I know is that these monsters don't just live in books and legends and that they kill innocents. They have no right to walk the earth. But I also know that my mother deserves justice."

"Don't lie to yourself, Gabriel. What you're seeking isn't justice, it's revenge."

"And why is that so bad?"

"Because justice leads to peace, revenge only to more injustices that others will seek retribution for. The cycle never ends. Don't you see?"

Twice I'd set myself on this route. The reason I was still alive stemmed from my first attempt at vengeance. I'd chosen to become one of the monsters Gabriel hated so that I could make the Hunter pay for what he took from me. I glared down at my palms held open in front of me, the comforter sliding down my body to the floor. These hands, their pale skin untainted, were such a lure. They looked like the hands of an innocent, but I wasn't one. Maybe I'd never been and that was why I'd fallen in love with Everett in the first place.

There was still a chance to save Gabriel from venturing down the same path as me. I stretched my hand to circle his wrist and yanked him to face me. He let me and I slid between his bent legs. Both our heartbeats went rushing from this new proximity, but I ignored the tingling of my senses and forged on.

"All you're trying to do is to make sense of something that doesn't. You lost your mom before you even had a chance to know her. It should never have happened, but still it *did*. What you've learned from Tobias, it gives a sense to your loss."

Gabriel tried to disengage from my hold on him, but I resisted. "If you go after your father, you'll put yourself at risk and if something happens to you, then your mother will have lost for good. Her death will have been for nothing."

"There's no life for me as long as he lives."

I laid one hand over his heart, the other cradled his cheek. "There *is* life as long as your heart beats. It'll beat much longer if you get away from this madness. Take Lizzie with you. Start a new life somewhere as far away from Scotland as you can. Save yourself, Gabriel."

He held me under his stare while his chest kept rising and falling. His mouth opened but no sound came from it. He pressed his lips together, shut his eyes as if to gather his courage to jump from a cliff. When he opened his mouth and his eyes again, his heart missed a beat under my palm.

"Will you come with me? If I leave St. Andrews…Scotland, my clan, will you come with me?"

His question punched the air out my lungs, making my shoulders slump. My chest caved in. I heard a whimper sneak out of my mouth. Images stole my whole focus, the ones I was drawing inside my head with the shredded pieces of hope I'd salvaged through the years.

The kaleidoscope of pictures told a sweet story of love and college. The tiny flat we would rent off campus. The shopping trips for cheap food. The mad cramming for our finals. First jobs. First mortgage for a suburban house. And one day a winter wedding in one of those cute mountain villages in Quebec. My dress would be one of those fancy lace and organza creations I'd seen in magazines. I wouldn't wear a veil. I'd want Gabe to see my every emotions when I walked down the aisle.

I'd stopped breathing while my soul indulged in those dreams but I had to take another breath, and with that breath, the movie of my dreamed life came to an end.

"I can't." The words fell between us like broken glass.

"Why not? You can stay in St. Andrews where some whackjobs have put a target on your head, but you can't take a chance and try somewhere else." He stalled there and blinked. "With me. You don't want to take a chance somewhere else with me."

"It's not that simple."

"What is it about you, Marie Aberdein? I'm baring all but I still don't know much about your life, except that you have nightmares so bad they keep you awake at night."

He'd reversed the momentum and it was about to hit me. "There's not much to say really."

"What are you trying to escape from?" Gabriel's voice faltered and became hoarse. "*A leanaigh*, let me in."

I didn't have to let him in because he was already there, in each breath I took, in the making of my every thought and every word. My lust for him had crashed against the barriers set by my long-lost love. But his smiles and his kindness were what had planted the seeds of his hold on me.

"Please let me in." It was a plea.

Panic swirled inside my head and made my tongue so heavy I feared whatever I said I'd stumble over it. I acted instead. My hand flew from his chest to the side of his face. I straightened so that my gaze was level with his and my breasts brushed against the cotton of his jersey. When I edged my face closer to his, our eyes read into each other. I was the one who kissed him, his lips still under mine.

He wanted words from me, not seduction, but I had to convince him otherwise. My tongue ran along his upper lip, then his lower lip—and again—until they both trembled under the tease. I slipped into his mouth and there again he objected, his tongue passive. I leaned further into him. His upper body mirrored my movement, bending backwards. He could go only so far without lying on the floor so he counterbalanced by gripping my waist. We were back to our vertical starting point.

I wasn't deterred, and neither was my tongue. It glided over the rim of his teeth—back and forth—then reached for the roof of his mouth. A low groan crawled from his throat. He sucked a harsh breath from me, his fingers flattened over my hips. Finally his tongue danced with mine. There were a couple of false steps but when they found their rhythm the rest of us started singing in unison.

While my fingers slid to the back of his head, threading into the thickness of his curls, his followed the lines of my thighs to end at the hem of my dress. They lingered there. I increased the pressure of my hold on him and triggered his own venture further under the material. Gabe's touch on my thighs was so delicious it hurt. He tipped his head, opened a new angle to explore my mouth, then pursued his discovery of my thighs. Up and up.

The silk of my underwear was the next frontier. The tips of his fingers skimmed the edge between my flesh and the material. Shivers rippled to my core, clashing with the heat already smoldering in the pit of my stomach. He deserted my mouth, tearing a moan of frustration out of me. A gasp followed when he palmed my bottom, then lifted me up, swinging my legs around his waist. He was hard against the point throbbing between my legs. His pull on me was brutal as if, despite the layers of material between us, he might still find a way inside me.

All I wanted was to sink into him but all I could do was rock against him. A raspy hum rumbled through my lips and he held me even tighter, grounding me. His eyes spied on me begging me to let him continue. I nodded, and a sharp intake of breath rolled through him. The kisses he rained down my throat softened his claim on my lower body.

He reached the hollowness demarking my neck from my shoulder, his tongue nuzzled the skin there and pursued the line of my collarbone. His hair had a clean scent, a blend of soap and bergamot and I breathed it in. I threw my head back for him to shift his kisses back to the depression at the base of my neck.

The tip of his tongue molded against the inward curve there and woke a fluttering line from my throat to my heart and all the way down to my sex. Strange how an innocuous parcel of skin could join a network of sensations, strengthening their bond. A buzz echoed now throughout my whole body, my breasts heavy and achy, the tendons over the back of my hands bulging out from my grasp on his shoulders, and the muscles in my thighs tightening around his waist. My lust for Gabe swamped me but my hearing—like my other senses—heightened.

Thump. Thump. Thump. His heart bumped madly against his ribcage.

Saliva filled my mouth. I swallowed but the familiar process was taking over once again. My gums itched. I ground my teeth. Rushed breaths pumped my lungs and I had to let the air out in messy pants that made me bend double. My fangs pierced through my gum. I bit my tongue—blood pleasing my taste buds—and collapsed over Gabriel.

The noise I made next morphed from a whimper into a yelp. I let go of him, and in a mess of limbs—his and mine—I disentangled myself. I'd have landed on my back if his strong hands hadn't caught my waist. He gently twisted me towards him and settled me on the comforter now crumpled over the floor.

I swallowed again and put the final burst of strength left within me into ignoring the sweet metallic flavor of my own blood. Gabriel caressed the sides of my face, his breathing as shaky as his hands.

"It's all good, *a leanaigh*. We're all good. You see, we've stopped."

My gaze landed on the bulge inside his jeans. That had to hurt. I trained my brain to focus on his pain—as intimately located as it was—rather than mine. It distracted me from the proximity of the twin points inside his wrists which had become my favorite part of his anatomy. Odd but true.

A slight tip of my head and I could indulge in him. He'd expect another kiss but it'd be a bite. Two clean incisions through the skin into the vein and a torrent of satisfaction would rush into me. So easy. So deadly.

Had he sensed the killing instinct shoving to the surface, scratching my polish? He retrieved his hands from me and put them clumsily over his lap, their fingers spread apart. My fangs reverted to their hidden place. Shame placed two heavy bricks on me, one on each of my shoulders.

"Marie?"

I kept staring at his hands.

"Marie?"

I swung my gaze to meet his, hoping it wouldn't waver.

"I'll take whatever it is that you have to give me." The rolling cadence of his voice smoothed the goose bumps that had broken out over my bare arms. "And I'll be damned if that doesn't make me sound like a bloody beggar."

His sorry smile creased the dimples at the right corner of his mouth. That dimple could steal years from his face. A minute earlier, I had Gabriel, the man, carving pleasure over my body. Now it was the boy right there in front of me. I thought of Hannah MacLeod, the price she paid for her son to be safe, and certainty struck me. I could never hurt him.

Denying what I was would be a lie too far, but with Gabriel I could also play with time. His soul bore so deeply into mine it extracted my humanity and wrapped it around me, so tight it melted into my skin.

"I don't want to push you. We won't do anything you don't want to do."

I stretched my hand to his. He threaded his fingers with mine as I knew he would.

That was the moment I blurted out, "I'm not a virgin."

Chapter 13 — New Dawn

There was a faint shudder, a tightening of his shoulders, but his fingers kept playing at intertwining with mine.

I waited until he decided to speak. "Why are you telling me this?"

To give you some of my truth. A tiny scrap of truth, but *my* truth nonetheless. "Because I know you have certain beliefs."

He chuckled again and the corner of his mouth twitched. I wriggled the fingers of my free hand as I yearned to trace the plump, curved line of his lips.

"I'm learning that beliefs are easy to harbor as long as they're not tested."

"You've dated before so they must have been tested."

He leaned forward and kissed the tip of my nose. "You North Americans get so hung up about the concept of dating."

"How would you qualify it then?"

"It's never mattered enough for me to put a name on it." His expression sobered up. He flipped over the hand he'd been playing with. The palm now faced up and he rubbed his thumbs over it with just enough pressure to bring the network of my senses out of its slumber.

"I hope you're not disappointed." My voice was so flat and low I was surprised he even heard me.

"I have no right to be disappointed in you."

"But you are a vir—"

"So far, I've made certain choices. Whatever my reasons, they don't make a better person of me." His thumb reverted to massaging my palm. "But you make a strong reason and a beautiful choice, and *that* will make me the man I want to be."

Emotion bubbled up inside me, burning my throat. I blinked. It was wrong, so wrong of me, but I let his words swell and coddle my heart. I almost didn't hear his next question.

"Have you been in love before?" His eyes now had a fuzzy glint about them.

"Yes" hushed from my mouth. "Yes, I have. Once."

His gaze passed back and forth between my hand and my face. It was his way of absorbing the blow. "Are you still in love with him?"

I snapped my hand out of his grip, sucked air into my lungs, trapped it within. My brain couldn't reconcile these two universes. My short time with Everett so long ago. My present with Gabriel. Their colors, tastes, sounds were so far apart I couldn't even fathom that the person experiencing them was the same. *Me.*

I'd married Everett and he'd fathered my child. He would be with me until my last breath. But was I still *in love* with him?

My lips parted and I released a rasping breath. But Gabriel had still not breathed in or out. At all until…

A knock at the door saved me from answering the question.

He stood and crossed to the bedroom door. When he opened it, it was on a still kilt-dressed Tobias. However, his dinner jacket had become crumpled, his bow tie hung open around his neck, and his hair was ruffled.

What wasn't tired, though, was how he stared at me over Gabriel's shoulder. His look was acute and not in the least bit friendly.

"It's done," he said.

"Did the men ask any questions?"

Tobias shook his head. "They made it to the hotel in half

an hour, but I followed them all the way to their boat. They loaded the bodies and off they went. Like last time."

Gabriel's shoulder relaxed. "Thank you."

"I hope we can trust those guys. It won't bode well for us if they start getting a conscience."

"They need the money. That'll keep their mouths shut better than moral principles."

"What about her?" Tobias flicked his head in my direction.

Gabe stepped sideways and blocked my view of Tobias and Tobias's view of me. "Marie is up-to-speed."

"Is she going to pack then?"

When had Tobias Svenson turned so strongly against me? He'd asked me out but my ego wasn't inflated enough to believe he resented my connection with Gabriel.

"*She* is staying here until further notice." There was so much coolness in Gabriel's voice I fully expected icicles to crystallize in the air.

"Nothing good is gonna come of this. We've already wasted enough time babysitting her. She's a distraction."

"I'll be the judge of that." Gabriel started closing the door. "Good night, Tobias."

The door hit the foot Tobias had wedged against the frame. "Can I talk to you…in private?"

"Very well." He turned towards me. "I'll take care of this quickly, promise."

Gabriel stepped into the hall, closing the door behind him. Of course, I could still hear their every words.

"I've come here to make sure Nathaniel pays for what he did to my dad. I won't leave until it's done."

"And he will pay for it. You have my word." Gabriel's even tone still held a threat.

"You wanted to check what my dad wrote with your own eyes. I understand. That's why we lost the chance to kill your father the last time he was in Scotland. But when he comes back—"

"He'll be a dead man."

And then something would die inside Gabriel. Provided he survived the confrontation. Killing his father would scar his soul and I didn't want that scar on Gabriel. I didn't want Nathaniel MacLeod to live either.

"I'm glad we're on the same page, cuz. That's why I want that girl out of the way. As much as I enjoy drilling through some vamps' hearts, we should focus on taking Nathaniel down."

"Nothing has changed."

"Yes it has, because your father will end up hearing about how you sent those bastards to hell. Then he'll know that *you* know." Tobias had delivered his little speech in apnea.

"You want him back in Scotland, don't you?" Impatience had crept into Gabriel's question.

"I do, but I also want us to be prepared and for you to be onboard."

"Don't forget why you came to me in the first place, *cousin*." The way Gabriel spat the last word out I knew the time for family bonding was over. Tobias didn't dare answer and Gabriel continued. "Because you can't take on my father and my uncle on your own. You can't afford a hitman good enough to do the job for you either."

"I fucking know you're my winning ticket. Why do you think I'm still here doing your dirty work?"

"Let me be perfectly clear." Gabriel articulated every word, each one sending a chill through the door. "You didn't do me a favor tonight. I was the one who put my life on the line. Not you. The day you can hold your own wooden stake and run them through, as you say, *then* you can ask *me* to dispose of their bodies. Until that point, that's how our teamwork is going to be, mate."

The balance of power had been reinstated and Tobias took his cue with a mumble. Gabriel shut the door after his cousin had beaten his retreat. He swiveled but his stare was cast down, one hand raked through the mess of his curls. He made his way back to our improvised camp next to the fireplace, bringing with him more warmth than the bright flames.

"You'd better watch your back with that one. His father betrayed your mother once. Apples don't fall far away from the tree." As figures of speech go, this was an overused one. Still very accurate where Tobias was concerned.

He sat cross-legged next to me. "He was rude to you. I'm sorry about that."

"Don't be."

"But he's right. It'd be better for everyone, starting with you, if you left St. Andrews."

It was out of the question. Gabriel could fight better than I ever could but I knew more about his enemies than he did. Lawrence, the Hunter, Stramos or Turned ones, I knew how they killed and how to kill them. I also knew that vengeance had a bloody taste, one that—when the time came—Gabriel might not enjoy as much as he expected. One second of hesitation on his part and he'd be dead. Nathaniel MacLeod wouldn't show any mercy to a traitor, even if that traitor was his son.

"I'm staying."

"Marie, please, for your sake—"

"I've got nowhere else to go." It was true, always true. "I'm staying. So stop asking."

Gabriel hadn't flinched against Lawrence's bodyguards or Tobias, but he did then. There was submission in his now stooped shoulders and bent neck. He stopped arguing too. In silence, he stood again to fetch the cushions from his bed and laid them next to each other on the floor. He grabbed the comforter and spread it over his lower body, keeping the corner lifted in invitation.

"So, *a leanaigh*, if you're so set on staying, it's my duty to keep a close eye on you. Twenty-four/seven. I can't possibly let you out of my sight, especially at night."

I arched an eyebrow and stole a glance at his bed and more importantly the mattress. "If I really do have to stay, wouldn't it be more convenient to sleep there?"

"Nah, let's not make it too comfy or you might get the wrong idea. You wouldn't want to deflower me on the floor, now would you?"

I choked. Anything I said would come out in a croak, so I crawled to the free space by the second pillow. I lay there and welcomed the comforter's warmth and his body next to mine. I faced the fireplace, his chest cradling my back, his arm over my waist, his fingers drawing circles on my stomach. We'd lain together this way one week before, but the tautness between our bodies had changed in nature. I still felt every inch of him but the rapport was fuller, tighter. There was something entirely new between Gabriel MacLeod and me that night.

Trust.

"Speaking of first times…" I let my sentence hang.

"Yes?"

"It wasn't your first kill tonight. When was that?"

"Last summer. Tobias and I, we followed my father to Edinburgh. I had to see what his so-called business trips were all about. That's when I saw the blond who's been after you. I wasn't in a good place then but my cousin was totally screwed up."

"I'm not sure he's fully recovered."

"His dad was murdered. I can relate to that."

"But you didn't kill La—" I bit my tongue in time. "You didn't kill the blond guy, then so who was it?"

"My father and him, they met at some club that vampires go to. There're some humans there, appetizer types, if you see what I mean. I wanted to get out as soon as our business was done, but Tobias lingered and got into trouble."

"He was about to become the appetizer."

"Yes. We were damned lucky because there was only one of them and it was a Turned. I'd never used a stake before." His fingers stopped their circular movement. "I'd never killed anyone before."

My hand covered his on my stomach. Our fingers intertwined again.

"It happened here in St. Andrews too." His nose nuzzled against my earlobe. "The night before the anniversary of my mother's death. I had to find a way to make the bodies disappear. That was when a few of my dad's former business acquaintances came in handy."

"Who are they?"

"Brothers whose family used to serve the MacLeod Hunter. Some of them are nothing more than mercenaries but they're more reliable fighters than some younger men in the clan. These two guys weren't cut out for it and they wanted out. My dad let them live, but he made sure they wouldn't find any other job. So they were more than happy to help me out for some extra cash."

"Will they be the ones taking care of your father's corpse?"

Gabriel ignored my bravado. He moved behind me, probably taking support on his forearm to hover over me.

"What about you and I pretend for the rest of the night?" His breath caressed my skin. It smelled of whisky, a comforting blend of spice and vanilla.

"Pretend what?"

"That we had a good time at the ball, that I chatted you up, bagged you. You came home with me and we proceeded to have drunken sex. Now we're about to collapse into post-coital comas."

"Talk about a romantic way to be deflowered."

His low-pitched chuckle tickled my senses. "Hearts and flowers are so overrated."

"What happens in the morning? You can't put me in a cab."

Gabriel scowled and ran his thumb over the line of my cheekbone. "In the morning, you stay here, with me, close to me. It's a new dawn, Marie."

The painful thing about Gabriel MacLeod was that he was so easy to believe. It was a double-edged quality for those who couldn't afford to believe. A sob climbed up from deep within me, its claws scratching the inside of my throat. My nose itched in that telling way and I was about to cry. A new dawn? How promising it sounded. But I'd never fare well with the light, at any time of the day.

"Thank you," I whispered, cocking my face so that it now rested against the palm of his hand.

"For what?"

"For telling me about your mom. For putting up a fight for me."

He gave me a shrug. "Killing those things is in my DNA, after all."

That hit me straight in the gut. I hissed and shut my eyes. I'd made my bed of lies, and now I had to lie in it. Those prickly lies punctured my skin.

"You fought for me to stay."

"*This* might end up being my most selfish fight." He lowered his head and tasted my lips.

The kiss was innocent with a touch of naughty. It was a mere brush with a teasing lick of his tongue over my lower lip. I swallowed and the heat of his kiss simmered down my breasts, my lower abdomen, and whirled between my thighs. With our bodies flush against each other, I couldn't miss his own arousal.

The kiss changed, not a mere caress anymore but a full-on meal of my mouth. His tongue filled me, suckled on my lips, biting the lower one, gliding beneath the top one. His hips settled between my legs as I spread them wider to welcome the width of him, my dress now bunched up around my waist. The roughness of his jeans scraped against my inner thighs, his cock so hard it snuggled against the folds of my sex. We could be naked, our skin so hot it burned through the layers of clothes.

When he abandoned my mouth, it was to rain hard kisses

down the length of my neck, along my chest. He cupped one breast—kneading, shaping it—and toyed with the hardened nipple with his teeth. The silk of the dress stole some of the heat of his mouth away from me. Frustration quickened my breathing and I lifted my breasts in a shameless plea for more. More suckling. More biting. More puckering. *More.*

Goose bumps broke when the tips of his fingers trailed along my collarbone. My hands clutched the back of his collar as I tried to pull him back to my mouth. The clenching of my sex begged for Gabriel's attention to move south but I couldn't let that happen. I couldn't have him inside me, not when I was still full of lies.

"Gabe." I wriggled under his weight. "We shouldn't do this here…" His fingers reached for the hem of my panties, sliding underneath them, brushing against the damp curls there. I reared up. "Not for your first time." The pad of his thumb parted my lips, simmering pleasure over my flesh.

He straightened and pulled on my underwear, sliding them down my legs. They were discarded without him tearing his eyes from me. They were hungry for me, his gaze glued between my legs. Heat from the exposure spread across my cheeks and I covered my face with the back of my hands.

"You don't want me to see you, *a leanaigh*?" His own hand cradled my bottom, his hips grinded in small circles against me.

I didn't answer, my throat so clogged up with lust.

"Do you want me to stop?" It was a challenge, one he could have addressed to one of his men. A taunt to stand up against him. To defy him.

I shook my head in surrender.

"I'm glad we've established you're still onboard."

A chuckle relaxed the delicious knot his touch tied in my lower belly. "I didn't expect someone as inexperienced to be so…proactive."

He swooped down, gathering my skirt in one fist, inching it higher and higher. He laid his palm on the top of my inner thigh and eased my leg further apart. I could feel the sleekness of my sex, its moisture inviting him in. My hands fell over my head and I dared a glance at him. His nostrils flared and his eyes were now all fired up.

"Never under-estimate the imagination of a twenty-year-old virgin. I ran so many scenarios involving my tongue and your lips I'm surprised I still have some free headspace."

I moaned, short and low, and turned entirely wanton. "Which lips?"

His mouth crushed against my sex in a grunt. The brush of his tongue sliding through my folds had my hips writhe, my hands flow to his head, grab his hair, tug on his curls. I rocked against his mouth, rode it in wild abandon. His tongue found the hub of nerves beneath my skin, licked it. One stroke. Two. The throbbing in my sex caught up with my heartbeat, pounding and erratic. His stubble grazed the inside of my thighs.

He sucked hard on the little mount, feasted on it. I whimpered and the noise mingled with the wet sounds his mouth made against my swollen flesh. The tip of his finger teased my entrance, sank into me, curled against my walls. He sucked harder. His finger plunged in and out of me, teasing me from the inside, awaking a forgotten spot.

When I came, it wasn't in a blind explosion. Pleasure trapped me inside my body instead. I could see and feel every part of me. I'd found a new truth, a truth that was his and his only. My chest kept lifting and falling. My heart thrashed inside my ribcage and the beat rippled through me. I was lying down but I could feel the world spinning all around me.

Gabriel shifted his weight, lacking his usual ease. After readjusting the comforter over us, he reverted to our initial position, my back to his chest.

"Thank you," I said in a quiver.

He cleared his throat, but his voice was hoarse. "Don't thank me, *a leanaigh*. I did it for myself as much as for you."

"Still, I'm the one collapsing into a post-coital coma."

He kissed the tip of my shoulder. "I told you you would. Let's get some sleep. We need some rest to face this new dawn."

Despite Gabriel's generous ministrations, I expected sleep to elude me. Electricity had been running through my veins since I left the ballroom. Images of the night twirled in front of my eyes and I had to blink. Twice. But I applied myself to following his breathing. It had such a regular tempo, as if our proximity didn't affect him. Other signs told me that he was, though: He was still hard against my bottom.

I smiled then. I sighed too and stared at the ballet performed by the flames. The show they gave enthralled me. The last thing I remembered of that night was the fluttering of my eyelids and the weight of Gabriel's hand over my hip.

***

I'm not sure what awoke me: the prism of light caused by the morning sun or the call of my bladder. It wasn't a brutal awakening, more like a progressive climb out of my torpor. What struck me though was that I hadn't moved, neither had Gabriel. Although the fire had shrunk down to no more than a few embers beneath a pile of ash, heat still wrapped around my bones. It all sprang from the large body cozied against mine.

I snaked out of Gabriel's grasp and sat up. The slash of copper in his hair clashed against the stark white of the cotton covering his pillow. I indulged in his profile, the straight line of his nose softened by the curves of his nostrils, the shape of his lips that a sleepy pout made plumper, the fan of his eyelashes and their almost feminine thickness.

My hand clasped my throat while the knowledge he was mine slithered through me. There was nothing permanent in this ownership, but that morning it was very real.

With caution, I stood and tiptoed out of his room. I made my way up to the bathroom where I did my business and brushed my teeth. When I saw Lizzie, I was ramming my fingers through the tangles in my hair and on my way down the stairs to his bedroom.

Had she seen me coming out of her brother's bedroom? In my now creased evening dress? How could I explain it?

But then I realized that Lizzie wasn't coming out of her bedroom on her way down to an early breakfast. She was on her way up and wearing her own evening dress, with its very own set of creases. Mascara was smudged under her eyes and her hair was an open challenge to a comb.

"You're awake." Her mouth remained rounded at the end as though it was a question.

"Just needed to go to the bathroom. I fell asleep fully clothed on my bed."

Lizzie didn't comment. Her gaze didn't meet mine either. She appeared in a daze that I attributed to one shot too many. I smelled liquor in her breath, in her sweat. And something else.

"Where have you been?" It was early morning after a busy night and I didn't have the energy to guess her thoughts.

"What do you mean?"

"I mean… Were you with Simon?"

Her eyebrows pulled together as if my question required consideration. "Yeah, yeah, that's where I was."

I kept referencing the effect of her night on her appearance without being able to pinpoint what troubled me. My aspect had to mirror hers too, so who was I to judge?

"Can I pass by?" she finally asked and I realized I was blocking her way.

"Of course." I stepped aside.

She hurried up and mumbled a 'goodnight', which didn't match the morning light sparkling through the window on the next landing. I stared at her while she retreated into her bedroom, trying to catch remnants of thoughts, images of her night stored in her mind. I failed.

Shaking my head at my own failure, I stumbled down the stairs. More sleep was clearly needed as I was off my game.

That was when I caught a lingering scent, musky and familiar. Cold saliva tracked down my throat. I brought my hand to my nose, sniffed, and ran my nose along the line of my arm.

Lawrence and his filthy smell were still all over me.

I eyed the door to Gabriel's bedroom. The yearning to snuggle back to his side warmed my inside, pulled at my heart. I ignored it and climbed back to the bathroom. There I started to undress, dropping my clothes on the floor.

I looked down at my naked body and traced the line of a hip. We hadn't made love last night, but my body was already his. Only I knew that his ownership of me wasn't like my ownership of him. From that day onwards, I belonged to Gabriel MacLeod.

It was my choice, and it was made for all the good reasons.

Chapter 14 — Hollaroch

I'd been at the MacLeod's ancestral home once before.

The place held a mythical dimension for my race. It's where none of us would have ever dared to venture until Gabriel MacLeod was slaughtered. I don't think any of us has taken the risk of returning since.

But here I was again, a Turned, at Hollaroch, invited by none other than the next hunter in the line. When Gabriel had driven through the gates of the estate, I'd fully expected to burst into flames. It hadn't happen but I wasn't yet counting my chickens.

Quite a number of us had been invited to spend the first weekend of December at the house. The MacLeod twins, Tobias, the irreplaceable Hayden and Fergus, and, unfortunately, Alice Cameron. Apparently the same group—minus myself—had made the trip last year and Lizzie had decided to turn the event into an annual MacLeod tradition. There were quite a few of those and this one didn't strike me as the most unpleasant.

I watched Gabriel feed the granite fireplace with new logs, and the definition of his back muscles under his jumper while he busied himself. I watched him from a distance because the flames were dancing to a mad choreography. I didn't trust their next move.

We stood in what used to be the common room. Hollaroch wasn't one of those Scottish castles that adorned postcards. The Hunter line belonged to a minor branch of the MacLeod clan, therefore their nest looked more like an upmarket farm than a noble estate. One hour north of Inverness, its land bordered the North Sea with long stretches of beaches endlessly battered by the wind.

"Are you scared of the fire?" Gabriel stared at me over his shoulder. He smiled and the dimple I adored was on full display. "Or are you scared of me?"

"No," I rushed my answer to defend myself. "I'm simply admiring you."

"Admiring me getting covered with soot?"

I shrugged because whatever tasks he was doing—even the most menial—I enjoyed the sight of him. I stored every image in the memory box I'd soon tuck away in a secret corner of my heart.

He extended his arm in my direction. "Can't you come and admire me from a little closer?" His voice tasted like single malt, warm and soothing with an unexpectedly sexy after-kick. "Please."

I couldn't resist its appeal, so I dutifully scurried to where he stood, making of his body a barrier against any flicker of flames. Gabriel engulfed me in his arms and I lodged myself between them. I rubbed my face against the rough material of his pullover. It was old and lint sprang from it, but it smelled of all things Gabriel. Of soap, bergamot, and of heather too, floral and infused with the spring.

"Miss Aberdein, I want to express my disappointment again with you not sharing my bed."

Since the MacIntosh Ball, I'd slept in Gabriel's bed every single night. We were getting acquainted but at a pace most of our peers would define as *slow*. After his oral ministrations the night of the ball, our explorations of each other hadn't ventured further than a kiss. We'd remained fully clothed at that. It was all my doing, although I wouldn't have minded skipping a few steps to satisfy my hunger for him.

But there were things I couldn't steal. As long as I lied to

Gabriel, making love to him would constitute theft. Or perhaps I was already a thief and the nuances I introduced were no more than hypocrisy.

"Mr. MacLeod, *I* am the one disappointed in your lack of concern for my reputation."

His hands journeyed down my ribcage, awakening hot sparkles on their path. They found their final destination cupped around my bottom. He drew me against him. The pressure he applied was gentle but enough for the softness of my belly to cradle around him. The feeling of him already hard and thick through the material of his jeans triggered the now familiar thrumming between my legs.

Over the past week, it was a part of my anatomy that had regularly reminded itself to me as if the two centuries of abstinence had merely been a hibernation of my senses. It was spring again and they were now in full bloom. The kisses he rained over the side of my neck felt like a practice run for my touch.

"What about we salvage your good name but I sneak into your bedroom tonight?" He whispered the question and the movement of his lips doubled with the faint stubble against my skin was a sweet tickle.

"You'll have to promise to come on tiptoes and not make the floor creak." My hands slid up his chest to cradle his face, lifting it away from my neck. His lashes shielded his eyes, his lips were parted, and all I wanted was to run the tip of my tongue along the edge of his front teeth.

When I did, a shudder broke his body. "I don't give a shit what the world will think about us." He rested his forehead against mine. "Marie, just be mine. In private, in public, on the moon if that rocks your boat, but be mine."

"Let's not waste any of our time together making announcements. I want it to be just the two of us for as long as we can make it last."

He inched forward and brushed the tip of his nose against mine. "I'll make time our ally, *a leanaigh.* I'll give you seconds and minutes and hours, enough of them to take us to the next millennium."

I shut my eyes and let his promise ripple through my soul, brightening the images that fleshed out my dreams. My dreams of a future, of a life with Gabe. The lump in my throat grew and I fought the need to choke. The only future—the only life—that mattered was his. There would be no *us*.

I wriggled out of his grasp before my lack of control overwhelmed me. My lack of control over time, the Hunter, of Lawrence. I had to come up with a plan more elaborate than sharing Gabriel MacLeod's bed if I wanted to ensure he could one day share that same bed with a woman he could have a future with. The self-image whipped me in the face. It slashed a cold dagger through the molten lava his touch had made rush through my veins.

"Don't get all scared on me," he snapped, his hands circling around my neck. He bridged the gap between us and tipped his head forward so that his eyes were level with mine. "I need you to believe as much as I believe myself."

"Believe in what?"

"In us."

I put my fingers around his wrists and tried to yank them away from me. He didn't budge but there was no threat in his hold, just a steady determination. "Gabe, you've known me for no time at all. How can you be so certain of your feelings?"

He pulled me against him, this time with the natural strength that was his, and I collided into him. The side of his thumbs aligned with my jawline, forcing me to meet his stare. His mouth straightened until he spoke. "Because for the first time I have something to fight for that is mine. Something, someone—" his voice unraveled but he swallowed, bringing it under control. "—who matters to me because I want her to, not because I have to or because I'm told to."

"How can you be so sure I'm all that?"

"Because you make me exist. Because you see me for

who I am and by doing that, you make me be…me." He chuckled at the last word, but the laugh toned down into a lopsided smile tainted by shyness. "You also make me ramble like a chick."

He was so wrong and he was so right. The reason I'd sought him was his name and his lineage. I hadn't known him then and all the quirks that were his: his economy with words, his few smiles that shone through me, his fierceness to protect those he loved, his grief for a mother he hadn't known, his playful way of making a child laugh. But all these things I now knew were his. They didn't belong to his clan. They weren't what was feared by my kind or what would make him revered by his.

They were just him. Gabe.

"At least now I know why you broke up with me."

Gabriel's hands shot down to my waist, pushing me aside, then behind him. I rolled my eyes. It was Alice Cameron, not a blood-deprived Stramos. I doubted she'd jump at my throat. The vibes I picked up from her across the room clashed with her still placid demeanor though. I cursed myself for not telling Lizzie about her brother and me. If she'd known, she might not have extended the invitation to his ex.

"Alice, I'm sorry you had to find out about Marie and me this way."

Her mouth twitched. Silence settled in the room and I rounded Gabriel, feeling pretty confident my life wasn't at stake. She managed to hurt me though.

"That girl is a nobody. What do you think your father will say when he finds out?"

I could answer that. Nathaniel MacLeod would be appalled to find out about my relationship with his son. However, his reasons ran far deeper than Alice could ever imagine. Next to me Gabriel spread his legs and placed his hands on his hips

The edge was undeniable in his voice. "I don't give a flying fuck about what my father thinks." Gabriel rarely used swear words. Alice had definitely struck a nerve. "However I do care about what you say about Marie in my presence. If you want to keep being welcome at Hollaroch or on the Scores, you'll apologize to her."

"I won't," she snapped.

I shifted from one foot to the other. This was getting out of hand. "Gabriel, there's no need for—"

"You and I, we're done. We could have stayed friends but I won't forgive you for insulting Marie. If you want to stay here and remain Lizzy's friend, you'll apologize to Marie. Right now."

Her expression frazzled. I knew that the prospect of becoming a social pariah outweighed her dislike for me or her heartbreak. Lizzie was a popular girl with an even more popular brother.

I didn't want to make more of an enemy of Alice so I rested my hand on Gabriel's forearm, the muscle tensing under my touch. "I don't need her to do that. I think this should be between you and her."

His gaze landed on me. When it did, warmth flickered through it. But they remained cool, focused. "I don't want you to go anywhere."

"I won't go far, I promise."

The nod he gave me was only a mild approval of my plan. I swiveled and bolted for the heavy wooden door opening onto the moor that surrounded the main building. When I passed Alice, she made a point of ignoring me. Since I was privy to her thoughts, I was treated to a fine collection of not-so-charming names. They didn't affect me and I left Gabriel in charge.

Our coats hung on the wall by the side of the door. I grabbed mine and an oversized woolen scarf. The fragrant patchouli emanating from it told me it was Lizzie's. I slid my arms into the sleeves of my Barbour jacket and stepped outside. A few loops of the scarf around my neck blocked the wind.

The land around Hollaroch was desolate. It was too close to the sea, and the sandy soil and permanent wind made it unsuitable for agriculture. The MacLeods used to rear sheep here but I couldn't see any around and I wondered from what sources the clan derived its wealth these days.

I was deliberating which way to go when a disturbing sight knotted my stomach. I blinked and blinked again. I scurried away from the house in the direction I believed to be north and the shore. Wisps of hair slapped my face over and over again. The wind brought moisture to my eyes.

The familiar silhouette marched ahead, perhaps fifty yards in front of me, the tails of his long coat flapping in the wind. I didn't narrow the gap between us until he reached what had to be his destination. The beach. I tried to block the sound of the waves crashing but it sneakered into my head and kept rolling there. It distracted me when I couldn't afford to be.

I hurried towards him, my feet now squelching in the wet sand. He kept his back to me, apparently contemplating the troubled waters. When I stopped there wasn't much of a gap between us. If he wanted me dead, no distance would spare me or prolong my fate. I wanted my first word to hurt but a plan had started to roam around my mind. For the plan to come to fruition I had to play nice. I took three more steps to stand next to him.

"Lawrence."

He didn't acknowledge my presence, which made no sense as he'd lured me here. His profile was set in harder lines than I was used to seeing on his face, his head slightly tipped forward, his mouth frozen. Lawrence had always played up his lackadaisical side, but I knew it was a lie. Underneath he was sharp and shrewd.

"For you to take the risk of venturing to Hollaroch again after two centuries, there must be something very pressing in the wind. What is it?"

He continued his mute game.

My temper rose up my throat. "You risked your life coming here, and as much as I'm intrigued you did so, I can't be seen with you."

His gaze shot to me. I couldn't help backing away because I'd just taken a glimpse into the monster he was within. The grey of his eyes had frozen into steel. His fangs had dropped. The change of expression was a fleeting eclipse while his face regained the semblance of humanity. "Seen by whom? The dashing, not to say reserved Gabriel MacLeod?"

I heard the snap of his canines retracting into his gum. The knot in my stomach loosened slightly. "Among others."

"It seems like St. Andrews is having a positive effect on your social life, or perhaps it's only about one person in particular." An arch of the eyebrow punctuated his insinuation.

"I'm glad I can have some form of social life because it means my heart is still beating. Should I remind you that you left me to die a week ago? Or maybe you issue so many death warrants, you've lost track of who you've condemned."

This was definitely not playing *nice* and I expected the full force of his anger to fall on me. Since we'd become reacquainted, I'd taken insolence to an unprecedented level where Lawrence Beaumont was concerned. But it failed to come to me again.

"I did not leave you to die. The next Hunter was at the door to rescue you. If I signed a death warrant, it was for my two Turneds."

Two highly trained, centuries-old fighters. I chuckled in disbelief. Lawrence bridged the gap between us, placing his body so close that in another inch we'd be touching. I tucked my head down. The move had my chin burrowed in Lizzy's patchouli-scented scarf. I squared my shoulders but that was my only pathetic show of defiance.

He lifted his hand to the side of my face. I anticipated feeling his fingers pierce through the flesh of my neck and my head torn away from my body. My eyes shut because what I wanted to see last was Gabriel's face, just like I'd seen him next to the fire inside Hollaroch.

But I didn't die.

Instead of snapping my head, Lawrence's fingers brushed along my cheek and I trembled half in disgust, half in relief.

"Do you think I could ever kill you?" It was Lawrence's voice that trembled now.

I felt my eyebrows pull together in dismay. Very slowly, I unburied my chin from its scarf hideout and risked a glance at him. He wasn't as tall as Gabriel but I still had to throw my head back to see him from so up-close. "Yes, I do."

Shock broke his usual cold features. Or maybe it was the mess made by the wind of his perfectly groomed hair. "Even after all I've done for you, after I killed the Hunter? You still can't see it."

"Can't see what?"

"That I love you."

My mouth gaped open, then shut again, and I giggled. It was a nervous, anxious giggle, not one of those free and dainty ones Lizzie broke into several times a day.

Lawrence's expression closed up. The steel solidified once again in his eyes. "Is my love for you a laughing matter?"

His question was followed by a tightening of his fingers around my neck, the pressure unmistakable even through the wool of the scarf. I didn't miss the threat.

"You're incapable of love."

"And why not? Because of what I am?"

I swallowed through a *Yes*.

"But we are the same, Marie, you and me, we *are* the same, and still you spat at me your love for Marsden. If you can love, why can I not?"

My answer erupted through a strangle. "Because you make love sound like an act of war when it should bring peace." The pressure on my throat increased but I continued, my voice vacillating. "Because you make love a final statement when it's all about the journey to get there."

"And what is that journey about? Do tell me."

"It's about cherishing, protecting, supporting. It's about giving the priority to someone else's needs. Or dreams."

He relaxed his grip on me. I breathed in the salty air of the sea while his thumb came to trace my lower lip. He lowered his face and ran his lips over mine. He didn't force a kiss but it was enough for me to taste him. His taste never changed, no matter how many times he inflicted it on me: copper and death.

He reintroduced inches between us. "What about telling the truth then? Is that also part of that mysterious equation?" I nodded. Dread pumped bile into my mouth because he *knew*. "Then allow me to question the sanctity of this new love of yours because it's love you think you have for the young MacLeod."

His words peeled off the layers of clothes I had on and the wind bit at my flesh. I was so exposed goose bumps broke over my whole body, making my skin itch.

"Don't take it away from me." I was now begging.

He winced, then his gaze deserted my face and got lost somewhere beyond me. When it shot back to me, I flinched. "So there is indeed something to take."

I heard the sadness. I didn't want to, but I did, and the power between us shifted from him to me. It wouldn't last but it was there for me to take, and take it I would. I covered his hand with mine, lifted it to my face, and tipped my head so that his palm now cradled my cheek. His attention was frozen on me as if I'd cast a spell on him.

"Lawrence, I lost my first love because of politics. It cost me my child too. I can't have it all taken from me again."

He gave no sign whether he'd heard me or not.

"I might not have a future with him, but please let Gabriel have that... A future."

"What makes you think it's in my power to spare him?"

"Because you're the chief of the European Council. Because you want to use Gabriel and Elizabeth as leverage against their father. But what you really want is Nathaniel MacLeod, not his daughter, not his son."

"I want Nathaniel dead indeed, but why stop there? Why would I leave his heir alive when he will pursue his father's crusade? And while I am at it, why not make their deaths as painful as possible? Why not play with their heads first?"

It was tempting to tell him the truth about Gabriel's own revenge plan. I didn't, though, because he'd confided in me and I wouldn't betray his trust. Plus Lawrence would always find a way to outsmart me. The less he knew, the better.

He jerked his hand out of mine. Next his fingers circled around my wrist, pulling me against him. I fought back, but against his ancient strength, it was no more than fidgeting.

"He's killed Louis and all your friends but now you're whoring yourself and spreading your legs so that a MacLeod can slide his Hunter's cock inside you."

He twisted my wrist, making me sway around in an attempt to relieve the pressure. I bent my knees, my body now awkwardly angled to his. It didn't alleviate the pain that pierced through the tendons and muscles of my arm.

"Let me go, Lawrence."

He didn't and twisted further.

I cried out, "Please."

He relaxed his grip on me and I collapsed onto the rock-hard sand, his polished boots filling my vision. I hurried back to my feet because remaining crumpled on my knees in front of him stomped on my pride. I hadn't much left that was mine but my pride. He wouldn't steal that from me.

I massaged my wrist where a red circle already marked my skin. He stared at it too with a shocked scowl as if he had no idea how his touch could have inflicted the bruise. The touch of a Stramos was hardly featherlike. I toughened my stance by aligning my arms along my body, the wind now hitting me from behind and throwing my hair in a myriad directions. I locked my gaze with Lawrence's.

"You wanted me to seduce him, remember? You were far

less judgmental then about whose *cock* I had inside me. I'm no whore but I also know what Louis expected from me."

His jaw tensed. "And what was it?"

"He wanted me to find a cure for the disease killing Turned ones like me, the disease that condemns us to either starve to death or drink from a human, risking murder when we do."

"And that is something that the high-minded Marie Aberdein would never do. But lying with her enemy, *that* you have no objection to."

I rubbed my lips together to keep myself from correcting him. I wasn't lying with Gabriel, at least not with the implications Lawrence had in mind. But once again volunteering as little as I could seemed to be the wisest choice. When I spoke, I channeled my self-control to avoid shouting. "I want Nathaniel MacLeod dead as much as you do."

"Not quite. I don't want him just dead, I want to make an example of him. Death, you see, can feel sweet if it comes after atrocious pain or incomparable loss. The loss of a child for example."

Dread coiled around my heart. "I beg you, Lawrence, I beg you: spare Gabriel. Don't make him part of whatever it is you have in store for his father."

If I had had any power during our confrontation, it had slipped through my fingers again. The terms of any deal I'd strike with Lawrence would likely now be on his terms. There wasn't much I wouldn't do to protect Gabriel, and the Stramos was very aware of it.

I hung on what he'd offer next but all I heard was the roar of an engine superseding that of the waves. It didn't trouble Lawrence who kept scrutinizing me. I dared to have a peek. A Hummer had stopped twenty yards away from us. A Hummer that looked a lot like those I'd seen at Saguenay the night before the slaughter.

"It seems like my carriage has arrived." One moment he

was there, the next he'd glided away with a smirk still curving his lips. He went so fast I almost stumbled into the space he'd left empty.

Anger welled up inside me. He couldn't leave me without an answer, without a promise that in this madness, Gabriel would be safe.

"I will consider your request, pretty Marie. And while I do that, think about what you can bring to the bargain. But always remember that I never make idle threats."

And with that he climbed into the car. I watched it drive away across the beach, branching soon into a path that led back inland.

I had wanted to reveal little, but I had in turn revealed too much.

Chapter 15 — No Idle Threat

I didn't know Hayden and Fergus sang—or played the guitar—but they did. Badly.

After dinner was served around the long table, the two of them had grabbed their instruments and treated us to a rendition of "We Will Rock You." It was so off-key my eardrums shriveled.

Gabriel sat by my side. He leaned against the back of his chair, one of his long legs reaching for mine under the table. His arm came to rest on the back on my chair. His fingers brushed my shoulder, but the contact was fleeting. It was enough for his silent claim on me to mark me. I followed his other hand when it stretched out to seize the stem of his wineglass, and watched its trajectory as he raised it to his lips. Saliva rushed to my mouth as my hunger for him overwhelmed me. I swallowed it, my fingers circling my throat.

Gabriel noticed my discomfort because his own fingers slid away from my shoulder and landed on my jeans-clad thigh. I glanced up at him and met his eyes. They asked me a silent question which I answered with a smile. That smile was so much of an effort my facial muscles ached. My gums itched as my fangs slowly pierced the flesh.

I was damn hungry. So hungry for blood.

Hayden and Fergus moved on to another tune, one I'd heard the crowd singing at the rugby game the day I officially met Gabriel. While they mistreated their vocal cords, I glared at my plate, where my untouched beef lay miserably. Whatever blood there was still engorging the meat, it wasn't enough to satisfy my needs. I should have dropped in at the hospital for a refill before leaving for Hollaroch. Instead, I'd pretended to be what I hadn't been for more than two centuries—human—and my lie had left me weak. Weak and making a spectacle of myself. Opposite me, Alice glared.

Before dinner she'd apologized to me. Her words had sounded so insincere there was no need for me to check on her thoughts. The truth was I didn't care about her. Next to the immediate threat posed by Lawrence, Alice Cameron didn't look like too much trouble. However I could do without her scrutinizing me when I'd reached a low point.

I stood and started gathering the remaining plates and cutlery. Lizzie had already disappeared into the kitchen to prepare the dessert with Simon in her wake. Gabriel's hand grabbed my waist when I picked up his plate. Heat simmered from under his touch and zigzagged from one hip to the other, leaving behind a happy trail.

"Sit down. You've done most of the work so far." That wasn't exactly true since my contribution had been setting up the table while the MacLeod twins had masterminded the whole night and weekend.

"That's not fair on Lizzie." Well, Hayden and Fergus were far too busy performing and Alice in sulking. Gabriel started to his feet but I ordered him back, "Stay put and relax. You cooked the meal."

His hand slid away from my waist but I enjoyed its journey across my bottom. The corner of his mouth curled up and the twinkles in his eyes told me he enjoyed the journey as well. If my hands hadn't already been full, I'd have pushed the rebellious curl that kept falling over his forehead and mingling with the tips of his eyelashes.

I took his plate and headed to the kitchen, praying my waitressing skills wouldn't fail me. In my peripheral vision, I noticed Alice leaving the table. She stole a glance over her shoulder to where Gabriel sat. Did the girl expect him to follow her? I listened to her and I was knocked over by disbelief: *yes,* she did. I shook my head because I believed he'd made himself plainly understood. I checked on him anyway while pushing the kitchen door with my back. Pleasure coddled my heart—and my ego—because it was me he was looking at.

"I'm telling you I'm fine, so can't you just take my word for it?" Lizzie bent to place a plate in the dishwasher. Her gesture was so brusque I feared for the safety of the piece of vintage Wedgewood she was holding. I heard it clink against another plate but nothing cracked, fortunately.

"Sweetheart, I'm just trying to help. You've been in such a foul mood."

"Please, Simon, don't *sweetheart* me. We're not yet middle-aged for fuck's sake." Lizzie raked her hands through the mess of her curls. Her cheeks were flushed with irritation, or maybe because of the woolen turtleneck she had on.

In any case, irritation was a departure from the rather gloomy mood she'd displayed since…well, since the Ball. I thought she'd be galloping like a wild horse across the field of first love. She'd finally got together with Simon after all.

"Why don't you go back to the table and enjoy the show?" I offered.

Lizzie seemed finally to notice my arrival. Her gaze struggled to focus on me. Perhaps there'd been one too many glasses of Bordeaux tonight. "You're a guest, Marie. You should be the one enjoying the music."

"I don't know what they're singing anyway," I admitted in a shrug.

"You don't know Queen? Shut up! I know they're ancient but everybody knows them." And Lizzie was back. "Seriously I sometimes wonder where you've lived all these years."

And my preference was for her to never find out. I gestured her towards the door and threw a "Have fun" at her.

Lizzie dragged the tension away with her. Simon let out a noisy huff and my gaze drifted to him.

"What's going on with her?"

He pushed his glasses up his nose. "Your guess is as good as mine." His tone was pitiful as he kept staring at the shut door leading back to the common room.

I laid the pile of plates and cutlery on the kitchen counter and started loading the dishwasher, rearranging its content. "The two of you are dating now?"

"We kissed."

I nodded and finished filling a row with the last dirty fork.

"She's gone all mysterious and distant since the Ball." He leaned against the countertop, his hands buried in his jeans pockets, his chin burrowed against his chest. "Maybe I shouldn't have pushed so hard. I've cornered her and now she's freaking out on me."

I closed the dishwasher and came to stand in front of him. I placed my hand on his shoulder and gave him a gentle squeeze. "Don't beat yourself up about it. Lizzie was ready to date. She told me so."

I could have as well said nothing at all because he pursued the same line, "I thought that with Gabe going out with Alice, she'd feel less guilty about the whole breaking-the-MacLeods-rules. But now that Gabriel is single again, maybe Lizzie is having second thoughts."

"She doesn't feel guilty at all, Simon. Chin up! Go back there and show her that whole moody princess thing she has going on isn't impressing you. Stand your own ground now."

His gaze flicked up to meet mine, checking if I was telling the truth.

"Come on, Simon!" I struggled to recognize that over-enthusiastic version of myself but I did have a soft spot for this boy, and underdogs in general.

He answered me with a nod of fake determination. "You're right."

I stepped aside and gestured for him to fly to Lizzie's conquest. He marched away. When I called after him, he had his hand on the knob of the kitchen door.

"I know you want to make Lizzie happy but don't forget to make yourself happy too." A crease appeared between his eyebrows so I explained, "It's great to be patient but make sure she treats you right."

"So you're saying I shouldn't *always* be at her beck and call."

"I guess that's what I'm saying."

"I'll try and find the right balance between managing Lizzie MacLeod's moodiness and my own sanity."

"Good luck with that!" I waved at him and his smile warmed me.

Left alone, I busied myself at tidying up the aftermath of the dinner preparation by Gabriel. He could certainly cook, but it wasn't an orderly process by any means. After switching the dishwasher on, I wiped the island top, then washed a few dishes. I was placing those dishes back in the imposing cupboard at the far corner of the room when I heard the voices.

They came from the common room that shared a door with the kitchen. They were so close that mere walls wouldn't have prevented me from hearing them well in advance of their arrival. But the lack of blood had weakened my abilities and I had focused entirely on my domestic tasks.

The female voice belonged to Alice. Her speech was rushed, her voice at a higher pitch than usual. She was enquiring about the identity of a newcomer. I wondered too who had joined our party. I couldn't remember any mention of an additional guest, plus all the bedrooms had now been assigned. Maybe Gabriel and I should come out as a couple and free up a bedroom. The thought of belonging to him—and for everyone to know it—had me fighting a smile of elation. A delicious flutter flew across my whole body.

That shadow of a smile froze and died when I heard the

newcomer. Fear grabbed and shook my guts so hard they dropped to the pit of my stomach. I threw, more than laid, the last dish on the shelf and bolted through the door to the common room. It was an impulse and impulses aren't an advisable *modus operandi* to avoid casualties.

Impulses weren't advisable either as soon as you entered within striking distance of a Stramos. And impulses became downright fatal when you entered within striking distance of Lawrence Beaumont.

The pace my heart pumped blood through my arteries would have put me in fear of a coronary, had I still been human. The internal thumping ripped throughout me, dropping in a cold shudder from my constricted throat down the lengths of my trembling legs.

"What are you doing here?" I barked.

My gaze bounced back between Lawrence and an Alice whose earlier gumption had evaporated. The wind blew from the opened window, billowed into the thick velvet of the curtains, and hit me. I wanted to fold my arms around my upper body to protect myself from the chill. I didn't because there was no need to emphasize my lack of weaponry. I swept my gaze around the room in search of some form of stake as defense, but who was I kidding? By the time I managed to break the leg off a chair, Lawrence would have torn my throat open. And Alice's.

"Are you out of your mind?" I yelled. The last thing I wanted was for anyone outside this room to come and check the reason for my shouting. Next I brought my vocal cords under control. "You're inside the Hunter's home."

Lawrence detached his attention from an awkward-looking Alice and nailed it on me. For any observer there was no change in his expression. I knew him better than maybe anyone else. The slant of his eyes narrowed, their corners crinkled slightly, and it wasn't in amusement. "I am indeed, and this statement does very much apply to you too."

"I'm a guest here."

"Do you know him?" Alice's voice was no more than a whisper.

I forced myself to keep watching the Stramos. He was here to hurt. It was too much of a risk to enter the walls of Hollaroch for his venture to be mere curiosity.

"Alice, please get back to the common room. I'm taking care of this."

Lawrence's glare swung back to her. She shrank under his scrutiny and stepped back.

"You will stay here, woman." Lawrence's order froze her to the spot.

Alice stilled and whatever spirit had inhabited her eyes vanished.

"What is it that you want?" Fear quickened my speech.

He edged closer to the girl, so close he bent his head to the inward curve of her shoulder. I could have sworn he was sniffing her. An invisible hand grasped my heart. On the other side of the embossed oak door the rest of the guests continued singing and clapping, oblivious to what was playing itself out here.

"Please don't hurt her," I begged. Begging was always my endgame with him and the knowledge brought tears of shame to my eyes. "She's innocent."

Lawrence's eyes flicked towards me over Alice's shoulder. His smirk made my teeth grind. "There is no such thing as innocence, Marie, except perhaps your own naïve belief in it."

He lowered his mouth to the pulsing spot along her neck. The click of his fangs stabbed my soul. When they buried into her skin, panic slapped me across the face and punched me in the stomach. Alice's passive whimper made me scream and propel myself towards them. I had no hope of stopping him, but it didn't matter because I couldn't stand and watch.

When he detached his mouth from her, I stopped midway. He ran the tip of his finger around the corner of his mouth and licked the speck of blood on it.

"Not as uniquely flavored as yours—" he shrugged, "—but nothing really is, unfortunately."

"Please don't hurt her," I repeated, stretching my arms in a prayer. "I'll do anything you want but don't hurt her."

"Anything?" He tilted his head sideways as if giving consideration to my request. "You see, this is the second time today you ask me to spare someone you care for."

And didn't I know that? Confronted with the obvious, I shut my mouth.

"I guess the moment has come for you to make a choice," he continued. I pressed my lips so tight together I feared the skin would vanish. "Who do you care for most?"

"Lawrence, she's not worth you taking the risk of coming here. The last time you did it was to slaughter the Hunter." I nodded at Alice's frozen form. "She's nothing to you, nothing at all."

"You are right, but she means something to you. The question is: how much?"

Lawrence couldn't understand that everyone mattered to me. Friend or otherwise. *Everyone*. With my concern for Alice skyrocketing, I failed to articulate that idea to him. I remained silent, once again scanning the room for anything, *anything*, that could, if not stop him, at least slow him down. The survey was no more a success than earlier.

"There is no point seeking an escape." He confirmed what I already knew. "The only resolution to the problem at hand is inside you."

"What can I do?"

"I have already asked, but I would indulge you and ask again: who do you care for more?" The saliva in my throat congealed, blocking any air from flowing in or out of my lungs. "Let me rephrase the question: do you care for that insipid girl more than you do for Gabriel MacLeod?"

I couldn't cry or collapse or even beg, because Lawrence's dilemma had already killed something deep inside me. The truth was that there was no dilemma at all. There was no choice to make either. If I'd felt shame before, it had been nothing in comparison to what was now shattering my conscience.

But I had to try and think this through because, as dumbfounded as I was, logic was missing in his action. Lawrence had always proved himself shrewd and calculating.

"I'm lost."

His eyebrow curved in genuine surprise. "And why is that?"

"You wanted to use Gabriel as leverage against his father by having me seduce him. Killing her doesn't take you any closer to your goal. If anything, you will alert Gabriel and the Hunter. They'll find out what I am."

"Do continue," he smirked. "Your mind fascinates me."

"Killing Gabriel now destroys any upper hand you stand to gain against Nathaniel. There's nothing to threaten or scare him with. Nothing to hurt him more than his own death."

Lawrence's hand slid up and down Alice's neck, forcing her head to stretch sideways. "So do tell me, sweet Marie, what am I really trying to achieve here?"

My mouth was dry when I spoke next, my tongue heavy and swollen. "You're here because of me."

He abandoned Alice, who swayed. He circled around her, clapping his hands as if we were at the opera. "Bravo."

"Each time you come here, it's really because of me." The realization had rendered my tone flat and bland. "Before it was to kill the man I held responsible for Everett's death. Tonight—tonight…" I had to kick-start my brain because the truth I was uncovering smashed against all I thought I knew of Lawrence Beaumont.

"Do continue." There was no more teasing. He hung onto my next word, his whole body immobile but still reaching out to me.

"You can't let me love again, so taking Gabriel's life will solve that problem. But by killing Alice—" I swallowed through a boulder-size lump, "—you'll make sure he can't ever love me because he'll know about me."

Because I wouldn't let Alice die, I'd give her another chance at life, just like Louis had done with me. But doing that would reveal what I was.

"You're seeing through me finally." He stepped back, always facing me, to stand where he had before. Behind that innocent girl.

There was no naïveté in my use of that word: *innocent*. She was a twenty-year-old girl who had a crush on her childhood friend. She was meek and sometimes mean but she was still an innocent.

"You do love me." Whatever the twisted definition Lawrence attached to it, he thought he was in love with me.

I'd never given any credit to his feelings for me, the ones he'd always hinted at or teased me with. My oblivion to them could very well be my downfall.

"I'll come with you." I hammered every word. "I'll follow you wherever you want me to. I'll give myself to you." I marched forward. "You can have my body and use it in whatever way you desire. I'll never try to escape. *This* is my promise to you but first you must spare them."

Humiliation burned my cheeks. What I had promised was my own enslavement. Still, just by looking at the disappointment sketched over his beautiful but chilling face, I knew it wasn't enough.

"I will not lie and pretend that it is not your mouth I kiss when I kiss random wenches, or your body I pound into when I seek my release in them. But as honey-sweet as possessing your body would ever be, that is not what I need from you."

"You want my soul but this isn't something one can steal. Not even you."

The corner of his mouth contracted. There was an ever-so-slight hunch of his shoulders. "I would settle for your heart."

I had hurt him but had no regret about it. Whatever I'd said, whatever *choice* I'd make now, he'd already decided on his next course of action.

"If I cannot have you, nobody else will. I am making certain on that." Hurt and anger burnt through his threat. "So what is it you are willing to do? Lose your love or lose *his* love?"

The name battled against the barrier of my lips. It wanted out but I fought back.

"Tick, tock. Which one is it? I'll count to five now. One, two." He taunted me in a fake melodious voice that tugged at my nerve endings. "Three. If you do not come up with a name, I will go after both of them, and I never issue idle threats." There wasn't even one alternative scenario emerging from the scrambled mess in my head. "Four. And fi—"

"Alice."

Chapter 16 — Downfall

His fangs plunged into the flesh of her neck.

It wasn't for a sample taste this time. I heard the tearing of her skin and of her artery that marked the start of the sucking. Blood poured out of the gaping wound. Alice's eyes rolled in their sockets and I was grateful she was already unconscious.

I stumbled forward. My hands covered my mouth like a gag. It was partly in shock, partly to keep me from launching myself at her throat and feeding from her. All I wanted was to place my lips on the gashing wound and indulge in the spurts of blood pouring from it.

I didn't want it, I needed it. My nostrils flared at the metallic scent flowing around me. I was thirsty for blood, hungry for flesh I could bite into, desperate for satiation. But it was into my own flesh that my overstimulated fangs planted themselves into. The taste of my own blood seeping from the inside of my bottom lip caused relief to pump tears into my eyes.

The lump that had filled my throat earlier expanded downwards into a heavy weight that filled my entire chest. It was like lead and pulled me down, my knees crashing over the rug. I choked, and although I'd have welcomed death, I sought my next breath. It was no more than a rasp. Seconds ticked by while all I could notice was how her body was turning slacker and slacker up to the point when she barely hung from Lawrence's arm locked around her upper body.

There was no tonicity left in her limbs. When he loosened his hold on her, she collapsed next to where I'd already crumpled. The thump her body made at landing brought bile to my mouth, but still my fangs refused to draw back. My hands fell from my face to my lap and I glared up to Lawrence towering over me.

Crimson coated what had been his starched white collar. His whole neck, chin and mouth merged into red. A fiery glint shimmered in his eyes, a direct effect of the feed. Alice was young, female and he must have emptied her. Emptied her while I'd watched.

"You killed that girl out of spite."

He nodded down at the corpse sprawled at his feet. "She is the choice you made."

"Lawrence Beaumont, I despise you." There were, in my words, vibrations I hadn't heard since I'd died. They stemmed from cells that had survived my mutation, that belonged to the girl I'd once been, the girl who knew right from wrong. It was that girl who now spoke. "Lawrence Beaumont, I hate you."

"If I cannot have you, nobody else will. Your broke my heart but I'll break yours in return."

I looked at Alice again, at her blank eyes now devoid of any sparkle of life. A shriek slithered its way from some hidden parcel of my being and clawed up my throat. It exploded in a howl piercing enough for Lawrence to double over.

He managed the next words, "It will be easier to live with your hate rather than the hope for your love."

How would anyone seek to elicit hate rather than love? But I shook my head: It didn't matter anymore. *He* didn't matter anymore.

"My visit to Hollaroch has reached its end. It was merely a detour. The destination is still the same. I want Nathaniel MacLeod to suffer and die. With my incursion into his stronghold and this incident," he tilted his head at Alice, "I am confident he will show himself soon at St. Andrews. I will be waiting."

"Get out," I growled. He had to go before Gabriel came in. Otherwise Alice would have died for nothing because Lawrence would slaughter Gabriel too.

He vanished. Behind me, the door opened wide.

I heard feet marching over the wooden floor, creaks replaced with the muffled sounds of those same feet stepping onto the rug. *His* scent mixed with the one emanating from Alice, which was pungent with blood and already-rotting flesh.

I stooped further down, dragged by the new weight of his gaze on me.

"Are you hurt?"

I shook my head. Air whooshed out of his lungs.

"What the fuck?" *Tobias.*

Silence. No other words. No voices. Bodies moving. A few gasps.

"What's going on?" *Lizzie.*

"Tobias, get out and close the door."

"Come on, Gabe, let me—"

"Come back in ten minutes to take care of the body. Fergus, step back too. Stay with Lizzie and Simon. Hayden, secure the perimeter. There's been a breach."

"Shit." At least, Hayden had sobered up.

The click of the door signaled the start of my fight was imminent.

Gabriel stood right beside me and slowly knelt so that his gaze leveled with mine. At least, it would have if I'd dared stare at anything other than my own hands twisted on my lap. His ran along my body, like he'd done after the first attack outside the house on the Scores.

Bone after bone, he surveyed my arms, my shoulders, my hips, and flew upwards to my skull. His fingers finally landed along my neck as he gently pulled it sideways to check for puncture wounds. He repeated the same gesture on the other side of my neck.

His erratic heartbeat pounded against his ribcage while

his fingers trembled over me, ransacking my own heartbeat. I had to put him out of his misery.

"I told you: I'm not hurt." I tipped my chin at Alice's form. "But she's dead."

Gabriel leaned over her body and gently—as if she could still feel—turned her on her back. Her head bobbed and blood leaked out of the wound. The gash on her neck wasn't wide enough to kill in the short time Lawrence had bitten her. But he was a Stramos and he could suck a human dry in a mere minute. Which he had. Almost.

With the tips of his fingers, Gabriel closed her eyes. At that moment, I knew there'd been enough lies. So far, my dupery hadn't cost any lives. It was in my power to keep it that way. Or to repair as much as I could the damage I'd caused.

"She doesn't have to be," I offered sternly.

His gaze swung back on me. It hit me like a punch. "What are you saying?"

"I think you know." The words burned my lips on their way out. They didn't conceal the twin culprits inside my mouth.

His focus was entirely on me but I couldn't read him. His face was closed up, his body immobile. No more trembling. His heartbeat dropped, steadying into a controlled tempo. He was an athlete, after all, and he knew how to train himself for a game. Or a fight.

I was scared of my own voice, scared of any words I'd utter next. If I couldn't tell, I could show. So show I did. I brought my wrist to my mouth and without any hiding this time, I bit into it. The sound of torn-apart skin and vein disgusted me but it also distracted me from the pain. Once I'd dug deep enough into myself, I drank from my wrist, swallowing hard. The familiar taste of my own blood descended into my throat like a snake of dread. What I had to do next already dried up any remnant of strength left in me. Of strength and courage.

I'd never been so scared than when my downcast gaze left the sight of my wrist and journeyed to meet Gabriel's. I expected to see in it the same disgust that ran rampant inside me. It wasn't disgust I saw though, but tears. They weren't shed, but floated along his eyelids. I'd caused those tears when all I wanted for him was light and laughter. I'd pulled him into my cursed darkness. Of all the dreadful things I'd done, it was by far the one that would shame me the most.

I extended my arm so that it hung over the girl's body. "Once I've drunk from her, some of my blood while she's still warm will be enough to turn her." He sucked air through his lips in a hiss. I swallowed again but the inside of my mouth felt parched and scratchy. "A few drops are normally enough but I haven't fed for a week so she'll need more."

He blinked and jolted as if my statement had been a pail of boiling water thrown in his face. There was no heartbeat, no air entering or leaving his body. When he opened his eyes again, his stare was glittering ice. So was his voice.

"You did not do this to her."

"I didn't."

"Who then?"

"Lawrence Beaumont. The Stramos who met your father at that Edinburgh club. The same one you saw outside your house, and the two Turned you killed at the ball belonged to him." My tone didn't betray the fear simmering inside my chest. "He's the head of the European Council."

Gabriel's only acknowledgement was a nod. His jaw and his lips were tight. His whole body was a solid block of stillness. I allowed myself to mirror that stillness, the corset that had kept me rigid and straight loosened and my shoulders curved in. My stretched-out arm came to rest back on my lap.

That was a mistake.

He switched from still to ferocious with the speed of lightening. His fingers grabbed the back of my neck. When he stood, I was pulled up with him. A hoarse squeal of pain escaped from me which he ignored. His grip on me didn't weaken when he rounded the corpse and marched to the door opening onto the moor. He was dragging me behind him, oblivious of my feet, which scrambled to match his pace.

Outside, the moon—round and full—sharpened the lines of the landscape. The strength of the wind had diminished with the arrival of the night and the roar of the North Sea filled the air. The thin wool of my jumper didn't offer much protection against the cold that burned my skin. He didn't give me time to notice or suffer from it as he bolted in the direction of the shore. One stride of his meant two of mine, and while his walk was assured, mine was all slouched. I wanted to call his name, to ask him to slow down.

To look at me.

But I didn't deserve even a passing glance from him.

So we continued our rush across the moor in silence. His grip strangled me and breathing was as much a challenge as moving. One hundred yards from the sea, he stepped away from the path that curled around a hill and led to the beach. The climb was steep. Twice my foot slid over a parcel of loose soil. When we reached the top of the mound, the wind and the sea fought for supremacy over my senses. The waves deafened me. The wind battered my skin so hard it rendered it numb.

Gabriel pushed me. I stumbled, and he shoved me forward another two steps until the tips of my feet were a mere inch from the cliff's edge. The rocks below me glittered under the moonlight. So did the crests of the waves crashing against them.

The mass of my hair fell in front of me, framing my vision and shaping the space beneath into a tunnel. At the end of it was death, even for a Turned. Gabriel's free arm looped around my waist and he slammed against me, his hips cradled mine. The intimacy of his touch disturbed me, even more so when his chest aligned with the curve of my spine. He had to be staring at the same void as I did. Any clumsy move by him and I could fall and drag him down with me. The thought scared me. I tried to shift back but hit the wall of his body.

"Are you a Stramos?" he asked through the curtain of my hair.

"Only a Turned."

"His?" I assumed he was referring to Lawrence and heard his dread to know the answer.

"No. My Maker was Louis Berthière."

"Was?"

"Your father executed him at the last summer solstice, him and twenty of my friends. Burned all of them."

The hand he'd looped around the base of my neck in a tight lock moved to my hair. He twisted several strands around his fist, baring my face to him and contorting my neck into a painful angle. His profile filled my vision.

"Am I supposed to feel sorry for you and your mates?" His lips were so close to my cheek his breath itched against my skin. "I wish I'd been the one who struck the match."

I jerked my body against his, straightening my upper half, and threw my elbow against his stomach. Gabriel's muscles were as hard as cement and my attempt at a fight didn't even make him flinch. "We were different."

"You're all variations of monsters and I loathe your kind as much as I do my father."

"None of us fed from humans. We kept ourselves away from them. We never wanted to hurt anybody and that's what cost my friends their lives."

His hold on me faltered ever so slightly and I managed to take in a larger lungful of air.

"What is it that you want from me?" he barked.

"Revenge."

He kicked the back of my knee. I stumbled forward. A thick wisp of my hair was still clasped inside his fist. I didn't fall into the emptiness but found myself suspended over it. My scalp burned and I shrieked. Tears blinded my vision and flew down my cheeks.

"I'm still alive, so there's more to it than what you say."

He twisted my hair more tightly, forcing my body

around, my back now to the sea. The void beneath me acted like a magnet. The only counterforce to it was Gabriel's grip on me. A tiny release and I'd plummet.

"I came to seduce and turn you against your father. Killing you or your sister wasn't a priority."

He yanked at my hair and I screamed, feeling infinite sympathy for Rapunzel. The mask of his face frazzled but the tightening of his jaw kept it on. "So why is it that you haven't fucked me yet?"

His words froze me, I blanked. My weight forced him to pull again at my hair. My moan wasn't born from my painful scalp but from the filth now wrapped around the bond I'd sealed with him.

"Tell me, Marie, why haven't you fucked me yet?"

I let my arms hang by my sides. I was setting myself for the final fall. By the twitches at the corners of his eyes, he knew that too. All he had to do to be rid of me was uncurl his fist and let go of my hair.

Of me.

"Because I fell in love with you."

Chapter 17 — Upstream

My truth floated in the wind, drifting between us.

He winced, as if my words had slapped him in the face. A gust of wind made him sway. I tensed to counter his movement, contracting my abdominal muscles. Gabriel had to put a foot forward to correct his movement. It strengthened his leverage over me but the pull on my hair increased further, making me hiss.

The soil on the edge of the cliff was loose and it crumbled under his weight. Gabriel collapsed on his knees and, with that, my precarious balance was lost. My own feet slid over the edge. Several rocks fell down the slide of the cliff beneath me. The pressure on my scalp blazed to my core, the pain blinding me.

With one yank he hauled me once more towards him. His hand grabbed the hem of my jumper, stopping my fall. But playing the acrobat had infused an aching fire into my muscles. My reflexes failed me. And his tug on my hair inflicted more pain than the blade of a knife slicing my throat.

I heard the sound of my jumper tearing. It set off alarm bells ringing in my brain. My fate closed in on me, but my eyes rounded in one last attempt to catch sight of him. My vision was blurred, the camera inside my head failing to focus. His hand clasped my waist at the same time as my upper body rolled over my knees. My forehead bumped against a wall—Gabriel's chest—and we twisted together in a tangle of limbs.

We crashed over the shrubs covering the steep ground. The shock of the fall knocked the air out of my lungs, as did Gabriel's body slamming against my back, pinning me down harder onto the wet blanket of grass. The moisture was already filtering through my woolen top, but the discomfort was chased away by the sheer relief of Gabriel alive above me. Gentle hands rolled me onto my back.

He aligned his face with mine, cheek to cheek. The curls of his fringe tickled my eyelids and his rasping breath my earlobe. I expected the contact to break. I expected him to switch to another means of achieving my destruction. I expected him to reach for a hidden weapon and torture me.

He didn't move and the chiseled ripple of his stomach imprinted itself upon my back. His chest heaved and the thumping of his heart against his ribcage was so violent I feared it would leap into my own.

The itch of my scalp receded. Gabriel lifted himself up by planting his elbow on one side of my face, then pivoted his torso, his hip now next to mine on the ground. His eyes roamed up and down my body, a scowl scarring the top of his nose.

"I'm fine," I squeaked, my voice having yet to recover.

He nodded in that ingrained military way of his. I knew him well enough to see the fear mingled with relief in the hard swallow he took. His Adam's apple bobbed up and down in slow motion, as if it had to push saliva through a human-size boulder.

His focus swept beyond us, down the steep decline leading to the sea path. Nothing alarmed him, and he reverted to his initial point. This time, instead of covering me, his body hovered over me. Our gazes met and I relaxed with the familiar sight of his slanted eyes.

His voice was rough when he asked, "Is Marie Aberdein your real name?"

"Yes."

His whole body slumped down an inch. His eyes

squeezed shut as if he had to reflect on my answer, as if knowing my birth name held a special meaning for him. I allowed my muscles to relax a bit and wriggled under him, trying to dislodge a small rock that pushed against one of my vertebra. His hand grabbed my hip and pushed me down, stopping any more movement. His touch didn't have the gentleness I'd grown accustomed to from him, but it beat the harshness he showed since finding Alice. Heat seeped from his palm, warmed the blood running through my veins, and soon pumped into my heart.

"From now on, I want the truth, Marie. One more lie and you'll die from my hands."

"If I ever have to lie to you again, it's the lie that will kill me."

"Did you kill Alice?"

There was only one true answer, but it was neither a *yes* nor a *no*. "Lawrence killed her to punish me. So her death is on me."

"Punish you for what?"

"For rejecting his advances. For refusing to be his little soldier in his feud with your father." I'd said the next words before, while hanging ten yards above the sea. Giving him those same words while he was pressed against me took as much courage as jumping from that goddamned cliff. "For falling in love with you." He flinched. "Take your pick."

"Was he the one who sent you to us?"

"No, that was my plan. I had nothing left to lose because each time I care or love, the MacLeods take it away from me."

"Who else have you lost because of us?"

I hesitated to say it out loud. "My husband was a Fiu. The MacLeod Hunter killed him at Culloden." There was something definitive about sharing with him that part of me, that very precious, very painful part of me. "When I was told, I went into premature labor and our son was stillborn. I would have died if Louis hadn't turned me."

A gasp of air rushed out from between his lips. My chin

was trembling so I coaxed it into stillness by grinding my teeth together.

His fingers clamped around my hip. "You had a child."

For the first time, I resented his weight, how he encaged me with the sheer width of him. I ducked my head sideways and searched the sky above for a sight that could distract me. Gabriel sat up on his knees, keeping my legs encased between them, then leaned again to take hold of my hands and pull me up to him.

He jumped to his feet and placed his hands under my armpits to lift me up. I didn't have time to check if I could stand unassisted because he promptly scooped me into his arms. When his warmth engulfed me, the wet chill that had filtered inside me evaporated in a shudder.

The climb down had to be a tricky exercise but I trusted his agility. My head bobbed down and snuggled against the curve of his neck. My forehead rested against the throbbing spot of his pulse, strong and steady, without triggering any feeding urge. And for that, I felt a tiny smile of pride tugging at my mouth.

I didn't pay much attention to our surroundings, but stole a glance when we diverted again from the path. Apparently, we weren't heading back to the house. Gabriel marched through the night as if it were the middle of the day, as if I didn't weigh anything.

After leaving the annex of the farm behind, we advanced along the shore, following its inward curve into a tiny cove. Steps were carved into the rock that snaked down into the sheltered beach. Nestled against the steep hill that merged into the moor stood a cottage. Its whitewashed walls shimmered in the moonlight. Gabriel didn't knock at the door.

After deposing me on my feet, he kept me leaning against him, one of his arms looped around my shoulder. I was grateful for his support because my legs were like jelly. He extracted a set of three keys from his jean pockets. They were all old and sturdy and I wondered why I hadn't noticed their bulging shapes before.

He slid the biggest one into the keyhole, turned it, then shoved the door, kicking it to open it wider. The creaking sound that followed spoke of rusty hinges and rainy winters.

"Come," he prompted me in a whisper, like a father leading his child to bed.

His fingers enlaced with mine and we entered the cottage. I expected the musty, stale smell of mold but the air inside filled my lungs with the scent of burnt wood and clean sheets.

"Stay here." He abandoned my hand.

He rummaged through the shelves that lined either side of a fireplace. I heard the sounds of a match being struck and the glimmer of a flame sparkled. He covered it with the glass body of an oil lamp and placed the lamp at the center of a square wooden table.

The halo of light revealed a single room filled with sparse furniture: an iron bed, the table, a rocking chair next to the fireplace, and a round basin with a porcelain jug next to it. The décor was Spartan but the grey wool of the throw placed over the mattress was smooth and thick. I fought the longing to sneak underneath it and gather its warmth around me.

The place reminded me of the room where I'd given birth to my son so very long ago. My hand flew to my stomach as if to soothe the child who'd been tucked in there. The sound of the door closing behind knifed through the memory and cut my survey short.

"There's no electricity here but I have another lamp stashed somewhere."

I shrugged without looking at him. "Most of my life has been spent without electricity or central heating."

The reminder of my age raised a brick wall in the narrow space between us. I cursed myself for it. Gabriel didn't need to remember how much older I was. Despite the fact there were far more urgent concerns, the thought chipped at my vanity. I didn't want him to see me as anything other than his peer, albeit one with fangs.

I observed him while he busied himself around the room, pulling one plaid blanket and a crumpled woolen form from the shelf. He then divested himself of his shirt in a swift grip of the back of his collar in that masculine gesture that didn't care about hair order and left it jutting out in weird angles.

The flame of the lamp threw enticing shadows over his chest and shoulders, each muscle highlighted into ropes and planes. My eyes followed the trail of russet hairs that ran from his navel to disappear into his jeans.

Now dressed in a rough navy pullover, he stood in front of me, blocking the modest light and hiding the details of his face. The exhaustion and my hunger had weakened my sight to an unprecedented level. Gabriel MacLeod was never easy to read but right then I'd have given a large portion of the cash hidden by Louis in offshore accounts to find out. I rephrased immediately: I'd have given all of it.

"Remove your top."

His tone made me jump. Defiance laced with a hint of reverence in a rough tremble that thickened his voice. I wanted to read in that voice of his what he wouldn't say in words.

"It's wet, and despite the resistance of your kind, it can't be comfortable."

The mention of my comfort clashed with my still throbbing scalp, which was all his doing. He unfolded the plaid in front of me and I let my eyes roam numbly over the material. The clean scent of summer air and lavender wafted from it, teasing my nostrils. Meshed with it, I also detected Gabriel's with that unique mix of earth and flora.

"Don't turn into a prude, lassie. I won't jump you just because I see you in nothing but your bra."

The nuances I'd heard in his voice earlier were now gone, or perhaps they'd never been there in the first place. My spine stretched and my chin rose, driven by that fleeting thing I had left in me: pride.

I kept my gaze locked with his while I lifted my arms

and pulled the jumper over my head. My hair fell back over my shoulders, very likely a mess of tangles. I fought the need to comb it with my fingers. How I looked didn't matter anymore.

Or perhaps it still did. Gabriel's eyes lost their single focus on my face to dive towards my heaving breasts. The swell of them blossomed when my nipples hardened against the lace of my bra. His gaze didn't settle there but its virtual touch wasn't elusive. It lingered long enough to trigger hot tingles. My lips parted. I sucked some of the air that floated between us. I might as well have stolen some of it from him because his own lips merged into a narrow line.

I stayed there half-naked in front of him, my head wrenched back to match his glare, the blanket hanging between us. MacLeods had no respect for weakness and I had no reason to expect Gabriel to show mercy.

What I definitely didn't expect was for him to stretch his arms and drape that blanket around me. He tucked the edges under my chin, leaving his fists curled around the wool, the knuckles of his thumbs lodged against the line of my neck. Time suspended until I swallowed, and the movement of my throat startled him.

"Hold on to it," he ordered and I obeyed, ignoring the brush of our fingers while I replaced his clasp on the blanket. "I'm going to make a fire."

While he took logs from a niche underneath the fireplace, I explored the limited space left in the room. There wasn't much to it once I'd eyed the crease-free linen spread underneath the throw and run my fingers over the ancient porcelain of the water jug on the sturdy vanity.

The heat reached across the room and warmed my back. It wasn't by any means as effective as central heating, but beggars can't be choosers. I'd hung by my hair over the North Sea and was left wet and chilled by the rescue. So some warmth—any warmth—would be welcome. I edged closer to the fireplace but stopped when I realized Gabriel glared at me over his shoulder. He was still bent forward, readjusting the logs with a poker. Even though my steps had been light, he knew better than to turn his back on a Turned. Even a cold, half-naked, female one.

"Why is this place so well kept?" I asked.

The wood was dry, as was the whole cottage despite being on the edge of the edge of the world. He reverted his attention to the fireplace, having probably dismissed any threat he thought I posed. I didn't know if I should be flattered or offended. After placing the stick against the side of the fireplace in a careful gesture that I was now familiar with, he leaned his forearms against the fire side. The width of his shoulders was in full display and I had to resist the appeal of snuggling against a body on which the tips of my fingers knew every line. Or almost every line. His square shoulders dipped into his back in a sharp curve that appealed to all the softness within me.

"When I come to Hollaroch, I always stay here."

My brainwaves had to be rewired as I had lost track of my original question. "Why didn't you come here this weekend then?"

He twisted his head, displaying a portion of his chiseled profile between his shoulder and his bicep. Our eyes met.

"You wanted to keep us a secret and I wanted to stay close to you."

So he gave up on his bachelor pad and chose the room next to mine inside the main house. The revelation made me wish I could turn back time and again be the full focus of his attention. Technically, his focus was entirely on me at that moment, but I dreaded how that attention would translate.

"What's the deal between you and Beaumont?"

So it would have to start with Lawrence. I was certain that wherever he'd regrouped after his show at Hollaroch, the Stramos would rejoice in the knowledge of Gabriel and me discussing him. I dreaded discussing him, I dreaded pronouncing his very name.

"Is he the one you were in love with?" Gabriel's words were stilted.

I'm convinced my eyes rounded then to the size of saucers. A giggle formed at the base of my throat and emerged in a croaked "No."

"I struggle to believe a Stramos would have taken the risk of stepping into Hollaroch for the sake of a girl who doesn't like him." Gabriel spun around to face me and rested his shoulders against the mantelpiece. His arms were now crossed over his chest, almost in a nonchalant way. His relaxed body language didn't fool me: I was his prey and he'd fall on me like a hawk on a scrawny rabbit.

"He's come here before."

"Impossible. Hollaroch is the stronghold of our clan."

"It was 1746. Your namesake, Gabriel, was staying at Hollaroch between hunting seasons. Lawrence struck by surprise and it paid off. Gabriel lost his head after Lawrence had bled him dry."

The squeeze of his shoulders told me *my* Gabriel had no knowledge of the event.

"And how are you privy to these facts?"

"Because I was there too." I forged on, prompted by his raised eyebrow. "Gabriel was the Hunter who killed my husband. The reason I accepted being Turned was to make him pay. But Lawrence knew me better than I probably did. At least he did back then."

I wanted to wipe off the disgust my confession had splayed over Gabriel's face. He looked as if he'd bitten into the sourness of a lemon, the furrow between his eyebrows expanding the ones at the corners of his mouth. But I'd sworn the truth and it was my truth.

"He knew I'd never be able to go through with the killing. I'd bought off one of the Hunter's servants and managed to have him slip a sleeping draft into his drink. But, although I might have been physically able to terminate him then, my mind wasn't geared up for it."

"What's that supposed to mean?"

I shrugged, but the blanket might have very well hidden my gesture. "I'm not a killer. I never was."

He pushed himself away from the fireplace and was in front of me in a fluid move. His body boxed me in, but I ordered myself not to flinch or wince. I suspected all he wanted was to put his fingers around my neck and strangle me. Instead he placed them over his waist, his knuckles white from the clench. The flesh there would end up bruised.

"You are a fucking killer, Marie. No matter how..." Gabriel squeezed his eyes shut and ducked his head. His chest rose when he breathed in a bucketful of air through his nose. When it whooshed out, it brushed against my face and I inhaled. His gaze shot back at me. "No matter how good you are inside, your very survival depends on the death of innocents."

My lungs burned, my throat opened, but my lips remained sealed. The truth, only the truth, even when it tasted like a lie. "And still I've never killed. I've never fed from humans either." Even when my life depended on it. "That's why Lawrence beat me and killed the Hunter."

"For you." Defeat tainted his voice.

"For me, yes, but everything Lawrence does ultimately serves only him. Shortly after that coup, he was appointed head of the European Council."

Gabriel abandoned his vigil over me and wandered around within the restricted space of the cottage. He rubbed his hand over his face, raked it through his hair, curled and uncurled it along his body. His steps kept tracing circles around me, edging along the side of the bed, the fireplace, the entrance door. And round and round again.

I pulled my blanket tighter together and bent my neck downwards. I wouldn't die tonight. That much I was certain, but I could lose more than my poor excuse of a life. What I had already lost ripped a piece of my heart away, the rest clung on in forlorn hope. The hope he could forgive me. So I waited for Gabriel to sort out the chaos inside his head.

Finally, the sound of his roaming steps diminished until it stopped entirely. He'd ended opposite me, midway between the fire and where I stood. I flicked my gaze up to steal a glance at him. His stance had lost some of its stiffness. The tension that had creased his eyes had eased. His expression had reached a level of neutrality that reminded me of my first weeks at the house on the Scores when I used to beg for crumbs of his attention.

But when he spoke, the sound was hoarse. The words stumbled over the barrier of his lips.

"You hurt me." He shook his head as in disbelief at his own confession. "Alice is dead and I've sheltered a Turned under my roof for three long months without once suspecting what you were. I've touched you, kissed you." His chuckle dripped with bitterness. "I should be angry and embarrassed, and heaven forbid, I'm all that, but more than anything else, I fucking hurt.

You lied to me and that's what bites at me more than the sharpness of your fangs."

A sob rushed up my throat, but it was so tight the sound died before reaching my mouth. My face ached with the trembling of my muscles: My eyes squinted and my lips puckered at the burn of his words. I'd sewn a web of lies, constructed excuses to stay near him. I'd knitted a warm blanket of dreams, indulged in its deceptive comfort. I'd fallen for him, but my love for Gabriel had been selfish. Just like Everett's love so long ago. His love had stolen so much from me. He knew it would and still he charmed and enticed, knowing I'd end up cut and bruised and burned. I'd done to Gabriel what had been done to me so long ago.

"You owe me the truth, Marie."

I tilted my head and fought the itch of the tears behind my eyelids. The unshed moisture robbed my vision of its sharpness and I was so grateful for the respite. The sight of Gabriel made me sore.

I caught my breath. "Why?"

"Because I need to know who you are to try to accept what you are."

"Maybe it's too late to separate the two."

"I don't want to believe that."

"And what will you do with this new knowledge about me?" Would he turn me over to his father? Jail me in a hidden dungeon somewhere on Hollaroch?

Could he still want me?

His throat worked. "I hope I'll do what is right."

The tension that had stiffened my spine evaporated. I shrank, and he seemed to expand. There was some level of freedom in relinquishing my fate to him. I trusted Gabriel and I was now ready to accept whatever he chose for me, whatever punishment he deemed appropriate. All I had to do was tell him about me, about the river that was my life. Perhaps that river had finally reached the sea.

He stretched his arm and I stared at his open palm. "I want to hear your story."

I wasn't a fool and didn't take it as a sign of his forgiveness. That extended hand was my salvation nevertheless. Now had finally come the time for atonement. All I had to do was remember when it all started.

When he led me to the rocking chair, Gabriel's fingers trembled against mine. He made me sit down. I couldn't relax against the back of the seat and sat upright instead. There was nowhere else for him to sit but on the stone tiles of the cottage floor. He rested his elbows on his knees, his whole body angled towards me. Seconds ticked by, filled by the crackle of the fire.

I sailed upstream on my river-life. I'd never taken the journey and certainly not shared it with anyone. In two centuries. I was glad I'd waited because Gabriel MacLeod was the only one I wanted to travel with.

I breathed him in, filled my lungs with his scent, and started to exhale. "I was born in Edinburgh in 1726 and Scotland was all I knew for twenty years."

Chapter 18 — A Gift

I woke to two sensations. Softness beneath my cheek. Heat caressing my face.

The latter penetrated the dread of the Saguenay dream. I jerked up, my body curling in to protect itself from a blow. The scream stayed buried inside my chest, my instinct managing to contain it. The only blow that hit me was the weight of Gabriel's gaze on me.

But it wasn't fed from anger or doubt anymore. He sat on the same rocking chair where my last memory of the night had taken place. Well, I must have dived into a deep slumber at some point during the re-telling of my life because light now pierced through the small windows. The lattice that hung from them dissipated its brightness, but judging by its intensity, the day had to be somewhat advanced already. I'd slept for hours on a bed Gabriel must have laid me on.

The bed was too narrow to accommodate both of us. The shadows darkening the half-circles underneath his eyes betrayed the fact that he might not have slept much, if at all. His hair was a rumpled mess of fiery curls. It softened the rigor of his jaw and the edge of his cheekbones.

My gaze traced the line of his stretched legs down to his bare feet. At least he'd made himself comfortable for whatever rest he'd managed to find. For an instant, I heard my fleeting worry that he might have gotten cold. But then my eyes tracked back up to his face and I forgot all about him being cold and gave in to the searing heat that sizzled between us.

He stared at my upper body, now covered by only a bra. The blanket had slid down when I sat up. Exhibitionism wasn't an inclination of mine but I didn't make a move or pull the cover back over me. I might even have lifted my breasts a fraction higher. The tingles that his gaze had elicited last night reappeared and spread across my chest. My breasts ached against the lace of my bra and became heavier, fuller. The muscles of my stomach clenched.

Gabriel swallowed hard. A gleam filled his eyes, eyes that narrowed as if the sight of me was a source of pain.

He hunched over his knees, making the chair rock forward. When his glare deserted me, I fought the sob that blocked my throat. For one moment, I considered begging him to look at me again, to acknowledge my very presence. But my needs were forgotten when I noticed how his chest arched in. His profile hardened, his jaw shut. I should have stayed put and waited for his inner storm to appease. I jumped to my feet instead, tucking the blanket under my arms.

The room spun around me and I fought a bout of dizziness. I was ravenous for blood. The ground was made of baked tiles and a chill seeped into me from the soles of my feet. It anchored me though, and I reached Gabriel without fainting. He didn't move but I heard his ragged intake of breath. I had an urge to extend my hand and rest it on the crown of his head. I wanted to caress his curls, run my fingers through them and comb his distress away. But I was a coward and did none of it. I waited, wriggling my fingers against my thighs and curling my toes to diffuse the cold.

I didn't see his own fingers flashing to mine and encircling them into his grip, both firm and gentle. He pulled on my hand, twisted it so the inside of my wrist faced up. The scars left by last night's bite were still visible. I was too weak for the healing to happen quickly.

The memory of Alice slapped me across the face. I'd

wanted to save her but there'd been nothing heroic in my action. It had sprung from guilt. My stubborn rejection of Lawrence had thrown her into the game the Stramos played. And when the moment had come to choose, I'd sacrificed her for the man I loved. A man who would have given his life to spare hers. Would Gabriel have to forgive me for that as well?

However, the touch of his thumb cured my body from any previous fidgeting. He kept drawing circles, keeping the two puncture wounds within their arc. When he stopped, my outstretched elbow ached from having held the same position for so long.

My tongue was numb. My teeth ground against each other. Last night I'd done most of the talking. My storytelling had been interrupted by his short requests for clarification, but he'd never elaborated or questioned me further. He'd simply listened. Listening was something Gabriel MacLeod excelled at. Maybe it was a natural side effect of his silent nature.

With a gentle tug, he drew me down and I knelt at his feet, my hands joined within his hold. I had to keep my arms close to my body to maintain the blanket tucked under my armpits. I was tempted to sway forward and seek the barrier offered by his denim-clad thighs bracketing me. But I had no control over my body anymore and my spine remained stiff.

The glint in his eyes, bright like the midday sun, opened the door to arrays of possibilities. The gravel of his voice draped around my heart. Although I'd resisted leaning against him, the sound was like coming home.

"Do all women your age need that much sleep?"

I frowned.

"My MacLeod gran, she used to sleep until well after noon. It used to drive my father crazy. He kept sending Lizzie and me to wake her up. We did it by jumping on her bed like drunken monkeys."

The comparison with his grandmother didn't amuse me as much as it seemed to him. I sucked my cheeks in and stared at the spot right at the center of his chest, at the bottom of the downhill slope from his pectoral muscles. The line there dented his skin. Even the thick wool of his jumper couldn't hide the definition of those muscles. The sight distracted me from arguing back. The tip of his index finger lifted my chin so I couldn't avert my eyes anymore. The humor there cooled my anger until…

"At least you don't snore."

I snapped his hand away and stood. He pulled me back down by curling his hand around the back of my neck. There was none of the toughness he'd demonstrated the night before, but I landed back on my knees nevertheless.

A chuckle rolled up his throat and his upper body bent forward until his forehead rested against mine. "Lassie, that was my poor attempt at comic relief."

He brushed the tip of his nose against mine. The sides of his thumbs ran up and down my temples and I could feel the agile lengths of his other fingers on my neck.

"Forgive me, *a leanaigh.*" The lines of his lips flattened, betraying the surge of emotions behind his words. Guilt. Pain. Need.

"Youth needs to have its day in the sun," I quipped.

He squeezed his eyes shut. "That's not why I'm asking for your forgiveness."

My next breath froze inside my lungs. Had the world gone topsy-turvy while I was sleeping? "You've done nothing to—"

His mouth crushed mine. He wasn't testing or seeking permission. His kiss was a claim. He nibbled at my lower lip with deliberate care, his tongue flickering along its edges. It felt like I was giving him even more of myself when he changed the angle of the kiss. I opened my lips wider to ease him in and a rumbling noise escaped his throat. Our tongues slid against each other. Heat kindled simultaneously at various ends of my body, down to my very toes. I moaned but the sound was lost inside his mouth.

A shiver had him tip further into me. My hands roamed

over his abdomen and traipsed down to the hem of his T-shirt. I lifted it to let the tips of my fingers glide along the twin dents that fell down into the waist of his jeans. He jolted away as if my touch had scalded him. My lips felt swollen and bare from his desertion. My heart shrank in apprehension.

Had I misread the signs of his attraction? He'd been the one initiating contact, hadn't he? I had simply followed his lead.

"I asked for your forgiveness and here I am failing you once again."

He'd said that but it could have been my line. It should have been. "I'm lost. You could have killed me last night, but you gave me a chance to defend myself, to tell you about me. But that doesn't change…who I am."

Gabriel inched back and his hands brushed down the sides of my face, my neck, and along my collarbone to end around the curves of my shoulders. A firmness settled over his face, his features now devoid of the humor I'd seen earlier. But he stared at me, through me, and across every parcel of my face, even my earlobes that I knew he had a particular fondness for. When he stopped his scrutiny, his gaze hooked mine. "That's all I need to know."

My confusion made my nose scrunch up. "What exactly is it that you need to know?"

"Who you are, not what you are."

I pressed my lips together to control a sob. My shoulders slumped, but his hold on me kept me from sinking onto my heels. I didn't have the nerve to stare back at him, so, instead, my eyes pierced through the floor.

Ironically, the cowardly breaking of the bond between us infused into me the courage to say, "Over two hundred years the line between the *who* and the *what* has become blurred."

"You're wrong, and if that's what you really think of yourself, then I won't rest until I've convinced you otherwise. Look at me."

And I did, because Gabriel's orders could never be ignored, on a rugby pitch, or here with him encasing me.

"I believe in you. I believe in you because, more than anyone I've ever met, you know the fine line between right and wrong. The truth about you is that you have never even trodden that line, even when your own life was at stake." The fierceness in his gaze almost made me jerk back. "And you *never* will."

"I drink blood," I spat. The anger at his delusion made my lips tremble. A jolt of adrenaline zapped through me. "I drink blood, and that is *never* going to change."

"You have never killed for it, and again, I know you *never* will." His next words were a mere whisper. "And that's why you're slowly dying."

"My motives aren't as grand as what you assume. They're born out of selfishness. I don't feed from humans because the guilt will kill me. Because I'm not sure I won't suck them dry. I haven't embraced *what* I am simply because I haven't the guts to do so."

"Is that how you justify killing yourself?"

There were no ups and downs anymore. I had revealed to him my deepest secrets. He was now throwing them back at me in jumbled pieces.

"I'm not committing suicide, it's preposterous. I never want to have to take or steal or rob to stay alive."

"It's not theft if it's given to you. Willingly."

Chapter 19 — Sustenance

Willingly.

That same word kept slamming itself against the walls erected around my brain.

"What do you mean?"

"You won't be stealing anything from me if I give it to you. Willingly." He ducked his head onto his chin to commit to his words.

"Why would you do that?"

"Because I want you to live." He swallowed. "Because I want you to thrive. Because I like who you are, I like it very much."

"To allow me to be who I am, you're willing to compromise who *you* are."

"I won't compromise anything. It won't prevent me from functioning normally."

"You'll compromise everything you believe in."

"Stop chanting that bloody word, will you? There's nothing to *compromise*—," he pronounced the word with an out-of-character roll of the eyes "—because I'll be doing something I believe in, for someone I have faith in."

"I'm not human anymore. I haven't been since the night I died giving birth to my son. Whatever goodwill my story awoke in you last night, you need to face reality head-on. Otherwise you'll get hurt."

And I'd crash when he finally came to his senses.

"It's a good thing you sleep like an old bag because I had plenty of time to face this new reality of ours." He rubbed his hands over his face as if to sweep the exhaustion away. His hands didn't return to my face but came to rest on his lap instead. "And I finally understood something that's eluded me since the moment Tobias handed me my mother's diary."

I summoned up some of the patience he'd shown me while I'd recounted my life's story, and let him explain.

"Mortality doesn't always warrant humanity. Kindness, fairness, self-sacrifice, they don't depend on physical traits, they're in the soul. You might have died once, but your soul is sparkling with life."

"What about Lawrence? How does he fare according to that new theory of yours?"

He tensed up and curled his fists.

"He never had a soul in the first place. Maybe because he's a Stramos, not a Turned—" he shrugged to convey he hadn't yet wrapped his head around all the implications, "—but there's nothing remotely human in him, not even that love he pretends to have for you."

Lawrence had killed Alice because of his feelings for me. He had damned me for it. But I wasn't him. He'd hinted at how alike we were, but my entire being rioted against that possibility. I'd never been like him and I knew—*I knew*—I never would be. If I had any doubts, I just had to look at Gabriel. His eyes were filled with my reflection. I saw myself like he saw me. A girl. *His* girl.

I had always laughed at the cliché of butterflies in someone's stomach, but there was a lot of fluttering currently going on inside my ribcage. The unease stopped when the new understanding of myself and of my fate planted roots. At last I gave myself, if not the right to believe, but the benefit of the doubt. It was a privilege I could never have afforded myself before Gabriel, and my chest expanded with gratitude.

"Louis spent two centuries telling me I wasn't a monster, but I never believed him. I thought he was trying to spare me or assuage his own guilt for turning me." I placed my fingertips to cradle the sides of Gabriel's face, the faint stubble there rubbing against my palm. "But maybe it was my own prejudice that kept me from believing him because he was a Stramos. I loved him like a father but I couldn't get over what he was. I didn't see enough of *who* he was, and I won't ever have the chance to."

Gabriel leaned his face against my palm. "Both of us were dealt one fate. You were turned and I was born a MacLeod, but what matters is what we make of that fate. I hope I can show as much fairness as fierceness, but you've already proven yourself."

"I haven't found a cure." That was a fact, an unavoidable fact.

"Then let me give you the time to." Once again my brain shut down, patching up the opening I had let Gabriel carve into it. "Allow me to do that for you and—"

"I can't do that to you, use you, exploit you." I stumbled to my feet but didn't reach my full height. Gabriel's grip on my waist was relentless when he pulled me back down.

This time his thighs surrounded me, pressing in on my sides, and our breaths merged as he spoke. "Allow me to do it for you *and* for me."

My next attempt at fidgeting out of his grasp was again cut short. I crashed against his chest, his hands now gripping my back. Panic had its fists around my heart and clenched. He wouldn't hurt me—that much I knew—but he wouldn't let me escape either.

I acknowledged my defeat and opted for stillness. When my words burst out, they had the speed of repressed rage finally let loose. They were vile and filled my mouth with the taste of bile. "Always so honorable, aren't you? Even when you're looking to get high on a vamp's bite."

His jaw locked, but the tension didn't last and his face eased back to its former calm composure. I raised my hands and slapped them against his chest, my fists, tiny and fragile, beating against his granite bulk. He didn't move an inch. I risked disentangling myself but only managed to end with my arms behind my back, his fingers circling my wrists.

"*A leanaigh,* there are a lot of things I want you to do to me and most of them aren't honorable. As far as what I want to do to you, none of them are." His cocky smirk loosened my limbs. While I collapsed further into him, he wrapped my arms around his waist, anchoring me to him. "I'm a virgin, not a saint, and I bloody well hope that my abstinence will end with you."

A whimper climbed out of my throat and broke through my mouth. The blanket glided along my body and crumpled on the tiles. My top half was bare again except for the bra, but this time my next breath had the tips of my breasts reach the wool of his jumper. Despite the barrier of the lace, my nipples reacted and hardened. They ached and tickled and distracted me from my anger.

Gabriel's lips parted, letting in a raspy intake of air. I fought the urge to inhale that very air back into me and pressed my lips together. But it wasn't my own flesh I wanted to feel, it was the plump shape of his mouth. My breathing rushed into a gallop. The friction of my breasts against his top sent a ripple all the way down between my thighs. The heat there simmered further when Gabriel leaned to place a kiss on my forehead.

It was a chaste kiss, given our situation, but my mind conjured images so suggestive, my skin ignited. I wanted his kiss on each of my nipples and for that kiss to lengthen them, to pucker them. I wanted him to replace the itch of the lace and wool with the wetness of his mouth. More than anything, I wanted his lips between my thighs.

Gabriel freed my fists and brought them to the sides of his face. He deliberately and precisely rubbed his thumbs against the twin spots where my blood pumped through bulging veins. His touch geared up the hammering tempo of my heartbeat.

But he sobered the mood by sliding his hands up my arms to my shoulders and straightening me up. "All these things I want to do to you, honorable or not, they won't happen if you die. And you *will* die if you don't feed from a human."

"Do you think I don't know that? I hid for forty years in Saguenay and spent every damned day in a lab to find a way for us to survive without acting like the blood-craving monsters we're designed to be."

"Then keep working until you find the cure, but for that, you need blood and I want to give that to you." He broke the taunt line of sight between us and sought inspiration somewhere in the narrow space separating us. When his eyes settled back on me, they were filled with purpose. "I want to give you much more than that, but I won't have the chance if you refuse my gift."

A lump clogged up, distorted my throat, but I couldn't swallow it.

"I don't know if I can do it," I whispered. "I've never…"

"Then share your first time with me." He cupped my face and tipped it up to bury his gaze into mine. "Please." A brush of his lips punctuated his plea. He feathered more kisses at the corners of my mouth and reserved the last one for the tip of my nose.

I wanted so many more of those kisses. An infinity and an eternity of them. I might be cursed for what I was about to do, but it didn't matter anymore. What else could God Almighty do to me that he hadn't already done? Kill me?

"Show me," I asked in a rasp, my voice an echo of the blend of dread and longing whirling inside me.

Gabriel drew my face closer to his, keeping the bond of our gazes tight while shortening it with every passing second. Our mouths were so close again that I expected another kiss, but he stretched his neck sideways instead. And there it was, the source of my survival, offered to me. *Willingly.*

I inhaled his scent that now permeated the air seeping

into my lungs. The earthy nuances had receded, overtaken by the spice of his arousal. His skin glowed like golden silk and I allowed my own arousal to break free. It throbbed between my thighs, then washed over me. When it encompassed all of me, my incisors tore through my gums. Saliva rushed up to my mouth and mingled with the sweetness of my biting fluid.

I had hardly tasted that sweetness before. It reminded me of candy floss, of melting sugar, sleek on the tongue but without the stickiness of it. For my kind, that fluid is a side-effect of lust or hunger. I'd never fed from a human and certainly never associated pleasure with the prospect of draining blood, so the taste had novelty.

I laid my lips over the throbbing spot on his neck, my lips tingling with anticipation. With my breasts pillowed against his chest, the thumping of my heart matched his in a mad staccato. His fingers shifted from the sides of my face and threaded into my hair, their clutch tight and impossible to ignore.

Before more doubts could shrivel my purpose, my needle-sharp teeth pierced through his flesh. I expected more resistance, barriers after barriers to vanquish, but reaching his carotid was a remarkably uneventful journey. The surge of pleasure didn't come from the blood itself but from the heat around my fangs. The sensation was unctuous and powerful, shooting to my head with dizzying speed. I would have tumbled or rolled over without Gabriel's gentle but solid hold on me.

Gabriel.

Gabriel, who hadn't even flinched at my bite. Gabriel, who kept me pressed against the hardness of his body. Gabriel, whom I'd hurt if I indulged longer in the pleasure-inducing feed.

I wriggled and started pulling my mouth away from his neck. Only to be forced back into it, my fangs planting themselves back into the twin set of punctures.

"Take it," he ordered me. His skin shifted against my lips

and the increased throbbing doubled my intake of blood and plunged me even further into his heat.

I had no shame anymore. No guilt. I took and took and took.

Gabriel's blood had none of the coppery taste and thin texture I'd grown accustomed to from plasma. It was thick on my tongue and with the aroma of cherry akin to an aged red wine. It rushed through my veins, strengthening and expanding them with the force of its flow.

My senses sharpened. My awareness of my surrounding became more acute. I didn't only smell Gabriel, but also the clean lavender infusing the bed linen and the salty air of the sea that filtered through the cracks of the windows. I didn't only see his skin, I could isolate every parcel of it. My own fingers that so far had dangled around his waist tightened their grip, my muscles powered by a brand new energy.

He winced under my grasp. I jerked back. My fangs renounced his flesh with reluctance, but I didn't care.

"Did I hurt you?" I forced my gaze to flick away from the blood trickling from his neck and checked the rest of him.

His heartbeat had steadied, with no inconsistency to its rhythm. His complexion wasn't abnormally pale. Heat radiated from him. And he smiled. He smiled not only with a curve of his lips but twinkles in his eyes.

That was when I felt the wetness of blood around my mouth. My hand flew to cover my reborn shame. His fingers were around my wrist once again and stopped my movement midair.

"Don't." The edge in his voice was unmistakable. "If you're ashamed of this, then you're ashamed of me, of us." He seized my gaze and held on it in a challenge. "Are you?"

"No," I cried out. "Never."

"Then don't cover yourself. This is us, not all of us, but I won't let it become our dirty little secret."

I wriggled, raising my arms to widen the brackets formed by his thighs around me. In vain.

"I have no shame with you. Do you understand? No shame." His voice and his eyes engulfed me with their fierceness.

Gabriel leaned towards me until his mouth was back on mine. The tip of his tongue traced the edges of my lips, millimeter by millimeter, erasing the remnants of his gift. Heat rocketed into me, setting my muscles on fire, boiling my blood. The graze of his stubble started a delicious itch that ran down my spine to my hips. I pressed my thighs together to contain their need to open wide for him.

Instead, my lips parted to let him explore my mouth. He sucked in a sharp breath. For a moment I thought he chose to ignore my invitation as his lips kept simply nuzzling mine. Frustration triggered a tremble in my hands and they roamed up his chest, settling on the swell of his pecs. This wasn't enough. I needed to rock against him, drown in him, fuse with him.

Maybe I said that out loud because Gabe palmed my bottom and scooped me up. I now straddled him. My core grinded against his erection. His tongue slid inside my mouth, teasing and tasting as if entwined with my own. He sucked on it. My moan got lost in our kiss. There was nothing tentative anymore. He drew me so close the contours of my sex molded around the length of his. My clothes suffocated me.

"Marie…" he mumbled in a rough whisper.

I clung to his lower lip, then ran my tongue along the tiny dent formed by the dimple on his cheek. The skin there, damp and salty, felt like the first step of my journey into him. I wanted to taste every inch of his skin, but his hold on me tightened and grounded me.

"Marie." The call was more insistent this time, the two syllables clearly pronounced.

"Yes." But my kisses became more urgent.

I didn't want to talk. I only wanted to kiss him, even though my heart clenched each time I did. My body ached when he tore his face from mine. His gaze sought me and when it did, I was trapped. There was no way to escape the dark gleam in his eyes that searched my face to memorize it.

"*A leanaigh*, would you do me the honor of being my first?"

A shudder of anticipation and pride and fear shook my soul.

He pressed his forehead to mine. When he spoke, his breath brushed over my face. "Would you do me the honor of being my first and only?"

Chapter 20 — First Times.

My answer might have come as a "Yes," or perhaps it'd been no more than a nod. I might have shouted. I might have whispered. But no matter how I accepted his request, it was clear enough for him to sweep me off my feet and carry me to the bed.

I stood now between his parted legs, him sitting on the edge of the bed. Without words or kisses, the air shifted thick and heavy between us while he held himself still, his fingers clamped around my waist.

Until then, he'd been the one showing me the way. The balance of power had reversed and I had no time to hesitate. No time to doubt or double-guess. Him. Myself. Our moment had come and I intended to seize it.

I stepped back and with swift, economical moves, drew on the zipper of my jeans and pulled them down to my feet. There was an almost tumble when I tried to extract my feet but Gabriel held me up. My throat closed up at the same time as my hands reached for the clasp between my shoulder blades and undid it.

Degree by degree I let the straps glide down my shoulders, the sides of my arms, dragging the cups of the bra with them. The lace scraped against the curve of my breasts, catching on the tender nubs. With the friction, they puckered, lengthened, and Gabriel's breath caught in a guttural growl. My thighs trembled. My hips writhed. He leaned in and nuzzled the valley between my small breasts. I didn't feel self-conscious to be so exposed; I couldn't wait for him to discover me.

When his tongue licked wet circles at the center of my breastbone, longing rippled from my heart to my core. His focus drifted down to my navel, and my breathing ratcheted up, morphed into choppy panting. There he explored the tiny maze of creases in slow licks and suckles. His hands slid to lie flat on my bottom and pull me closer to him while his fingers slipped under the lace of my panties. His calloused palms grazed against my skin while he kneaded my cheeks.

I arched my back, offering more of my flesh for him to cup, and a low rumble rolled out from his throat. The hot breath he released against my belly had me thread my fingers through the thickness of his curls. I heard his loud inhale and I drew him tighter against me, thrust my hips against him.

His long index fingers hooked around the lace of my panties, pulling on them until they reached my ankles. I stepped out and he threw them away. The air that brushed against the curls at the top of my thighs did nothing to cool me off. His gaze devoured and consumed me, its dark and hungry glint making my toes curl. His eyes ended their exploration, meeting mine, and blood rushed to my face, burning every cell on the way.

"I have never seen a woman completely naked before." A smile tugged at the corner of his mouth. "At least, not in the flesh."

"I hope you're not too dis—"

"You're beautiful." He breathed in through his nose, his nostrils flaring. "You are so beautiful I can't think straight anymore."

"Then don't." My plea was a whimper of sound. "Make me yours."

"The thing is—" his throat worked on a swallow, "—I don't like words. They never feel like enough, so I act instead. I play, I fight, I *do* because that's my only way to prove myself." His hands skimmed over my skin, away from my waist, down the lengths of my thighs. One of them glided between my legs, grazing up and up to reach the crease at the top. He pressed his palm there, his finger rubbing along one of my lips.

"I've never wanted something—someone—as much as I want you. But I'm scared that whatever I do now, it won't be enough to make you stay." Pink worked over his cheekbones and the sight was like a light stroke over my heart. "I'm already yours but I have no idea where to start to make you mine."

"Anywhere." Like an invitation, my breasts quivered with the heavy breath I took next. "Touch me, kiss me. Anywhere. Every inch of my skin is yours to claim."

His lids fluttered and I was shaking when his tongue rolled around the bead of my nipple. He captured it, flicked, plucked, and my head tilted backwards. I was squirming by the time he let go of it with a loud pop and switched to the other. My legs limp, I held straight only with the support of his palm now cupping my core. I curled my hands around his shoulders, grabbing them tight while a wash of emotions punched me, making me weak and greedy for more of him.

He lifted my leg and placed my foot on the bed by his side. If I hadn't already given up on any propriety, the position would have made me gasp in embarrassment as my swollen sex was now open and fully exposed to his exploration. And explore he did.

His tongue replaced his palm, skimmed along one lip, the other, thrust deep inside me. My moan choired with the muffled humming that came from him. There was nothing delicate in the way Gabriel touched me. He kissed, licked, lapped at my sex with appetite. He drank me with undisguised thirst, thorough in every suckle. When his teeth buried gently around the little nub of nerves, I shuddered. Rapture fell over me, making me cant my hips and swivel them against his face to chase its heat and oblivious darkness.

I collapsed against him. It was only with his solid arms wrapped around my waist that I didn't crumple at his feet. The taut skin over his shoulders was damp with sweat, so was his hair when I rammed my fingers through it once more. His face was nudged between my breasts, our scents mingled, their musky aroma a balanced blend of male and female. But it was all ours now, tantalizing my senses to have a taste of my own.

I pushed away from him and he frowned at the sudden gap between us, fear flashing through his eyes.

"Your turn." Impatience had me lift up my chin, but my voice came out strangled.

"Aye."

Without any artifice, Gabe yanked the pullover over his head and it landed somewhere at the foot of the bed. He was so beautiful my heart ached. Freckles splayed along the hard swells of his shoulders and I struggled to reconcile that almost boyish attribute with the testosterone sipping out of his every pore. His chest heaved and the rasp of his breathing filled my ears.

"More," I coaxed him.

The cockiness of his smirk told me that as unexperienced as Gabriel Macleod might be, he was back in control. Of me. Of us. He uncurled himself to stand, aligning his body with mine. I licked my bottom lip when all I wanted was to run my tongue over the imaginary line running between his nipples. With his big palms back around my waist, he guided me down to the edge of the bed, the exact spot where he had sat.

He snapped the button of his jeans, pulled down the zipper, and that single sound vibrated in the quietness of the room. My focus narrowed on the bulge of his crotch slowly revealed to me. Gabriel Macleod didn't bother with triviality like underwear whether he wore a kilt or not. The hard, thick length sprang out of the restraint of his jeans that now hung low from his narrow waist. His cock was glorious, silky with just a drop of moisture glistening on its head. I breathed him in, all musk and spice, and my tongue ran along my bottom lip again.

His hand reached down, giving himself a light stroke,

and his sex jutted out. He kept his fingers at the root of the shaft, his grip raw, the muscles of his stomach clenching in rhythm with the heaving of his chest. Lust swamped back over me, and I rubbed my thighs against each other. My skin there was slick from his mouth and my arousal.

"A word of warning." There was no threat in his voice, it came out husky instead and he cleared his throat. "If you give me the same little treat as I just did to you, it's likely I'll explode in your mouth."

"What makes you think I'll mind?"

His chuckle was low, but the humor was absent when he answered, "The first time you make me come, *a leanaigh*, I'll be inside you." He gave another stroke of his cock as if to tame its visible eagerness.

Gabe matched his promise by hauling me to my feet. With a firm grasp of my bottom, he lifted me against him. My legs twined around his waist when he pivoted and sat back on the edge of the bed. His sex cradled against my stomach and I grinded my hips against its root. I felt it harden, its silky heat turning into a magnet to my core.

My move triggered a helpless groan from him. "I might be a rookie, but I'll be damned if I don't make it good for you." His features twitched as in pain. "Or if I embarrass myself by shooting too early for you to even enjoy it."

I lifted myself up to release some of the pressure on his sensitive parts. That didn't seem to appease him. He pulled me back against him, grinding his hips against my core. "Don't think you have to spare me, lass."

I should have reassured him, reminded him that first times were always awkward experiences, a necessary step that had to be taken before the real deal was sealed. But I kept my mouth shut.

I kept my mouth shut because I had no doubt Gabriel Macleod would take me on an unforgettable ride the instant I welcomed him inside me. I had to share my absolute trust in his abilities, so I grabbed hold of his hair and licked the inside of his upper lip. In return, he sucked on my tongue, traced the roof of my mouth, the edge of my teeth, bit my lower lip, and repeated his assault until my hips had climbed onto the tip of his cock, hot and thick for me.

It had a will of its own and twitched against my opening. All my senses converged to this spot but he slowed down and I had to force myself to look at the rest of us. My breasts crushed against the hard muscles of his chest, his arms ironclad around me, mine still clutched around his shoulders, my nails now biting into his flesh, which glistened with sweat.

He kidnapped my gaze with his. For one second I forgot my need for him. His eyes burned with lust and darkness and uncertainty.

I cupped his cheek. "What is it?" I heard fear in my voice, fear he'd change his mind and withdraw so far away I wouldn't be able to reach out for him anymore.

But he leaned into my palm and the reassurance in his gesture loosened the knot that had formed in my belly. "This is it." His gaze was riveted on me, nailing me, trapping me with its intensity, his voice low but firm. "This is it for me."

"What is it?" I repeated in a faint croak.

"*You* are."

I collapsed inside, the dam I built so long ago around my heart destroyed with his two words. They filled every recess of my soul with the flush of a promise, and tears blurred my vision. My lips felt numb when I struggled to part them but no sound came out from my mouth.

He covered it with a kiss, silencing any attempt at an answer. "I thought you should know that before we get even more wet and messy."

I laughed. It bubbled out from deep inside me. A trail of joy followed it. For one moment, my muscles relaxed and I returned his kiss. There was no sensual intention in that kiss of mine but by leaning into him the rounded tip of his cock slid further into me. He sucked a gulp of air, drew it deep into his lungs, and released it with a groan. His hands moved to the small of my back, then to the plumpness of my bottom. He clenched my cheeks and his mouth nuzzled against the hollowness at the base of my neck.

"Open up my eyes." He licked the shallow dent there. "Show me how it is done." Small kisses rained against the line of my throat. "Ride me and set the pace."

I sank onto him in one smooth glide, my sex stretching around his invasion, my need to be full with him superseding the pain. We shuddered but my push down his cock was relentless until I settled down with him as far into me as I could take. We stayed still, chests heaving in shared falls and rises, while our bodies acclimated to each other.

But he'd asked me to show him the way and I couldn't wait any longer. My sex clasped his cock in my claim on him and I started undulating. My hips rocked against him, our foreheads now touching, and my breasts jiggling against his pectorals. His lidded gaze remained on my face as if I was his lifeline. I knew he was mine.

When he surged to meet my downstroke, I gasped. My entire body tightened. But I didn't stop or slow, I forged on, carried by the matching strength of his thrusts. His stomach muscles strained with each one of those and we kept colliding halfway.

As he moved, a low moan rolled out of his mouth and flowed down my spine. My head fell back as I plummeted into a void carved in pleasure. The heat of his mouth around my nipple drew me back and I bowed over him.

"I—I need you to take over," I begged.

He swung me onto the mattress, leaving me with my legs wide open, my core still throbbing. The mattress dipped with his weight, and I heard the sound of foil tearing before he rolled on a condom. He stole a glimpse at me over his shoulder. "Sorry, I got carried away and forgot to wrap up."

"I'm not sick. I mean, I am sick but not in a way that could affect you when we… I'd never put you at risk, you must know that."

Gabe didn't answer. He crawled back between my legs, levering himself up on his arms. I eased with relief into his heat. With the pad of his thumb, he brushed my temple, threading his fingers in the wisps of my hair now spread over the pillow.

His face expressed an almost puzzled wonder. After the frenzy of the past minutes, the slow tempo tipped me off-balance. I resented the silence but resisted the urge to babble, and let him nibble at my earlobe instead. It was a challenge not to indulge in the softness—the kindness—of his touch. But there was something unsaid between us and I wouldn't allow a misunderstanding to taint whatever would happen next—what already had.

"You must know that," I said again. "I would never hurt you, whatever my intentions were at first. I'd never put you at risk, knowingly or not." I bit on my lower lip to keep it from trembling.

His body tensed along mine. He lifted himself entirely, severing any contact between us, a plank of unyielding muscles hovering over me. I could read the beginning of a scowl in the way his brows drew together. My limbs turned into lead, soon to be swallowed by the mattress. I wanted to take my words back, jumble them around in any way that could make him come back to me.

I didn't have to because he swept the scare away. "This isn't about you hurting me, but me hurting you." Peppering featherlight kisses around my mouth, he didn't seem in a hurry to elaborate. "I hope one day you'll have another child and I pray I'll be the man you want it with. Until then, you must stay free to choose your own path and I won't do anything to take that freedom away from you."

Something cracked deep inside me, not the protective wall I'd built because Gabriel had already destroyed it, but the very thing that had hidden behind that wall. The mute but throbbing pain born from the loss of my son. A loss I'd never recovered from but carried with me, buried and left raw to fester. I saw that pain, I visualized it. It took shape and color.

But instead of drowning me, the strength to face and wrestle with it shot through me for the first time since the night my baby had died. I saw hope. It rushed through me, lifting me up. I struggled to catch my next breath. It mingled with a sob and tears prickled at my eyes. By reflex I started curling inward, but Gabriel's grip on my hip stilled me.

"I want you to be mine, Marie, but my love for you isn't a trap or a fence. It's made of everything you are and it goes wherever you go."

I shuddered and gulped, but hunted the truth in his eyes nevertheless. It was all there in the unwavering way he stared back at me, and I feared *my* love for him would cripple me right then. So I grabbed his head and brought him down for a kiss. I spread my legs further apart and he settled against me, *inside* me.

Him inside me had an odd familiarity now. He rocked his hips, filling me in, filling me out, and I let him please me without racing towards the end this time. We took our time, melting into another, until he found a rhythm and a swivel of his own.

But—eventually—there was no way to prevent our shared pleasure from ratcheting up. I dug my heels into the firm globes of his bottom and arched up beneath him, taking in even more of him. The silent order had him lose control. He pounded into me, bucked, thrust. The sound of his flesh slapping against mine sizzled my senses. I thrust back.

My closed eyelids were the backdrop for a firework of red and purple sparkles. But it was pitch black in my head when I fell. Nothing else existed, nothing else mattered but the primal joy exploding out of my every cell. I danced and swirled and glided over waves of ecstasy. And I sang his name.

I was left blind by it—blind, breathless, and deliciously beaten. His low groan stretched inside my head and I pulled him even closer to me, cradling him with my legs wrapped around his waist and my arms around his neck. His body strained against mine as he came deep inside me.

Aftershocks of pleasure still shook him when his cheek came to rest against mine as we both recovered, sucking air into our lungs and panting unevenly.

When he spoke, his mouth brushed against mine.

"Will you stay with me, Marie Aberdein?"

"I will, Gabriel MacLeod, I will."

Chapter 21 — Moment of Truth

"That's not right." I squeezed Gabriel's hand hard and stalled.

My warning hadn't much value since he'd already drawn the same conclusion *and* jumped to the next step. His jaw was locked rigid. His gaze surveyed the moor that spread around Hollaroch under the dull light of the midday sun. The space would have been deserted if only for the SUV parked randomly in the driveway leading into the property. We'd left our own cars in the garage when we arrived the day before.

He spun to me and his hands folded over my shoulders. "Listen to me." His voice had gained a military edge. "You're going to the cottage now. If I'm not back within an hour, you'll find a set of keys underneath the mattress. On the keyring there's an address of a flat in Inverness. Go there, hitchhike to the train station if you have to, and wait for me."

I stared up at him. Time was against us but I had to find a way to get the message to him. Loud and clear. "Whoever's waiting for us inside—" and I had a pretty good idea of his identity, "—we're handling it together. I'm not fleeing to a goddamned hideout in Inverness while you stay here and face the music. Alone."

Impatient anger swirled and darkened the emerald of his eyes. "I won't be able to think straight if I know you're at risk. So for both our sakes—"

"For both our sakes, you'd better get your act together

because this isn't how the two of us are going to work, you acting the hero and me skulking in the rear."

"You're in no shape to—"

"*You* listen to me now, Gabriel MacLeod. I've managed to look after my own skin for two hundred years and learned a few tricks along the way in dealing with psychotic Stramos and over-trained Hunters." I might not have won battles, but I'd survived nonetheless. "Besides, you told me I could take our love wherever I wanted to. Well, I'll make it stand by your side."

He inhaled sharply. His mouth thinned. But with a loud release of air, his shoulders slumped and the shaded gleam in his eyes betrayed his capitulation. "Fair enough."

"Great that's settled then. Now why do we have to get inside in the first place? We're not armed, have no element of surprise…"

"Because the others are there too. Lizzie, Simon…and because he already knows we're standing right here. He probably also knows all about you by now."

"He wouldn't harm Lizzie. She's his daughter."

The arch of his eyebrow enlightened the naïveté of my comment. His words pointed at it. "He had no qualms killing the woman he'd vowed to love."

My instinct was to run away, not to save myself but keep him out of danger. The thought slammed against the plan to fight I'd professed earlier. But there was no life for us, no space for our love, unless we made it happen together.

"Fine." I gave him a purposeful nod. "Let's do it."

His wide hand cradled my head, clutched at the wildness of my hair. He pulled me in and I crashed against his chest, his lips devouring mine. His tongue swept inside my mouth, called for mine, and they collided with each other as if they were at war. I tasted his now familiar flavor, a hint of mint and spice and freedom. The kiss was brief but left me gasping my next breath. When his touch left me, a chill sent shivers trickling down my spine. Panic hit me with the thought it could be our last kiss, our last contact. My mind turned foggy.

"I'm no hero, *a leanaigh*." His throat worked through a swallow. "But I'll die before I let anything happen to you. *He*—" The word dripped with disgust. "He has some*thing* to fight for, but I have some*one*."

His promise cleared my mind by giving me a weapon. "And I you."

My heart lurched and my eyelids fluttered to keep my tears from welling up. Now was not the moment to give in to my overemotional self. Gabe stretched out his hand and I took it. Our palms flat against one another, we marched towards the main house.

"I can't detect any heartbeats in the surrounding buildings."

We'd reached the twenty-yard perimeter. "And from inside the house?"

My focus narrowed in on the manor, channeling my hearing without much success. We were too far away and there were many of them. "At least four."

We reached the entrance door, solid wood embossed with the MacLeod's coat of arms—its girth slicing through the moon. Even if it hadn't been his ancestral home, there was no need for Gabriel to knock. We were expected.

The creak of the door opening grated on my ears and distilled dread into my blood. My feet froze at the doorstep but Gabriel's advance was relentless and I scurried forward. The inside of the manor hadn't changed much since the night I'd ventured inside the Hunter's stronghold to kill him. I could almost smell the scent of the melting wax from the candles. Memories flashed in front of my eyes but I gave them a mental kick. Gabriel's hold on my hand tightened as if he'd felt my weakening spirit.

We reached the door to the dining hall, which was the largest in the house. I could hear the beating hearts behind it, but Gabe had been the one leading me to it. Maybe MacLeods had a sixth sense drawing them to each other. There was no doubt we'd reached our destination.

"Let me lead, will you? I've known the man all my life and all his mind-fucking tricks."

"And I've known Hunters for two centuries. So I guess we both have our own areas of expertise."

"Damn, woman. You're little but you're fierce. All right, but let me kick off."

My acceptance came in the steady gaze I shot back at him. I'd experienced fear before, the morning Everett left for Culloden, for my friends in Saguenay on the last solstice dawn. Never had I felt its tremor ransacking my whole body like a sub-polar wave, beating my heart, punching my guts, and making my skin itchy, my palms clammy. And with that fear mingled guilt and even more fear because, at that very moment, I realized I'd never loved anyone as I loved Gabriel MacLeod.

We stepped into the central room, where we'd had dinner the night before. The layout hadn't changed. The long, rectangular table at its center, the framed portraits of past MacLeods hanging on the walls at regular intervals, they were still there. The rest of the room was in disarray. The upholstered chairs where we'd sat and suffered Fergus and Hayden's recital were scattered around. The remnants of our dinner were splashed over the hardwood floor, and broken pieces of the Wedgewood pottery created a broken rug of glass topped by cutlery.

My assumption had been almost accurate: five heartbeats in addition to ours. Tobias was the first I noticed since he was lying two yards from us, his arms bound behind his back by makeshift manacles. I guessed the ropes of the curtains. Blood oozed from a gash on his lower lip, and the flesh of one eyelid was in the early stages of bruising. He was alive so I didn't linger long by him. As was Simon, although his dilated pupils and quick breathing revealed a heightened level of anxiety. But again, the still-alive box could be ticked for him.

Hayden and Fergus were leaning against bare parts of the walls with mirroring body languages, arms crossed over their chests, heads hanging forward. I didn't have long enough to dive into the intricacies of their minds but I picked on the same emotions: shame and remorse. Lizzie was nowhere to be seen.

My gaze flicked back at Gabe. If he'd taken note of how his friends showed no sign of physical harm, nor had their hands tied like his cousin, he didn't show it. Gone was the tenderness I'd read in his profile while he worshipped me that morning. The lines were now cut and chiseled into an unreadable mask. His focus was solely on the fifth man sitting on the single upright chair at the opposite end of the table.

That man didn't give anything away as to his inner thoughts. His heart beat steadily. I didn't pick on the revealing smell of sweat. On the contrary, he inhabited the chair as if it were a throne, and he a king facing a hall full of despised minions.

"Right on time, son. I just arrived half an hour ago and took care of that cousin of yours. Not that it took much effort to neutralize him. From now on, choose your allies with more care, won't you?"

I'd heard Nathaniel MacLeod's voice only once before. Last solstice dawn in Saguenay. Curt orders roared at his troops and the final insults he'd spat at my friends. At Louis. A heavy weight settled in my chest, one I tried to shake away: his voice reminded me of Gabriel's. Same timbre, low, gravelly, only with the highland brogue more pronounced.

Gabriel chose to ignore the welcome. "Fergus, Hayden." His tone didn't carry any accusation but the two bears acknowledged him simultaneously by lifting their heads. "Were you the ones who called him?"

They exchanged a sidelong glance, pushing each other to answer. Fergus was the one who finally manned up.

"I'm sorry, mate. You know we had your back right from the start, but we couldn't—we saw the bites on Alice's neck… It had to be her doing." He nodded in my direction. "She had to be one of them and you've been eye-fucking her since she moved into your house." Gabriel hissed at the word and Fergus shrugged with defeat. "When you decided to stay with her after what happened to Alice, we figured the vamp had you wrapped around her middle finger. We had to call him."

There was no reprimand, no outraged cry. Gabriel seemed to have already taken the new development in his stride. "What about Lizzie?"

"She's gone," Simon cut in. He was slumped in one corner and I could feel the constriction in his chest, the clenching of his heart. "It was all very chaotic after we found Alice's body—after you stormed out with Marie. One moment Lizzie was with me, the next she wasn't." I hated the tremble in his voice. "I've tried to call her mobile, but she's not answering."

"I'm having it tracked," Nathaniel said in a curt tone. "I'll send some men after her as soon as we've found where she is. I've come on my own and my preference would be to keep all of this between us. I don't need anyone else to know about my son's fuck-ups."

Despite the urgency spinning around us, I couldn't help comparing father and son, not only their voices, but the similar shape of their faces, from the square jaws to the high foreheads, their sheer size, broad chests and hard shoulders. However their complexions differed: Nathaniel's darkness sucked in the surrounding light, Gabriel's inner fire reflected it.

For the first time since we'd stepped into what felt like a trap, Gabe's eyes betrayed some emotions although I couldn't pinpoint exactly which ones. Anger? Hate? Fear? Until then, it'd been as if the very presence of the Hunter was nothing to worry about, not even a blip on Gabriel's radar.

"When you find out where she is, *I* will be the one going after her."

"She's my daughter." He still had that same relaxed pose, but his stillness chilled my organs. It was lethal and I couldn't help swaying towards Gabriel.

"I'm her only family."

"From the way your life has unraveled in my absence, I have reason to question your professed sense of family duty. After all, you sheltered a Turned under the same roof as your sister for three months." Nathaniel straightened up in his chair. It wasn't much of a move but the threat coiled around my muscles.

There was a controlled pull on my hand that had me slide behind Gabriel. He parted his legs, widening his stance, hiding a portion of me from his father's glare.

The Hunter forged on. "It seems you've now gained a premature understanding of our world, but your instincts are in dire need of sharpening."

"She didn't kill Alice. Lawrence Beaumont did."

Nathaniel narrowed his eyes. At last, a genuine reaction from him. "Beaumont was here? That's impossible."

The satisfaction of seeing him annoyed instilled some much-needed warmth in me. I'd have gloated if my throat hadn't been so closed up.

"Just like he was in 1746 when he slaughtered my namesake. Yes, father, he was the one who committed the deed then."

The Hunter's fingers curled around the end of the armrests, turning his knuckles white.

"Didn't you know that?" Gabriel taunted.

His father shifted position, leaning a few degrees forward. "How would I? I haven't fucked your girl."

Gabriel moved to bolt, but my grip on his forearm held him back.

"Because that's all it is. A fuck." Nathaniel had infused so much filth in the last word, bile rose up to my throat. "You got caught in her clutches. She blurred your mind with her sweet piece of arse, but that's all there is to it. No matter what she convinced you of."

He meant it, but it was meant more as a provocation than anything else. I wouldn't rise to it. Neither should Gabriel. I had no clear vantage point of his face anymore, but there was no missing the squaring of his shoulders and his fiercer grip on my hand.

"Is that how you look back at my mum? A fuck that turned into a big mistake."

His father jumped to his feet and slammed his fist on the table, the vibrations rocketing across my own body. "How dare you talk about your mother like that?"

"How dare I?" Gabriel shook his head in what I assumed was a genuine display of shock. "I've got some news for you, *Dad*. I've played catchup in more areas than one. I know what you did."

A moan made everyone's attention shift to the crumpled form at my feet. Tobias was sitting up, blinking. Finally he opened his eyes wide and took in his surroundings.

He zeroed in on Gabriel and a frown of guilt appeared on his battered face. "I'm sorry, Gabe. I tried to fight back, to hold him off but...I didn't even hit him once."

"That's fine, Tobe. You tried and I shouldn't have left you on your own anyway."

But the young man stared down in embarrassment. When he tried to stand, a groan rumbled out of him. I rushed to his side and knelt down, taking hold of his elbow. He recoiled at my contact.

"Don't—you're one of them."

"I'm sorry I lied to you and everyone else." I meant it, although telling the truth would have resulted in one of them skewering my heart or burning me.

I was about to stand straight again but Tobias surprised me. "I believe you and we have the same enemy anyway." He tipped his chin towards his uncle.

I answered with a silent nod, extended my hand, and helped him up. I proceeded to untie the cords binding his wrists.

"Enough!" Nathaniel didn't seem concerned by the wellbeing of his nephew. Well, he was the one responsible for Tobias's condition after all. "What is it that you think you know about your mother's death?" He stepped out from behind the table.

Gabriel left our side and advanced towards his father. His gait reminded me of a feline stalking its prey. It took nerves to come close to the Hunter that way. Even most Stramos would keep clear.

"She didn't want me to be raised as the next Hunter, so she took us and tried to get away." Gabriel passed his father, his shoulder bumping against the older man. "But you couldn't let that happen, so she had to die."

Nathaniel reacted like thunder. He spun and rocketed forward, grabbing Gabriel by the collar and nailing him against the wall. My fangs slid through my gums and I shot forward. A solid arm looped around my shoulders and held me back.

"Let him," Tobias whispered into my ear. Let him what? Die? Not a chance. I fought against Tobias's grip, but he managed to keep me from rushing to Gabriel's rescue, which saved my life. If I couldn't defeat a concussed human, I had no hope against a fully-conscious Hunter.

Not that Gabe looked very flustered by his father's attack. He smirked back at him, a glint of hate simmering in his eyes.

"You're out of your mind, son. I should kick your arse for spreading lies like that."

"I'm not the fucking liar here. You are."

"Don't you dare—"

He didn't have time to defend his good name. Gabriel head-butted him.

The crack I heard was like a caress on my scarred heart. So was the blood that spurted out of Nathaniel's nose. He hunched forward. "Fuck!"

Next, Gabriel shoved him back against the table, forcing his chest to hit the surface with a loud thud. With his own chest now plastered against his father's back, Gabriel twisted the man's arm behind his back.

"How can you live with yourself, you bastard?" Gabriel

shouted. Nathaniel wriggled but only ended up with his cheek pushed harder against the wood. "You'd married just two years before. She'd carried your children. She just wanted to protect us, to give us a chance at freedom." His voice shook with unshed tears and his sorrow stabbed me. "And you killed her."

I expected more denials, more fighting back, but Nathaniel MacLeod gave up and froze. His body turned limp and there were no more recriminations. His panting was the only sound emanating from him.

And finally, "You're wrong. I'd never have hurt your mum. We had our problems, that's true. They had everything to do with my family and our duty. But I loved her and I'd never have let anything happen to her."

"So you're saying that it *really* was a car accident and that you had *no* idea she was taking us to the States." Gabriel shoved his father's head harder against the table. "Try again."

He winced. "That's the truth, dammit. Your mother is the only woman I've ever loved."

A shadow crossed Gabe's face. Doubt mingled with relief. His grip slackened and he let go of his father. However he seized a dirk that must have been hidden in his father's jacket.

He retreated two steps, pointing the weapon at Nathaniel. "Turn slowly and face me. Your hands where I can see them."

"Are you out of your fucking mind?" As much as Tobias had wanted to keep me out of the fight, he wasn't inclined to do so himself anymore. He left me behind and took two steps forward. "The bastard tells you he's innocent and you believe him. No questions asked."

"Tobias, stay back," ordered Gabriel. "The questions are coming but I want to see his face when he answers."

"Has he been the one poisoning your mind?" Nathaniel didn't even reward Tobias with a look.

"I've not poisoned anyone, asshole. You killed my aunt eighteen years ago and then you had my dad murdered."

Nathaniel raised his hands, palms forward. "Guilty on one count."

Chapter 22 — Moment of Choice.

At least we were getting somewhere.

"Which one is it?" Gabriel's voice was gruff.

I dreaded whatever was coming next. It was one thing for him to contemplate his father's involvement in his mother's death, quite another hearing it straight from the horse's mouth.

"I sliced his father's throat."

The tone was mild and conversational. I wanted to retch. I would have if I hadn't heard the sharp intake of air combined with a painful whimper. It came from Tobias next to me. Without thinking, I grabbed his hand and squeezed it, triggering no reaction from him.

"Not that I think there's ever a good reason to *slice* your brother-in-law's throat, but please do indulge us with some form of explanation." Gabriel's tone matched his father's, but his facial features were taut.

"Svenson had built a lucrative business selling vampire's blood to junkies. Of course, they didn't have a fucking clue what they were getting high on. It was laced with heroine or incorporated in various pills Svenson was known to deal. The man was shrewd, I give you that, and it took us a full year to track him down."

"That's bullshit." Tears strangled Tobias's voice. "And even if he was a dealer, that didn't give you the right to tear him apart."

The Hunter's gaze jumped to Tobias, acknowledging him

for the first time. "Drugs were the bread-and-butter of your father's business, and you know that. But he wanted to expand his activities beyond dark back alleys. He decided Spring Break was the perfect opportunity for that and he started selling the shit in Cancún. One college boy OD-ed on it, and for the record, OD-ing on Stramos blood for a human means going homicidal first. He went down but only after bludgeoning his girlfriend. They were both twenty. Your very age, boy."

"I don't believe you." I stepped closer to Tobias, who was now shaking his head. He pushed me away and wandered towards the table hiding his face in his hands. "I don't believe you."

"I understand why you don't but I have a recording of his confession before I…"

Before he murdered him. Nathaniel showed some mercy by not finishing the sentence. "You can also check your facts and you'll find he was in Cancún at the time of the deaths. We have witnesses, although I'm sure you'll say they're working for me."

"So very kind of you to volunteer all this information." Sarcasm coated Gabriel's words. "What an upstanding guy you are."

His father's mouth twisted, with displeasure or hurt, I wasn't sure. "I don't have anything to prove to him, you or myself. I've killed many over the years, but I value human lives more than anything. I wouldn't have killed Svenson if I didn't have the irrefutable proof he was putting lives at risk."

"How dare you say that?" I was done listening to the man. "You slaughtered twenty of my friends in Saguenay. All they wanted was to live in peace and find a way to survive without hurting anyone. That made them better than most humans. You knew that and still you burned them. *All* of them." A single tear traced its way down my cheek and I swept the back of my hand over my nose.

The Hunter pinned me with a look, scanning my body

from head to toe. His gaze didn't meet mine and I lifted up my chin because his scrutiny felt like a slap.

"You're Berthière's daughter." Finally our eyes clashed and I wish I could have destroyed him with all the hate that filled me. "The apple of his eye, I've been told. I've been looking for you since that night in Saguenay. Little did I know that Marie Berthière was actually Marie Aberdein, my children's new housemate. You fooled us, little girl."

"Don't patronize me, MacLeod. I've got two hundred years on you." Sometimes the age difference didn't hurt as much.

"If that makes you feel better, I didn't enjoy burning your Maker. To his credit, he was trying to give some purpose to your pathetic filthy race."

"Then why didn't you just let us be?" My question came out in a faint trickle. I hated myself for it.

"Pay attention to the adjectives, lass. *Pathetic. Filthy.*"

"There's nothing pathetic in just trying to live." My gaze circled the room. "That's all we're trying to do after all, human or not."

"What a poignant statement."

He clapped his hands. Gabriel parted them with a swift sweep with the side of the dirk's blade. "Enough."

"You're right, that's enough. All I'm interested in right now is what you know about your mother's death. Because if it wasn't an accident, then I'm going after whichever motherfucker was involved. You can count on that."

Gabriel remained silent for several long seconds. He tilted his head forward in a silent assessment of his father's truthfulness. He must have passed the test. "Svenson had kept mum's diary. She'd made sure they'd get to him if something happened to her. Then after his dad's death, Tobias received an envelope from him. It contained the diary and a letter that pointed to you and Malcolm for what happened to his sister. And to himself."

"Malcolm?" Nathaniel's question cut like a diamond. "How is he involved?"

"According to Svenson, Malcolm was the one who sabotaged mum's car for you and then covered up his tracks by buying off the police."

"Why would you believe Svenson? He was hardly a man of his word."

"At first, I didn't. Nor what was in mum's diary. I hunted down the copper who was in charge of the investigation." He gave a one-shouldered shrug. "I was persuasive enough for him to spill the truth and he acknowledged his connection to Malcolm."

"But not to me."

Seconds ticked by. "Not to you. But why would Malcolm have her killed, unless you asked him to?"

Nathaniel leaned against the table for support, as if the revelation had finally taken its toll. His shoulders were slumped. His eyes opened onto a frightening new reality. If I didn't already hate him with my all being, I'd have pitied him. But this emotion didn't last long because the man was already back on his feet and in the game.

"We'll get justice for this, Gabriel. I promise you, we will."

"*I'll* get justice for her, and so will Tobias for his father if we can't prove that whole story about Stramos blood and Spring Break. I don't believe a word you say, but I want absolute proof before I kill you."

"Fair enough. I'll lure Malcolm here and you'll see what he has to say about this. *I* won't let him get away with it if your story checks out. Now would you please be kind enough to stop threatening me with my own blade?"

"Don't." Tobias had recovered. "He killed my and Marie's fathers. Are you going to let him get him away with it?" He sounded like a boy. "You promised me, Gabriel, you promised me."

Gabe's gaze darted to me, begging me for an answer. His arm was still straight and pointed at his father's heart. Knots twisted my stomach. My saliva brought an acrid taste to my mouth. I had to press my lips together to keep from gagging, shut my eyes to lock up my raging emotions.

One word, one nod, one look, and Gabriel would execute my command. Louis would be avenged, Odette, Vincent. They were the reasons I'd come back to Scotland. The reasons I'd wriggled myself into Gabriel's life.

But not into his heart. My hands flew to my neck to loosen the imaginary rope that was tied around my throat. The sound of blood rushing through my veins hummed between my ears. It morphed into a buzz, making my face twitch. I focused on taming the madness swirling inside me, ran my palms along my thighs, in a soothing gesture.

My eyes popped open. I saw Gabriel and it was like seeing him for the first time. The fiery curls, the slanting eyes, the fleshy lips. The elegant line of his nose I peppered with kisses when we woke up in each other's arms. I wouldn't rob him of his soul and burden him with sin and sorrow. He wouldn't be my weapon, my means to an end.

"Gabriel, stop listening to your dick, will you?" Nathaniel MacLeod didn't waste much time on poetry. I wouldn't hold that against him. "First of all, you need to get rid of her. She's with you to make me pay. I'm sure she's a good shag—Turned often are—But you must be an example to your men. You made a mistake and it needs to be corrected." Silence bounced between the upholstered walls of the dining hall. "*Now.*"

Two-centuries of saving my skin had fine-tuned my perception of danger. The little hairs on the back of my neck rose. Without making a show of it, I stole a glimpse at the path to the door. It was clear. I could also throw myself through the window. We were at ground level. The broken glasses would tear my skin, but I'd heal. Beyond the window were the moors. After the moors… They'd catch up with me. I'd fed, but they were MacLeods. They would definitely catch up with me.

"I will never hurt Marie." Gabriel sliced through my

escape plans. "And if you even come close to trying, I will destroy you." His eyes circled the room and settled briefly on each individual in turn, apart from me. "And so that it is perfectly clear, I will end anyone who even contemplates hurting her."

Tension whistled out of me like air out of a burst balloon.

"That's a chivalrous promise made by your cock." Nathaniel was persistently concerned with one specific part of his son's anatomy. "First, you're forgetting some of us can fight back, unlike that cousin of yours."

"I'm not the one whose nose is pissing blood." The edge of Gabriel's mouth lifted. "But do proceed to your second point, father."

Nathaniel clenched his jaw, causing a spot similar to his son's to throb there. The shift in power made the air between the MacLeods crackle.

"Second—" the Hunter spat out the word, "—you'll never be anointed next March if our clan knows you're sleeping with a Turned. It's bad enough you broke your vow of purity, but with one of those creatures, it's simply unforgivable."

I'd never contemplated this possibility. Gabriel not becoming the next Hunter because of...me. Gabriel's mind had opened to new possibilities; he didn't condemn my race as a whole anymore. But I'd be burying my head in the sand if I ignored this stark fact: some of us killed. They stalked, hunted and sucked innocents dry.

While there were humans just as murderous, there was human law enforcement to contain them. In our world, there was no one but the Hunter and his troops.

I forced my gaze to drift to Gabriel. The dirk was still pointed at his father with unshaking aim. But he stared at me and his stare was as unshaking as his arm. It probed my soul, tested it, searching every recess for an answer to the question he addressed silently to me. My spine stiffened, making me stand up taller. A warm ball of love bounced inside my ribcage, and every thump knocked my selflessness down one more notch.

I should let Gabriel go. I really should. He was a good man. He'd redefine his duty with fairness and never kill blindly. One day he would marry a girl. They'd grow old together.

Together was the operative word here. Me, I was stuck in this same unchanging body.

But the ball inside me burst, releasing the heat of my love for him, of my dreams with him. My lips trembled and smiled weakly at him. He accepted it with a nod.

His focus reverted to his father. "If the clan can't accept her, then I'll have to step down. She's a nonnegotiable part of me."

The gauntlet had been thrown down. Nathaniel welcomed it. A sharp intake of air made his chest swell. He wiped his nose with the back of his sleeve. The man I was looking at now had lost all arrogance. If anything, he seemed to have shrunk, his gestures were choppy, and I smelled the sweat bleeding from his pores.

"We'll go away. We'll leave St. Andrews, Scotland, and never show our faces again if that's what we have to do to be together."

Reality slapped me. "Gabriel, don't. This is going too far. We—"

Nathaniel cut me off. "I can't let you get away either. My authority will be questioned. If you give up on your duty, the next Hunter will be Lizzie's firstborn male. Until he reaches 21, I'll remain the acting leader and I can't show weakness even to my own blood."

Gabriel nodded. "We'll have to fight then."

"To the death."

Chapter 23 — One Blade.

I shot forward, my fingers around Gabriel's wrist, shoving the blade away.

"I won't let you die. I won't let you kill your father either. Not for me."

He yanked me by the elbow, dragging me out of the direct line between them. If I had feathers, they'd have been ruffled. But I didn't care for the treatment. I would argue, I would seduce, and I would convince. But he was *not* going to die in the name of our love.

A melody echoed across the hall. Not a lullaby, or a piece of classical music, but a mobile phone ringtone. Gabriel's brow arched but his focus narrowed on his father.

"I must answer. It might be about Lizzie." Nathaniel's voice had reverted to its initial mundane tone. "My daughter has gone AWOL, right after a murder was committed in her home. I, for one, would like to make sure she's safe and sound."

"Take the call," Gabriel barked.

Nathaniel extracted the phone from the back pocket of his jeans and brought it to his ear.

"MacLeod. Have you tracked the signal?"

I listened to the exchange and its content knotted my stomach. Something was off.

Nathaniel didn't lose any time after ending the call. "Apparently, your sister's phone is still here. We need to search the house again. She called an unknown number shortly after eleven last night. There was no cellular activity after that."

"Has anyone searched her bedroom?" Gabriel kept his eyes pinned on his father.

While Hayden and Fergus exchanged powerless glances, it was Simon who chimed in, "We looked for her there, but we didn't look for her phone."

"Fergus, Hayden, get your arses up there. Turn the place upside down if you have to, but find where she left her bloody mobile. She might have left other clues."

They started to scurry out of the dining hall.

"I want to go first, Gabe," I cut in. "There're things I may be able to pick out—smells, even remnants of thoughts— they'll miss all that."

Gabriel nodded in approval.

"If she goes, I go too. I'm better trained than anyone here *and* she's my daughter."

Nathaniel had a point.

Finding Lizzie superseded anything else, even our vendetta against her father. And the truth was that if there was ever a good tracker out there, it was the Hunter.

"Let him go," I said in Gabriel's direction.

"The three of us will go upstairs. You two—" he gestured at Fergus and Hayden, "—start a perimeter around the main house. I don't want him to get any more support. There are guns in the cellar. Go and grab them. Fire only if they fire first."

With the tip of his dirk, Gabriel gestured for his father to leave the hall. He followed with the dagger pointed at Nathaniel's back. Trust wasn't back on the menu quite yet.

I followed them up the spiral staircase leading to the upper floors. Lizzie's room was next to the one I'd been allocated. Nathaniel pushed the door open and stepped into the room. I caught my first glimpse of it, and it struck me as all things Lizzie. Powdery pink wallpaper covered the walls.

The furniture was painted in a creamy shade of white and there was a four-poster overflowing with lattice. The bed was unmade, the pillows in a messy pile.

"Look inside her bedside table," Gabriel prompted me and I followed the instruction.

I rummaged through the mess inside the drawer—hairbands, a bottle of body lotion, pens of various colors, a pair of scissors—but no phone. "Empty."

"Father, any brilliant ideas?"

The Hunter lifted up curtains and rug and cushions on the twin bergère chairs on both sides of the window. I wasn't as active and efficient in my search. Instead, I remained rooted to the side of her bed, my eyes fixed on the soft linen. It was crumpled as if she'd tossed and turned before finally jumping out of the bed. I sat on the edge of it, ignoring the noises made by Nathaniel or how Gabriel kept him at weapon's length.

I closed my eyes and summoned every ounce of my senses. I ran the flat of my hand over the linen. The cotton was all soft. You could expect Lizzie to choose the highest thread count money could buy. I stretched out my hand to one of the square pillows on top of the mattress. My fingers slid underneath it. Their tips touched a flat, rectangular shape, which I extracted.

"I found the phone." Whatever father and son were bickering about, my announcement ended it. "It's switched off." I remedied that and the screen lit up.

"There's no information on this phone my guys haven't retrieved already."

"Lizzie is glued to her mobile 24/7. I can't believe she'd go anywhere without it. She has to be close."

"Let's search the rest of the property." Nathaniel was already bolting out of the bedroom. Gabriel—and the dirk—blocked his way. "Come on. It's your sister we're talking about. Bury the hatchet for the time being, will you?"

"Don't leave my sight." Indeed, even when he addressed his next question to me, his gaze was on Nathaniel. "Can you detect anything else? *Anything?*"

I shut my eyes again and leaned over. After resting my head on her crumpled pillow, I joined my hands in front of my chest, holding the phone tightly. I knew Lizzie would have lain exactly like this. She'd dialed the number at eleven, but there'd been no answer. She'd waited for the callback, waited and waited. Hence the tossing and turning.

I twisted to my side and buried my face in the pillow. I drew her scent into my lungs and kept it there. My whole focus narrowed on each of its components: her cherry-scented shampoo, the aloe vera of her face cream, the patchouli in her perfume. I pinpointed every single one of them. They were all hers. I'd lived with the girl for three months and was attuned to her.

But it wasn't enough. I released a deep breath into the pillow, then inhaled another one.

"Why is your Turned acting like a sniffer dog? We need to get going."

"Shut up."

Hopefully Gabriel would keep his faith in my abilities a little longer.

I tuned out their voices. Something was here, flimsy and fleeting, but still here. I had to catch it before it vanished. So I ignored the cherry, the aloe vera, the patchouli, and dived deeper.

When I found it, I realized it'd been there all along. My brain had simply refused to associate it with Lizzie. I jolted off the bed and back onto my feet, letting the phone drop. It landed with a thump. The room spun around me. This time it had nothing to do with my illness. It was my brain catching up with my senses.

"What's up?" Gabriel stepped towards me, keeping his dagger pointed at his father.

My stomach was churning. Adrenaline shot saliva up into my mouth. I barely managed to swallow its acrid taste. My gaze roamed the rest of the room in search of any other clues. On the back of one of the bergère chairs lay the turtleneck Lizzie had worn the night before. I grabbed it and brought it to my nose. Now that I was looking for the musky scent, I also found faint hints of lemongrass in the cashmere.

"Goddammit." The pullover muffled my swearing.

I checked the pullover for any other signs. When I found them, my body temperature plunged. Inside the high collar of the jumper, twin dark spots bore witness to puncture wounds.

Nathaniel yanked the pullover out of my hands and checked inside the collar. His voice was strangled. "Who?"

I couldn't meet his gaze and sought out Gabriel's. He spoke the name, the sound of which reverberated within the walls of my skull. "Beaumont?"

"Yes."

"What the hell?" Nathaniel threw the pullover onto the floor. His hands covered the sides of his head, he pulled on his hair, kicked the foot of the bergère. It fell backwards. "How did he dare go after her? In my own home?"

"It's my fault." Gabriel's arm had lowered, the tip of the dagger pointing down. He was shaking his head in disbelief, his eyebrows drawn in a scowl.

"You brought all that shit under my roof." The Hunter dug his index finger into my chest.

I scrambled backwards.

His hand was inches from my neck when Gabriel's body bounced against him. The force of the impact threw the Hunter onto the floor. "Don't ever touch her again."

Gabriel was about to kick the older man in the ribcage. I pulled him away. "I'm not hurt." My arms clasped around his chest. "He's scared. He's scared for her." So was Gabriel. So was I. "Your father is right anyway. I knew about Beaumont's plan to use you and Lizzie as leverage." I couldn't hide the quiver shaking my voice. "I assumed I was his only way in. I'd never have imagined he'd dare go for Lizzie himself."

"Do you think she's still…" Gabriel's breathing quickened, "Do you think she's still alive?"

"I do. I'm not saying death isn't his endgame, but he has other motives before getting there. Holding power over your

241

father, torturing him, even blackmailing him, that'll feed his power."

Nathaniel was already back on his feet. "Why now?"

"Because you slaughtered the whole North American Council two weeks ago and he's expecting you to try and slice his throat next."

"So he's taken my daughter as insurance?"

I nodded. "This is his rehashed version of Culloden. Lawrence is going after the last line of Highland Hunters and wants to finish the job he started two hundred years ago. But why simply kill you when he can make you suffer first? Lizzie was an easy prey."

"My daughter is a MacLeod. MacLeods fight and don't fall easy."

"She's a twenty-year-old girl who is looking for love and romance. A motherless girl whose dad has pretty much checked out of her life. Lawrence might not even need compulsion. He's a monster with an unfortunately endless amount of charm."

"Shut up, you whore! I—"

"I'm calling him." Gabriel grabbed the mobile from my hand and sat on the edge of the bed. The dirk lay on Lizzie's messy sheets.

His fingers scrolled on the screen. I already knew what he was up to: retrieving the last number Lizzie had dialed. Lawrence would never have left the phone behind for us to find if he hadn't wanted us to use it. He wasn't the kind to leave any loose ends.

"The hell you are," Nathaniel shouted, but Gabriel didn't even spare his father a glance. "I refuse to play that SOB's mind games. I won't let him blackmail me and hell if I ever negotiate with a Stramos."

I begged to differ. "You signed a truce with him not so long ago. What's that about negotiating?"

"Because I wanted him off my back while I focused on America. I was buying time before pursuing him."

"Did you seriously expect him to fall for it?"

"Well, he did—"

"Until you slaughtered the whole American council. After that, he kind of put two and two together. You underestimated Lawrence greatly and that might cost Lizzie her life."

Hatred flickered across Nathaniel's dark eyes, but he dismissed me. His focus narrowed on his son instead. "Whatever it is you have in mind, just drop it."

Gabriel's eyes flicked back and forth over the screen of the phone, ignoring his father's order. "She called that same number ten times last night." His thumb ran over the screen. "From what I can see, the first time she dialed that number was a week ago. Last Friday."

The revelation punched me straight in the plexus solar. "The night of the ball."

The lines at the corners of Gabriel's eyes deepened. "Lawrence was there."

I'd thought he had only been there for me, to play with my mind, my heart. I'd underestimated him too.

"Lizzie didn't spend that night at home. I thought she'd stayed with Simon because she was acting all cagey about it afterwards. So I didn't push her. But Simon told me…" my voice weakened, "…last night he told me nothing had happened between them."

"She was with Beaumont." Gabriel buried his face in his hands. "I'm such a fool."

"She's been acting moody lately. Maybe that's because she fed on his blood."

"My own daughter is whoring with a Stramos and you still want to go and rescue her."

I didn't pay much attention to Nathaniel. He'd shifted somewhere behind me. I felt the warmth of his body, smelled his anger seeping out of every pore. But I only saw Gabriel and his lost gaze. His hand had fallen on his lap, his fingers clenched the mobile. His options were few. None had a clean outcome. There would be losses.

But Nathaniel kept pushing and pushing. "She made her choice, Gabriel. Just like you did."

"Can you just shut up?" Frustration had me spinning around. All I wanted was to bark at that man and make him shut up.

I didn't see what he had in his hand until it was buried deep inside me.

Chapter 24 - Freedom

The first jolt of pain was a burning sizzle that twisted my heart.

My eyes hunted the source of the discomfort. They found it right next to my heart. Only the handles of the scissors could be seen, so far into my chest were the scissors buried. Lizzie's scissors. From her bedside table. A scream gurgled out of me. It was more like a pathetic little shriek. Nothing dramatic. A tiny wheeze of air out of my constricted lungs.

My legs gave way beneath me. I collapsed into a heap of limbs on the floor. My head struck the hardwood floor. The thump echoed in my head. The impact was so blunt it made my stomach lurch.

I heard him call my name. But all I was able to do was lie still on my side. My hands grasped the handles. Blood spurted from the wound. The wetness coated my fingers. The blades of the scissors hadn't pierced my heart—I'd be already dead if they had—but they'd hurt me badly. If I moved, the blades would cut my heart and I'd find out whether there was a place of solace for creatures like me. Once we were truly dead.

As fragile as my predicament was, I couldn't ignore the mayhem swirling above me. I forced my eyes open. I even risked angling my head towards the window. Both bergères were now on their sides. Two silhouettes circled around them in a wild ballet. Their movements blurred my vision.

I closed my eyes. They felt all gritty. *I* was all gritty. For a few seconds I let myself go. I summoned up all my energy to open my eyes again, because danger roamed around the room. I struggled to catch up with what was happening. There was no more circling, no more lunging and kicking. Only one man was left standing. Relief had me take in a gulp of air. The movement hadn't been advisable: The edge of the scissors sliced into the edge of my heart. It skipped a beat. There was a spasm. It started beating again in a sporadic rhythm.

I tried to get back to the man standing. Gabriel had the dirk pointed at his father's throat. I heard the Hunter's ragged breathing.

"Come on, son, get on with it. Or maybe you don't have the balls to kill me."

I saw the hate flashing through Gabriel's eyes. His resolve. I saw the start of his lunge forward.

"Don't!" Gabriel froze. "Don't kill him now. You can use him as bargaining chip." And I didn't want him to have his father's blood on his hands.

"He hurt you."

"He did, but you need to think of Lizzie, of how we're going to get her back."

Gabriel's expression closed. He'd spent his life protecting his sister, he wouldn't stop now. Not even out of fury.

His stance relaxed slightly. "Get up." There was all his hate dripping from the order.

Gabriel was already looking in my direction. He didn't see the tiny blade Nathaniel extracted from under the leg of his combat trousers.

Fear struck me deeper than the scissors had. "Watch out!"

Gabriel reacted faster than thunder. The tip of the dirk disappeared into Nathaniel's body. I heard the air whishing out of his lungs. His last breath. But I couldn't check with my eyes. The back of my head had bumped back against the rug.

I felt a hand sliding under my neck. My name kept

bouncing between the walls of the room. But inside my head, it was no more than a faint echo. I held on to it, though, to my name being called again and again, to the face that now filled my vision. The warmth of his fingers against my cheek brought me back to life. I tuned to his touch. To his voice. To the tears in his eyes.

"Don't cry," I croaked.

It felt like the effort made by my throat had contorted my heart. I guess it was a good sign.

"You need to tell me what to do."

I knew him well now. He'd mastered his voice into a sharp military tempo, but it sounded broken to me, as if shards of glass had slashed through his throat.

"You're a bloody doctor, Marie, so tell me what I should do."

I tried to swallow but my mouth was so dry it turned into a strangle. "If I move, the blade will go deeper into the heart."

"I'll call an ambulance. The paramedics, they'll know how to get you to a hospital safely."

My head bobbed. I moaned and froze. "Too late. I'm losing too much blood." I rolled my eyes to try and catch a glance at the rest of the room. "Your father...I'm sorry." His eyebrows drew together in confusion. "I never wanted you to be the one...killing him."

"Don't waste yourself. He's not worth it."

There was some movement behind him. Steps made the wooden planks of the floor creak.

"Shit." *Simon.*

More expletives followed, coming from Hayden and Fergus. I couldn't see any of them. I had to let my eyelids flutter and close. Keeping my eyes open had drained my last remnants of strength.

The air shifted next to me. Someone else was there. To my right.

"Find the mobile. It must have slid under the bed."

More shuffling. Gabriel's fingers cradled my cheeks. His

kisses on my eyelids were featherlight. "Stay with me, *a leanaigh*. Stay with me a little longer. I'll make it right for you."

"Here." It was Tobias.

"Dial the last outgoing number, then give me the phone." Gabriel's fingertips traced along the edge of my cheekbone.

"What are you going to do?"

"Please, Tobe. No questions. Just get my car ready. You'll drive."

I tried to blink. I couldn't even do that. My brain had to play catchup with the ping-pong of words exchanged above me. It failed. Below me the floor seemed to open into a void. I was falling into it.

"Marie." The tips of his fingers trembled now. "Stay with me. Please, stay."

I wanted to hush the tears that cracked his voice. "I'm sorry."

Did he even hear me?

The void swallowed me.

***

I woke to a humming sound and faint vibrations rolling along my body.

That wasn't how I expected hell to sound or feel. Perhaps the Almighty force up there had looked down on me with pity and granted me a nicer destiny than purgatory. A place that smelled of heather and earth, and of the glens.

And I should really take another deep breath of this scent. I inhaled. Maybe I took in more than a gulp of air and my lungs might not be functioning anymore, wherever I now was. But, goddammit, it hurt. Only it wasn't a stabbing pain anymore. More like a fist pushing against my breastbone. Relentlessly. I protested with a groan and turned my body to diffuse the pressure.

"Don't move."

Steely arms stifled my attempt at movement. But I had to try and release the pain. I checked I had still control over my fingers by wriggling them. It worked. So I tried to lift them, but I didn't have enough strength. Instead, I slid them up to my hipbone, over my belly, and to the source of the pain. They circled around what was a fist.

"What the he—?" My eyes popped wide open.

They opened to Gabriel's face. He inched towards me and peppered my face with soft kisses.

"I'm alive." It was either that, or something had happened to him. I wouldn't contemplate that possibility.

"I'm going to keep it that way." He cradled me tight against him. Moisture dampened my dry lips as I tasted the salt of his tears. "Your breathing had slowed down so much I thought you were gone, so I took the chance to remove the scissors. But I keep applying pressure to the wound. I've heard that in so many fucking movies and it's working. There's less blood."

I had already lost so much of it, my shirt was soaked and heavy.

"Keep holding me, Gabriel." My head bobbed against his chest. The tip of my nose snuggled against my favorite part of his body, the valley formed by the swell of his chest.

This man was a warrior and he had to keep fighting. Up to the very end. So I let him fight for me one last time. I'd be gone by the time we reached a hospital. I didn't care if we were packed on the backseat of his car. I was in his arms, coddled into him, and there was no sweeter death for me.

The fleeting memory of Louis crossed through my consciousness. I'd never been more grateful to him. He'd given me the lease of life that had allowed me to meet Gabriel MacLeod.

"Thank you." I addressed the words to Gabriel.

"Don't thank me yet. Do that once I have you all mended."

I tried to shake my head but failed. All my muscles were

numb again, and Gabriel's heat didn't permeate the barrier of my skin anymore. "Thank you for seeing me."

His eyes narrowed in confusion.

"For seeing what I couldn't see in myself anymore." I paused and steadied my breathing. "With you, I'm a girl again. Only this time I fell for the good knight, whose armor was so shiny it brightened every dark part of me."

"I know what you're trying to do, Marie. Stop."

"What is it?"

"You're saying goodbye. Keep up your strength. I intend to shine so much I'll give you the worst fucking headaches."

I giggled. The giggle shot blood up my throat. I spat it all over his jumper.

"We've arrived." Tobias shouted from the driver's seat.

Where? The hospital? I blinked to sharpen my eyesight and catch a glimpse through the window. There was no sign of urban life, only a vast expanse of sky. The brakes squeaked. The car came to a stop. The back door opened.

"I have to move you. It's going to hurt." He grabbed my hands and linked them over the wound. "Try to apply as much pressure as you can while I carry you."

He had to let go of me. I was bleeding internally. My vitals had crashed. I'd reached the end and I wanted it to be peaceful. With him only. But I had to indulge his despair. Later he'd know he'd done all he could. That would give him peace and his peace mattered more than mine.

It didn't hurt so much when he took me out of the SUV. We were on another one of those long stretches of beach on the coast north of St. Andrews. A lot like Hollaroch. There were far worse places to die.

Gabriel soldiered over the thick sand. I snuggled my face in the nook of his neck. Tobias flanked us. I wasn't applying any pressure to the wound and the blood was trickling from it. I wanted him to stop his march, to lay me on the sand, and let me fly away.

Finally, he stopped.

"What have you done to her?"

I thought everything had already frozen inside me. I was wrong; that voice congealed my still faintly functioning organs. I moaned something that sounded like a *no*. My brainwaves kick-started. "Why is he here?"

Gabriel ignored my question. "My father did it."

"He should never have gotten close enough to her." The voice broke in a strangle. "She is always putting herself at risk. I would never have let it happen. *Never*."

"I lowered my guard." The tendons along Gabriel's neck tensed and contracted. "That's my fault."

All I wanted was to shake the guilt out of his soul.

"The hell it is."

I'd never heard Lawrence swear. My impending demise had to be rattling him. I was laid out on the sand, my body molded against its soft mattress.

"The blade missed the heart but it must have been by no more than half a centimeter." Gabriel had regained some composure. "But the blood loss is taking her away."

I averted my eyes when Lawrence's scanned my body. I'd shrivel if I wasn't already fading away.

"She's almost gone." Lawrence whispered as if the statement would be less final if pronounced in a hush.

At least, someone here wasn't completely delusional. That was when I heard the muffled sobs. They came from behind Lawrence.

My eyelids felt like they were glued together but I managed to open them anyway. "Lizzie?"

Her face was stricken with tears, her cheeks reddened. It was like I was seeing her for the first time though. Her fiery curls were dancing in the wind. There was a new glint in those slanted eyes of hers, a new presence behind them. Gone was the girl. She'd been replaced by a woman. A troubled woman.

"I'm so sorry, Marie. I'm so sorry my dad did that to you."

"That's not your fault. I'm just so glad you're alive."

Gabriel ignored our exchange. "It's not too late?" His question was a plea. "You can still save her."

"I still can, but only because I'm a Stramos." Lawrence had regained some of his composure. "She's too weak for a Fiu or a Turned to even try."

"Then get to it, will you?"

The words bounced and ricocheted of each other but I couldn't make sense of any of them.

"I have one condition."

"Spit it out."

"Afterwards, she'll come with me." His next words were rushed. "My powers will protect her, and I will die rather than anyone hurting her again."

I went into shock. Spasms twisted and shrank my muscles. My lungs tightened, pushing off the little air they'd contained. My mouth gaped to suck some back into me.

"Please calm down." Gabriel wrapped himself around me and the weight of his body forced mine to relax. He kept whispering and hushing and combing my damp hair away from my face. "It's going to be all right."

"Get off me." I didn't have enough strength to breathe anymore, but I managed to shout at him. "Did you hear me? Get off me."

Gabriel's features stilled. He frowned but obeyed. Carefully, he disentangled himself from me. He kept my upper body cradled tight against him. His arms encased me and he rocked me gently.

"I'm not going with him."

Gabriel murmured sweet words into my ears, but I didn't catch their meaning. My command of Gaelic was now rusty.

"Marie, take the offer." *Lizzie.* "Lawrence will look after you...he's in love with you." I heard her pain.

I ignored her and focused on Gabriel instead. "I'm not going with him."

"*A leanaigh*, it's the only way, *my* only way to keep you alive." His lips trembled against mine.

"If I live, it's to love you."

"It won't change that."

"It will change everything." I raised my hand to his face. It shook but joy seized me when I finally felt his warm skin and his familiar stubble of russet hairs. "It will change everything. I have compromised so many times, this will be one time too many."

The onset of tears grated his voice. "I need you, Marie. I need your sparkle to keep lighting me up. Even if it's from far away."

"I'm sorry." The tip of my thumb brushed against the sharp line of his cheekbone. "I'm sorry. I only want to be your girl, even if she has to die."

His grasp on me strengthened in despair. For several long seconds he was the one clinging on to me and I was the one supporting him. He shut his eyes but the tears escaped and ran down his face anyway.

The nod he gave me was stiff with grief. "We'll do it your way then."

"Thank you."

"I told you my love will never trap you and I'll keep my promise, *a leanaigh*. I'll set you free."

Gabriel's gaze remained on me, warming me, consoling me. He didn't even look at Lawrence. "We won't need your help, after all. So get the hell away from us."

My hand slid down Gabriel's neck and settled along the swell of his shoulder.

I felt more than saw Lawrence kneeling next to me. His hand covered the wound that tore my chest.

Epilogue
Gabriel

My clansmen formed a half-circle behind me.

Rows of them spread down the steep hill leading to the cliff. The anointment of the next hunter follows a millennium-old protocol—a protocol I'd completely disregarded tonight. First, the rank directly behind me was made up of my friends instead of the most senior MacLeods. Second, two foreigners were among them. Tobias stood next to Simon. Hayden and Fergus flanked them. They all wore the MacLeod tartan.

These were the only four members of the gathering who knew the truth about my father's death.

No guilt twisted my guts each time I relived the moment I plunged the dirk into him. None whatsoever. My only regret was not to have ended him right when I entered the dining hall. If I'd killed him then, he'd never have hurt her.

I'd failed so many times over the past months. Lizzie having gone AWOL with a sadistic Stramos ranked only second. Surely that in itself should compete with killing my own father on the ladder of guilt. But what I regretted the most was failing my girl. She'd looked up to me as her knight in shining armor. When the moment had come to up my game, there'd been no fucking knight, no fucking armor.

So I stood on the edge of that bloody cliff on the first night of the full moon after the Hunter's passing. I'd play the game and pretend to follow in his footsteps. Because there was strength in numbers. Because I'd need an army to get my sister back and punish my uncle. I'd need an army to protect innocent lives. I'd lead that army.

To protect what was mine, I'd delegate to nobody.

I raised the ceremonial dirk above my head, its tip pointed at the moon. I knew the Gaelic words by heart and I recited them without hesitation. They spoke of light and darkness, of good and evil, of courage and perversion. Tonight was a formality to please my clan. The Hunter's powers had moved from my father to me the instant he took his last breath.

My voice was booming to cover the crashing sound of the waves below. Once done, I turned to face my clan, still brandishing the sword towards the starry night. My men mirrored my gesture and began to chant my name. Again and again.

I lowered the dirk and started the descent, my people parting as I moved among them. It was like Moses crossing the Red Sea. That level of reverence had gone to the heads of more than one of my ancestors. It didn't boil my blood. All I could see were the faint lights farther down the coast, on the other side of Hollaroch. They were fleeting, but they were *there*. I repeated them to myself like a mantra and that knowledge kept my heart beating steadily. The lights were still shining and I'd be there soon.

Tobias was the first to catch up with me.

"Lead the men inside the main building," I ordered him.

"How long will you be?"

"Don't know yet. As soon as they're drunk, they won't be looking for me."

"I'll be generous with the whisky then."

"Thanks, mate."

I didn't want the rest of the clan to know where I was going in such a hurry. But Tobias's hand circled my elbow, holding me back.

"Gabe."

I frowned. All I wanted was to get the hell away, not chat with my cousin. But judging by how Tobe was shuffling on his feet, there was something he had to say.

"What's on your mind? Spit it out."

"Listen, I wanted to thank you."

"For what?"

"For taking me in. I'm not part of all that…" He tipped his chin at the sea of men behind us. "But I want to. After what my father did, it's my chance to make up for—"

"Your father's mistakes aren't yours. The truth is I need someone I can trust, and you've proven yourself to be loyal to me."

"I couldn't put up a fight against your old man."

"You'll get better. I'll train you. So will Hayden and Fergus."

The nod my cousin gave me was stiff and his eyes glimmered. "Go now. I'll buy you time by getting all these Highlanders acquainted with tequila."

"I'm sure you'll fulfill your mission beyond all expectations."

I marched away into the darkness. My uncle Malcolm had vanished after the news of my father's death had spread. A death we had to manufacture by faking a car crash and bribing a policeman. I was learning the ropes pretty fast.

When I branched off into the small path that led away from the manor down the coast, I checked over my shoulder one last time. No one followed. I reached the steps carved in stones and the sand of the tiny cove. The waves lapped gently against the beach. The soft sound was like a melody and it made me think of her. Of how silently she moved, her steps light, her gestures swift and precise.

I couldn't just walk to the cottage, I had to run now. It was like racing against the time I'd spent away from this place. I couldn't stand another wasted second. I knocked at the door three times. A pause. Two more knocks. Steps approached. A lock was unlatched. A sliver of light peered through the narrow opening of the door. I slid inside and closed the door with my shoulder. Suddenly, it was like I'd shed all my clothes and was standing naked like a newborn. My heart bumped and thrashed. She would hear its every beat. I didn't want to hide it anyway. As far as getting naked, it was my plan for the night. The earlier the better.

The hand that came to rest on my chest was tiny with lithe fingers. The touch was featherlight. It steadied my heartbeat, grounded me. But a jolt of energy sizzled from those fingers, melted through my skin and bones. It dashed into my veins and shot straight to my dick. Aye, abstinence was a distant memory and how happy that made me.

Because I'd make her mine in that small bed of ours. It was so bloody narrow there wasn't enough space for us to lie there and make love on it. No complaint on my part. It gave me the excuse to come up with positions that didn't involve lying down. Like her bent forward over the edge of the bed, her hips lifted in the perfect angle for me to pound deep into her.

The image made my dick thicken and poke against the wool of my kilt. *That* she'd have noticed even if she wasn't who she was.

"Are all these new powers of yours going to your head?" Her gaze was pointed at my crotch. The arch of her eyebrow was a perfect curve. Her mouth was puckered in the cutest smile.

And I loved her. What I felt made me forget myself. It made me fly out of my own body, even when that very body was totally fired up. My chest expanded and I filled my lungs to the brim. I needed that extra weight to bring me back down to earth, to remind me I couldn't ever let go. Nothing and *no one* would hurt her again. As long as I breathed, as long as I lived, I'd protect her. I'd do anything to make sure of it even becoming what she was and keep sheltering her.

My throat clogged up. My fingers curled. I grabbed her waist and pulled her, lifting her up against me. My hands ran along her spine, her face buried in the nook of my neck. She wound her arms around my shoulders and let me carry her to our bed. I sat on the edge, her legs on both sides of me. I couldn't talk.

All I could do was rock her body with mine. Gently. Like I'd do to console a child, but in truth I was the one who needed comfort. I nuzzled my face between her breasts. It wasn't even me fondling her. It was just me feeling her softness, hearing her heartbeat, breathing in the jasmine in her scent.

She wriggled against me, sliding her hands between us, along my abdomen to my chest. With the flat of her hands, she created some space. I resisted. She cupped my face and forced my gaze to hook with hers. Her eyes were the warm color of a single malt with speck of gold floating within.

"I'm fine now, Gabe." She rested her forehead against mine and repeated, "Thanks to you and Lawrence. I'm fine."

I shut my eyes. The tension in my face made my jaw ache.

"You can't be thinking about me all the time, worrying about me," she said. "You have to look forward now. Your clan is going to look up to you... There's Lizzie."

The name made my eyes pop wide open. "Beaumont has her wrapped around his little finger." He'd kept my sister after saving Marie, but he hadn't needed to use compulsion for her to follow him without putting up a fight.

"He's going to make you pay." This time it was Marie's turn to avoid my gaze.

I lowered my head so that she couldn't escape and start on the same guilt trip. "It's not your fault she's with him now. Even if he hadn't given you his blood, he'd never have let go of her."

"She was supposed to be a weapon against your father. Now she'll be a weapon against you."

And didn't I bloody know it?

"I can't help thinking that she made her choice. No

matter the blood he's feeding her or the compulsion, there's a part of her that wants to stay with him. To love him."

The seconds stretched out. I felt the shame of my words heating my face. I didn't want to be like—or to think like—my father. I shouldn't doubt my sister this way. It shouldn't matter. What mattered was how I'd extract her from the clenches of that prick.

"Lawrence is complicated." Marie's voice had lowered to a whisper. I resented its intimacy because it told me of the history she shared with him. I fucking hated it. "Maybe there's still something good inside him, something redeemable. Maybe that's what Lizzie sees."

I lifted her chin to stare right at her. I had to know. The doubt had eaten at me since Beaumont had chosen to stay.

"Do you see it too?"

She rubbed her lips together, a sure tell I'd hit a point. Next she'd be reaching for her throat. I knew every single tick of hers. Something in my stomach twisted. She was fucking killing me.

"Do you see it too?" I hated hearing my fear.

She stiffened against me but the tip of her thumb brushed the line of my cheekbone. "I do." The two words broke and slapped me all at once. She wasn't done with me though. "I do see it. I hope for it, but I won't fall for it."

"Why not?" I was a glutton for punishment.

"Because I've already fallen." Her lips caressed mine and my chest caved in. "I've fallen. So deep. Into you."

She pulled away but I drew her back to me and crushed my mouth on hers. My tongue hunted hers, mated with hers. I invaded her and made her all mine. My free hand fell on her hip and curved around her arse. I'd grown hard again and she was all warmth and curves against me. I nibbled at her tongue, traced the edge of her teeth with mine, nipped her lower lip, suckled on it. And she was making those little squeals that made me want to lick her all over.

I swung round and lay her on her back. Her legs were

wrapped around my waist. I rested my weight on my forearms to keep from smothering her. All I wanted was to cover her completely, hide her from the world with my body, breathe air into her lungs. I wanted to be her everything.

I broke the kiss. It took all my willpower but I managed it. No matter the amount of tequila Tobias would pour down my men's throats, I'd have to go back to them. Before that, I'd make love to Marie. But first she needed to know something, something I hadn't had the guts to say yet.

"Marie?"

Her breathing was choppy as she chased my mouth. I pulled away and she frowned.

"*A leanaigh*, do you remember my promise? To keep you free…that my love for you would never be a cage or a fence."

She nodded and there was moisture in her eyes. I didn't want to make her cry, but I had to tell her my truth.

I swallowed a big gulp of air and took her gaze in mine. "I don't want the same from you. I want you to own me, Marie. I'm yours for life."

"And I'll keep you, Gabriel MacLeod. I'll keep you for as long as you want me to."

A Note of Thanks

My heartfelt gratitude goes to my beta readers on the other side of the Pond. Heather Fellows, your love for all things *vampires* took me to the end of this story. Laura, my *Voluptuous Book Diva*, you opened my eyes on many of my characters and Lizzie has to thank you for it. Chanpreet Singh, there is no word to say how much I value your generous support and your genuine faith in me from one book to the next: You are an absolute gem... and you can save lives! Jocelyn Conway, I feel privileged to have met you and your family on that rainy London afternoon. You are a true Lady and have a special place in my heart.

Najla Qamber, you beautify my stories and turn them into the most exciting covers. Thank you for your professionalism. There are not that many people like you out there.

Deb N., I keep your edit letter in a safe place. I've learned much from it and not just in relation to this book.

Last but not least, I want to thank my husband and my daughters for inspiring me to be *more*.

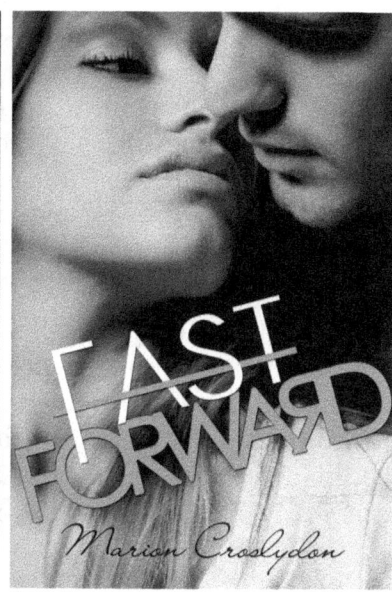

*Want to know **more about Josh and Cassie**?*
Top 50 Amazon Bestseller.

Reviews

"I FIERCELY loved this book."

~ Goodreads Top Reviewer, 5 Stars

"I relished this story."

~ Good Choice Reading, 4 Stars

"I fell in love with their relationship."

~ Schmexy Book Blog, 4 Stars

"It is a 'feel' book."

~ The Autumn Review, 4 Stars

A girl who needs to undo the past.
A boy who wants to forget it.
In love, there's no way back.

At high school in Steep Hill, Kansas, Cassie O'Malley and Josh MacBride were the poster couple for quarterback/cheerleader romance until they starred in their own tale of teen pregnancy. No need to say: their shotgun wedding was low-key. But when there was no baby anymore, they went their separate ways.

Five years later, Josh has breezed through Georgetown and is about to finish his post-grad degree at Oxford University. He is set to join a lobbying group on Capitol Hill, owned by his new fiancée's father. For Josh, the sky is now the limit… only he must first take care of a tiny legal matter: technically, he's still married to the girl who broke his heart.

Meanwhile, Cassie has been waiting tables in Steep Hill to pay for her sick grandmother's care. On the day of the old lady's funeral, Cassie is served with two sets of papers. Josh is asking for a divorce. Her heart squeezes, but, well, he moved on a long time ago. But the second envelope shakes Cassie to the core. So, for the first time, she leaves Kansas and heads to good ol' England.

There, Cassie finds that Josh has not just "moved on," he's freakin' engaged to some blue-blooded heiress. The feelings Cassie had buried deep rush back to her. But no matter if he keeps thrusting the divorce papers under her nose, she needs him to save the only person she loves more than Josh, more than life itself…

** You can order *No Reverse* here: **

Smashwords
https://www.smashwords.com/books/view/344900

264

About Marion

Marion loves to share happy vibes, talk book crush, fictional boyfriends and sexual chemistry with like-minded people. And because she spends most of her days on her own deep inside her London writing cave, you are welcome to come and say "hello" from time to time. Just to make sure she doesn't sink into insanity. Her friends, family and arch-enemies (there are quite a few) will be forever grateful for your help.

Her debut novel, *Oxford Whispers*, a New Adult paranormal romance, won the IndieReader Discovery Award, 2013. Her contemporary romances, *No Reverse* and *Fast Forward*, were Amazon bestsellers, both in the New Adult and Kindle Top 50 charts.

To be the first to know of upcoming releases, please join Marion's Newsletter (there will be no spamming and no drowning your inbox).

Marion's Newsletter: http://marioncroslydon.us9.list-manage.com/subscribe?u=58f138f1a8e9a9395c7360c5b&id=a8c6babca7

You can talk to her here:
Facebook https://www.facebook.com/MarionCroslydon
Twitter https://twitter.com/MCroslydon
Goodreads
https://www.goodreads.com/author/show/6455086.Marion_Croslydon
http://marioncroslydon.com/
Email: Marion@MarionCroslydon.com

PROLOGUE
JOSH

Steep Hill ~ November, six years earlier.

The dozens of eyes set on me don't make me break a sweat.

I don't give a shit about what those people think right now. The church could just as well be empty since the girl I love isn't here. Mom didn't send out any invitations after I proposed to Cassie two weeks ago. Still, half the town has found its way to the church where Reverend Beasley will marry us.

That was supposed to happen twenty minutes ago.

"She won't screw this one up, Josh. She loves you." Woodie, my best man and wide receiver, whispers in my ear. His chubby face is all flushed. He's embarrassed. That's how I should be feeling. Only I don't.

"She'll be here soon," I answer back. "Cass's never been on time for anything. She won't start with her own wedding."

When I try to reassure Woodie, my eyes meet those of my dad, dark and stern, just like mine. His tight jaw screams a loud and fat "I told you so." Good Ol' Jack MacBride has never been Cassie O'Malley's number-one fan, even back when we were kids and she used to climb the cottonwood tree to reach my bedroom window. To him, Cass has always been bad news.

269

He's the only one who knows the price I'm ready to pay to take care of her and our unborn baby.

But the truth, pure and simple? I would risk everything to be with her. Cassie is the only future I want. Whether I take her and the baby with me to Georgetown, or to our community college, it only matters that we go there as a family.

"Jesus. H. Christ," Woodie bursts out. "Her grandma's arrived."

My lungs can't help puffing out some of the air I didn't know was trapped inside. Mrs. O'Malley has finally arrived, and, with her, hopefully Cassie. Mrs. O. is the gentlest of all ladies. Acute diabetes makes her look older than her sixty years. Her skin has always had that same waxy complexion and she's underweight. But now, she smiles back at me and answers my silent question with a nod. Mrs. O. and I, we've always understood each other.

Judging by where Mrs. O'Malley's gaze is directed—somewhere behind the half-open door of the church—my girl is about to walk down the aisle.

Woodie hyperventilates. "Okay now, look ahead and only turn back when I tell you to do so."

As if he's the one getting married to Cassie, and maybe he wishes he were, Woodie glues his eyes on the whitewashed wall behind Reverend Beasley, who clears his throat. A drop of sweat tracks down his temple. Clearly everyone has been freaking out thinking that I'd been dumped at the altar.

When the organist starts playing, my heartbeat breaks into a home-run sprint and a lump fills my throat. I have to see her.

Three.

Two.

One.

I look back and steal a first glance at her. The sight punches me straight in the stomach. She's so beautiful in her gran's wedding dress. The look is '70s, I guess. Her hands hold a bouquet of daisies and her hair, the color of a cornflower field, cascades over her shoulders and down her back.

She doesn't smile but instead, her eyes dive into mine as if I was her anchor, not Mrs. O'Malley who walks by her side. I answer Cassie's silent plea by nodding. An intake of air makes her shudder.

Whatever Cassie says about not caring for marriage, she isn't telling the truth. Her dead junkie mother couldn't name the bastard who knocked her up at seventeen. So getting married in front of God and Steep Hill is the first step to show Cass our child won't know the same fate.

She's by my side now and I grasp her shaking hand to give it a squeeze. We turn and face Reverend Beasley. A broad smile breaks out not only on my face, but in my heart and in every cell of my body.

I have my girl and I'll never let her go.

ONE
CASSIE

Steep Hill ~ Present.

Drops of rain smashed like marbles onto Gran's coffin.

I always knew I'd end up burying her. Only I didn't expect that the day would be so damned wet, or for it to come so soon.

Plus I hated umbrellas, and the water had now filtered through my cotton dress. I shivered and goose bumps broke out across my bare forearms.

Woodie, on my right, sent me a worried look every other minute. I wasn't going to cry. I'd keep that promise to myself. I wouldn't provide any more real-life entertainment to the good people of Steep Hill. And I wouldn't break when their honorable mayor, Jack MacBride, raked me with his gaze across the gaping hole of my gran's freshly dug grave.

For sure, my tears would make him happy, kind of an indirect payback for all the "trouble" I created over the years. That jerk should be thanking me. Six years ago, I covered his ass big time, so he could keep his precious family intact.

And where did that grand gesture leave me? A high-school drop-out turned bartender in the middle of Nowheresville, Kansas. But the truth? MacBride wasn't the one I should be angry with. I made some very bad choices and I deserved to pay for them for the rest of my life.

Reverend Beasley turned towards me and waved for me to join him at the head of the coffin. I put one foot in front of the other, my shoes squishing into the muddy grass.

"Cassandra, here, would like to read a prayer to honor the memory of her grandmother, Iris. As you'll all know, Iris raised her after the death of Cassandra's mother, Jeanine."

Was he talking about me or poor Cosette from Les Miserables?

Reverend Beasley moved aside, making me now the focus of attention.

"Th- This is," I stammered, but seeing the half-smirk on Jack MacBride's mouth I squared my shoulders, cleared my throat and started again. "My grandmother wanted me to read these words translated from Gaelic." My voice was as steady as my sinking heart would allow. "May the road rise to meet you; May the wind be always at your back; May the sun shine warm upon your face."

Breathe in, Cass. Don't collapse now.

"May the rain fall softly upon your fields; until we meet again; May The Lord hold you in the hollow of his hand."

Tears welled up in my eyes but I couldn't let them flow. I couldn't. When I got back to Woodie's side, he took hold of my hand. The contact shot warmth through my skin, and I was so grateful to him for showing me—for showing everyone—his friendship.

I didn't even know where the man I wanted by my side was. Would he have come, had he known? So, I settled for Woodie's friendship instead. I managed to break a smile, and he squeezed my hand.

Yes, I was lucky to have him in my life. I hoped I deserved him.

By the time the service ended, the rain had stopped. Rays of sun pierced through the fat clouds, but they weren't enough to warm me while, one by one, I received condolences from the line of familiar faces.

When Jack MacBride made it to the front of the line, I

curled my fists. God, how I wished I could punch his sorry face.

"We're sorry for your loss, Cassandra."

No, you're not.

"Thanks Mr. MacBride." I turned away from his hazelnut eyes, the same color as Josh's, and focused on his wife, Miranda, a deep-to-the-bone nice lady. "Gran was always fond of you, Mrs. MacBride. She would have been delighted to know you came today."

"She can see us, Cassie. She can see you, and she's proud of how you're handling yourself."

Miranda wrapped her arms around me, and I breathed in the scent of sweet tea. It reminded me of my gran. Heaven, afterlife, angels and demons, I wasn't sure I believed in any of it. If God existed, he wouldn't have let my sweet grandma suffer through all those years, let the disease eat her alive.

"I hope you're right," Now wasn't the time to share my spiritual doubts.

"As sad as Iris's death is, you need to see it as a great opportunity." Jack's words made me and his wife gasp at the same time.

I was the first one to recover. "How so?"

MacBride had the decency to let out an embarrassed cough. "Well, you can leave now, pursue your own dreams... turn the page on Steep Hill."

And get out of your life for good.

As much as it cost me to acknowledge it, the jerk was right. "I could do that."

I could also blackmail his treacherous ass and syphon away his cash, but as tempting as it would be, this was not the girl Iris O'Malley raised. This was not who I was.

"Don't hesitate to visit us if you need anything, darling."

"Thank you, Mrs. MacBride."

Five or six more people to greet and thank, and I'd be done. I lifted my chin and glued a smile over my face.

TWO

Woodie and I were the only ones left in my gran's house.

Empty cups and plates filled with cake remnants covered every surface in her tattered living room. The taillights of the last visiting car disappeared down the muddy road leading out of our farm. The farm I'd have to sell to pay back our medical bills.

I rushed to the closest window and pulled the frame up, then moved to the next.

"Do I stink?" Woodie asked from the plaid couch, his wide-framed body spread all over it.

"You don't, but hypocrites do."

"Come on, Cass, don't go all paranoid again." He took a swig of his Bud then wiped his mouth on his sleeve. "It was nice of people to come and remember your grandma."

"I wish they'd remembered her when she was still alive… when I needed someone to look after her while I was on a night shift at Teddy's."

After five years in that damn diner, working nights to pay the bills and caring for Gran during the day, I never wanted to see it again. Woodie leaned forward, resting his elbows on his thighs.

"Get over it. With the little money your grandma left and the sale of the farm, you're leaving this shithole for good… and debt-free"

I let the spring air flow into the stuffy room and into my

lungs, closed my eyes and let my mind fly towards my new life. The life I would start tomorrow when I boarded the first Greyhound bus to Nashville. I'd never given a chance to my singing. But with my sweet Gran now gone, nothing—nobody—would chain me to Steep Hill.

I busied myself and tidied up the house. Gran had drilled order and cleanliness into me, making me totally OCD. I checked on Woodie, bringing him one last slice of pecan pie, but he had dove into ESPN, so I set the pie down in front of him on the coffee table.

The lights of a car parking in my courtyard invaded our bubble.

"Expecting anyone?" The arrival intrigued Woodie enough for him to abandon cable TV.

No, I wasn't expecting anyone. I clutched my hands and risked a glance through the window.

A short man in a suit stepped out of the car a large envelope in his hand. Fear kicked me to the porch. God, did Gran owe someone money? Someone else than the bank? Have they come to collect?

I dried my hands on my apron and introduced myself. "Cassie O'Malley. Can I help?"

Little Man bridged the distance between us. "I'm looking for Mrs. MacBride... Cassandra MacBride."

That was also me. No one ever called me that though. I started to confirm my identity, but the words got stuck mid-throat.

"That's her," Woodie chimed in. I felt him close behind me. "What do you want?"

"Mrs. MacBride, I have a document to hand-deliver to you."

The envelope hung from between his fingers. I stared at it but didn't budge.

"Please, Mrs. MacBride," the man in the suit prompted me and I had to slap myself mentally to grab the document. "I also need a signature to prove you've received the document."

I nodded and took the pen he held out.

"You can't sign the paper on the porch..." Woodie slid the porch table over to me.

The return address had the name of a local law firm. I'd dealt with them before: The guy who owned it was Jack MacBride's best buddy. Holding the envelope tightly against my chest, my fear palpable in my shaky voice, "What's that about?"

The man started walking back towards his car when he threw me a backward glance. I saw pity in it, and my heartbeat hitched up a gear.

"Everything will be clear once you open the letter." With one last nod, he got back in his car. I watched him drive away, forcing myself to stay still.

"Are you gonna open it?" Woodie side-stepped me. Maybe it was the cold of the early night or my gut betraying me but a shiver ran through my body. "Should I do it for you?"

I shook my head. I had a pretty good idea what was in that envelope. Six years I'd been waiting for it to come my way. Hell, I was the one who'd asked for it in the first place.

With Woodie in step, I walked back into the house and collapsed on the couch. He grabbed the TV remote control and put Michael Kim on mute. He was really serious about the letter.

I grabbed the knife Woodie had used to slice his pie and tore the envelope open. My eyes flicked through pages of legal jargon until the end when I recognized the signature, Woodie peering over my shoulder the entire time.

"What a douche! And he chose today... of all days." Woodie's voice cracked.

I replied with a shrug. "His dad probably didn't mention about my gran."

"Still, he could have given you a call, or something... to make it easier. I don't know. He should have waited until he came back from England and…" Woodie left his sentence unfinished.

"What would that change?" I patted his thick thigh. "Josh is asking for a divorce. That's it."

So it was official. I had no family left on planet Earth. Today I buried my blood and when I signed this paper, I would cut off the only bond that still linked me to Josh MacBride, my husband.

"What are you going to do about it?"

I stifled the anger that threatened to burst. "I'm going to sign it and set him free. For good."

And set myself free? I needed more than a piece of paper to forget about Josh.

I threw the damned document onto the coffee table, then looked around for a distraction. That's when I noticed the letters I'd let pile up since Gran's... departure. I began to sort through them. All bills or bank statements, except one.

That letter was addressed to me, or rather to Mrs. Cassandra MacBride. The handwriting was familiar. With the same knife, I tore the envelope away and pulled the letter from inside. It was only one page long and at the bottom, the name of a man who had always been nice to me.

"Whose writing is that?"

I ignored Woodie's question.

He shifted on the seat next to me. He was the only one to know the truth with Gran and Jack MacBride. I didn't tell him right away, but since we shared the misfortune of staying behind, here in lousy Steep Hill, I figured I needed someone to share my burden with. Someone my own age.

A couple of words in the letter hit me hard. The heat I felt vanished and blood froze in my veins. My gaze shot back to the top of the letter, scanning the lines again.

"Oh my God." My hand flew to my mouth and a wave of nausea rushed over me. "Oh my God."

Woodie's arm circled over my shoulders and he pulled me against him. "Please tell me what's going on."

I shook my head as fear tightened my throat and belly while twisting every one of my organs into knots. Words finally broke through my lips.

"I have to go…"

Woodie leaned backwards to stare down at me. "I'm lost, Cass. What's that letter about?""

The tears I'd managed to keep inside at the cemetery edged at my eyelids. I didn't have time to cry. I sniffled and a plan started to build in my head.

"Cassie, I hate seeing you upset, but, I swear, if you don't tell me what this is all about, I'll slap your silly head until you explain everything."

Another sniffle. A swallowed sob.

"I'm leaving for Kansas City tomorrow."

And I'd fly to England if I had to.

THREE

I checked the address against the number on the door in front of me against the details I'd scribbled on a Post-It note. Number 36, Compton Road.

Josh lived here. According to the divorce papers at least. Judging by the volume of the music exploding from the three-story house, he was already celebrating his freedom.

Party time.

And Sweet Jesus, it was the mother of all parties. A girl stormed out of the house, passed me, and stopped between two parked cars to puke.

I shot my head back towards the front door and ignored the retching sounds. Throwing up was the main reason I drank so little. I had spent the first half of my pregnancy bent over a toilet seat and I'd sworn I would never, never, go through the same shit again.

The girl had left the door of the house half-open and I took my chance to get inside without having to give any introductions. Hey, I'm Cassie, Josh's wife, the one he wants to get rid of.

The hallway was packed with a crowd of people about my age. Boys and girls shouting at each other, since the music could have deafened the deaf. I side-stepped a couple involved in a tongue-swinging make-out session.

Oxford parties were pretty much the same as in Kansas.

Still, even if the scene was familiar, I couldn't shake off

the unease deep in my belly. Maybe it was the jet lag. I'd landed at London Heathrow that same morning. Or maybe it was simply the after-shock of the crazy week I'd been through. My gran had passed away six days ago. Then there'd been the quick visit to Kansas City, the wall I hit with Social Services… and now I was in Europe.

An expensive last-minute plane ticket wasn't how I'd planned to spend the small inheritance Gran had left me. It was supposed to settle me down in Nashville. But what I had to do, I had to do it face-to-face.

"Wine? Jack and coke? Beer? Tell me what could put a smile back on that sexy mouth of yours."

A lanky guy stepped in my way. I lifted up my chin so that I could stare into his eyes. "Nothing, thanks."

I moved to the side, but he followed my trajectory. "Lovely accent. Are you a friend of our oh-so-popular host?"

I smelled beer on his breath. The guy had obviously been throwing them back all night.

"Maybe."

"I've never seen you around here before. And with those baby-blue eyes of yours, I'd remember." He extended a hand, which I grabbed and shook automatically. "I'm Frederick. But everyone calls me Freddie."

"Cassandra."

"Cassandra," Freddie echoed, not letting my hand go. "The notorious Cassandra."

I nearly choked. Had Josh told this guy about me?

"What do you mean?" I managed.

"Cassandra, daughter of King Priam… Apollo granted you the gift of prophecy."

Relief. He had no idea who I was.

"You know, Greek mythology, Helen of Troy and all?"

"Sure." I forced myself to smile back at him. I had made it to my senior year in high school. Plus I'd watched the movie. Gran was a Brad Pitt-fan.

If I could predict what level on the scale of "pissed-offness" Josh would reach when he saw me, that would come in handy. Or scare me off. Maybe Freddie could give me some insight into the new Josh MacBride.

Freddie grabbed my hand and pulled me behind him as he passed through a door. "Come on. Have a drink."

We entered what must have been the living room. The sound doubled, so I assumed we were closer to the epicenter of the party. I felt a pang of jealousy that Josh should have the best sound system, while all I had was a basic MP3 player and some half-assed barely audible speakers. I untangled my hand from the guy and shoved it into my pocket. The table next to us was filled with used and unused plastic cups, along with bottles of vodka, O.J, and a single bottle of white wine.

Freddie grabbed the vino and filled a glass to the brim. "Not a big fan of Australian chardonnay but I guess it'll have to do."

I took the cup and gulped down half of it in one go. The prospect of seeing Josh for the first time in five years smashed my resolutions. Or maybe it was simply the effect of Freddie. The guy seemed kind of creepy.

"So, Cassandra," When he pronounced my name, a fake American twang replaced his stuck-up English accent. "Did you meet Josh here in Oxford?"

Hearing his name in the mouth of this stranger shot an arrow straight into my heart. My chest tightened. A tingling sensation swept up the back of my neck and spread across my face. The guy had taken a step into my comfort zone. He towered well above my five foot one and my back was against the wall.

"I know him from back home." I skirted around Freddie so that he'd be the one with his back against the wall.

"You know him from Texas." Freddie poured himself a screwdriver—three-quarters vodka/one-quarter O.J. by the look of it—and the drink vanished down his throat in five sips. The guy was going to blow his head off.

"Kansas."

"Euh?" My answer had him spilling some of the liquid over his chin.

I took a mostly-clean napkin from the table and handed it to him.

"I know him from Kansas, not Texas."

"Same thing," he dismissed my correction with a wave. "Big space, burgers, and cowboys."

Was this jerk for real?

"Cassie?"

My heart squeezed real hard.

His voice was the same, but it still felt like centuries had passed by since the last time I'd heard it. I forced myself to turn around and tried to ignore the tornado swirling inside me.

Looking at him was like time-travelling. Josh hadn't played ball since high school, yet his shoulders were strong and well-muscled. Same square jaw, same Coca-Cola brown eyes. Only I didn't see me in them anymore.

What did I expect? The guy had gone to college, not Mars.

"What the hell are you doing here?"

My mouth shaped into a "oh" or maybe it was an "ha." It didn't really matter because I only answered his question with a croak. For the first time in my life, my legendary wits failed me.

Josh bridged the space between us and grabbed my elbow. His fingers burnt through my leather jacket. I felt his warmth seeping into me, and I focused on his touch while he dragged me away from the party.

"I was talking to Cass—" Freddie shouted from behind.

"—Later," Josh cut him off.

We climbed a staircase and stepped into a bedroom on the second floor. Hanging from a chair, I recognized his old Chiefs cap.

I was out of breath. Josh freed my arm and crossed the room, creating an area of safety between us. He stared at me as if I were a two-headed monster.

"You could have mailed the divorce papers. No need to hand-deliver them."

I swallowed hard. I'd spent a fortune and crossed a fucking ocean to see him face-to-face. There was no chickening out now. I shuffled on my feet so that I could hold myself straighter.

"I need to tell you something. Face-to-face. I… I'm not ready to sign the papers. Not yet. We need to talk. And then, if you still want me to sign, I will."

When I'd told Josh I was pregnant, his mouth hadn't dropped open nearly as wide as this. But, credit to him, he recovered quickly. "You've been begging for one for the last six years. Now that I'm ready to give it to you, you change your mind. Have you dedicated your life to ruining mine?"

Those sweet words of love… I shook myself. This wasn't about me, or Josh. I had to think straight, "big picture," and work at reaching my goal.

"What happened between us, it's sad." I moved toward him until we were nearly arms' length away. "But we can work things out, try and get over what happened when…"

"When you killed my child?"

I shuddered.

"When you went behind my back and had an abortion?"

His words pierced into me like icepicks. I couldn't hold his gaze, so my eyes focused on the tips of my shoes instead.

"Or when you forgot about our vows and went on tour with your new rock star boyfriend?"

Josh was now close enough that I could smell him, and he smelled the same. All man now, but still with some of the scent of the boy I grew up with. He smelled like the lemons from his mother's award-winning garden. I wanted to throw myself into his strong arms, have them wrap around me and make me feel like he did when we were younger—when love was easy.

"I did what I had to do, and I did it for you."

His body jerked backwards and his hands flew up to his face. "You have absolutely no shame."

His words should have floored me. Instead they fired up frustration. "No shame? Do you think you'd be where you are now, Ivy League and all, if I had burdened you with a baby when you were seventeen?"

First, Josh didn't react. Then I saw the thoughts processing all over his face, as if it were the first time he'd looked at the past that way. So I hammered my point home. "If I'd had the baby back then, you'd still be in Steep Hill, and not even close to getting your butt out of there. Just like Woodie and me."

When Josh finally talked, it was like a judge passing a death sentence.

"You did not have the right to make that choice for me. But you did and now there's no way back."

Whatever the "real" truth was, Josh was right.

"Maybe you're right." I gave in, my voice cracking. "But you had so much going for you. I knew I had to let you go."

"Why?" His eyes widened. "We could have made it work."

We'd already had that conversation. For someone that smart, Josh had always lacked common sense.

"Really?" I cocked my head. "You'd have stayed in Steep Hill, so that I could look after both my sick gran and the baby"

Josh opted for silence again. Seriously, had he ever extracted his head from his butt and looked at a situation the way it really was?

I took a deep breath to focus on tidying my thoughts. Now was the time to share the truth with him. If he was to be angry with me, better make it for the right reason. I bridged the space between us. He didn't budge. Good. I extended my arm to touch his forearm. He didn't react. The contact filled me with hope.

"Josh," I whispered, "I came here to tell you... I didn't—"

The background sound of the music downstairs burst into the room, then receded when the door behind me slammed shut again.

"Darling?" A girl's voice.

Josh stepped back, his jaw tightened. Before he had been looking down at me. Now he wasn't looking at me at all. That was when I noticed the bottle of fancy perfume on the table next to the double bed.

I spun around. A stick-thin brunette stood two yards away from me, all designer jeans and turtleneck top. Her hair cascaded down her shoulders in a way only a professional's blow-dry could have delivered.

"I've been looking for you everywhere." The girl's accent was East Coast, all clean and polished.

"Sorry, Lenor." Josh struggled for his words. "I bumped into a friend from home."

"How sweet." Lenor approached me, her manicured hand extended for a shake. "I'm Eleanor, Josh's fiancée."